## About the Author

Born and raised in England, Linden Carroll currently resides on the West Coast of Canada. As a former writer and editor of environmental publications within Environment Canada, she now nurtures her interest in the natural environment by beachcombing and spending part of the year in the North Cascade Mountains in Washington, USA, where she has enjoyed many years hiking the trails with her rescued canine companions and howling to the moon with the coyotes around the camp fire.

# Dedication

To my daughter with heartfelt thanks for her unending support, advice and patience throughout the writing of this book.

Also remembered is my wolfie/northern canine companion. Part of my life has been devoted to the rescue of dogs and the one in the photograph on the book remained by my side throughout the writing of this and my other books. He passed upon the completion of *Deadly Assumption,* having walked the trails with me for almost 14 years.

Linden Carroll

# DEADLY ASSUMPTION

AUSTIN MACAULEY PUBLISHERS
LONDON * CAMBRIDGE * NEW YORK * SHARJAH

Copyright © Linden Carroll 2024

All rights reserved. No part of this publication may be reproduced, distributed, or transmitted in any form or by any means, including photocopying, recording, or other electronic or mechanical methods, without the prior written permission of the publisher, except in the case of brief quotations embodied in critical reviews and certain other non-commercial uses permitted by copyright law. For permission requests, write to the publisher.

Any person who commits any unauthorized act in relation to this publication may be liable to criminal prosecution and civil claims for damages.

This is a work of fiction. Names, characters, businesses, places, events, locales, and incidents are either the products of the author's imagination or used in a fictitious manner. Any resemblance to actual persons, living or dead, or actual events is purely coincidental.

**Ordering Information**
Quantity sales: Special discounts are available on quantity purchases by corporations, associations, and others. For details, contact the publisher at the address below.

**Publisher's Cataloguing-in-Publication data**
Carroll, Linden
Deadly Assumption

ISBN 9798891553880 (Paperback)
ISBN 9798891553897 (Hardback)
ISBN 9798891553903 (ePub e-book)
ISBN 9798891555204 (Audiobook)

Library of Congress Control Number: 2024908560

www.austinmacauley.com/us

First Published 2024
Austin Macauley Publishers LLC
40 Wall Street, 33rd Floor, Suite 3302
New York, NY 10005
USA

mail-usa@austinmacauley.com
+1 (646) 5125767

# Acknowledgements

I wish to acknowledge and thank my editor, Dania Sheldon, who worked so diligently and patiently within a short time-frame to complete this project. Her attention to consistency, flow, and overall correctness to ensure a literary product of quality has been both inspirational and motivational. Thank you, Dania. I look forward to working with you on my next project.

I also gratefully acknowledge the work and support of my publishing team through the production of this book to its fruition.

# OTHER BOOKS BY LINDEN CARROLL

**OLIVE—Austin Macauley Publishers, UK**

Olive is a story of human endurance spanning four generations from the end of the nineteenth century through WWII during the almost total destruction of Southampton, a port city in southern England. Olive is the spine of this historical novel. Ostracized at birth by her family, Olive's life is that of an opportunist and black marketeer. She uses her sex, guile and music skills to move up, but there is a price to be paid, and her children bear the cost.

Olive demonstrates the impact one woman had on those whose lives she touched.

**FULL CIRCLE—Austin Macauley Publishers, UK**

This is a story of the indomitable spirit of a youth into manhood; his earliest years spent growing up in the war-ridden city of London, England.

Twelve years old and orphaned following WWII, he follows a clandestine lifestyle on the streets of London while England rebuilds after the war. His rescue of another teen from the streets and their liaison cause him to experience the pain and intensity of first love and parenthood subsequently separating them.

Becoming a seafaring adventurer, he spends many years travelling across England and Canada finally returning to his homeland to re-claim his lost love and their daughter.

This novel follows the path of an orphaned boy and all-consuming undying love, spanning more than 50 years, ebbing past the physical, flowing into every hidden corner of the mind and flooding the very soul to eternity.

Visit lindencarroll.com
info@lindencarroll.com

# Table of Contents

**Preface**   13

**Introduction**   15

**Prologue**   16

**Part 1**   19

   *Chapter 1: Deadly Reunion*   21

   *Chapter 2: Rose and Stewart*   32

   *Chapter 3: Sarah*   44

   *Chapter 4: The Meeting*   56

   *Chapter 5: Mönchengladbach*   63

   *Chapter 6: Jonathan Reflects*   70

   *Chapter 7: In Search of Sarah*   78

   *Chapter 8: The Exuberance of Youth*   86

   *Chapter 9: Memories for the Treasure Chest*   95

   *Chapter 10: Germany, Here We Come*   102

   *Chapter 11: France and the White Horses*   112

   *Chapter 12: The Aftermath*   125

   *Chapter 13: Gina and Ronald*   138

**Part 2**   147

   *Chapter 14: Luke*   149

| | |
|---|---|
| *Chapter 15: A Major Predicament* | *160* |
| *Chapter 16: Luke's Best Friends* | *168* |
| *Chapter 17: Susan* | *179* |
| *Chapter 18: Anne Arrives in Vancouver* | *189* |
| *Chapter 19: Food for Thought* | *200* |
| *Chapter 20: Held in Custody* | *212* |
| **Part 3** | **221** |
| *Chapter 21: Germany and Thoughts of Home* | *223* |
| *Chapter 22: Forgiveness* | *235* |
| *Chapter 23: The Homecoming* | *245* |
| *Chapter 24: We'll Meet Again* | *258* |
| **Epilogue** | **266** |

# Preface

The initial inspiration for writing my novels came from listening to the seniors I have mentored over the years. Their true-life accounts, and those of their parents, formed the basis for my first two novels, *Olive* and *Full Circle.* Seniors have much to say and all too often there is no-one to listen, which is a shame as they are fonts of information, particularly on the history and life of bygone days.

My first two novels, *Olive* and *Full Circle* focused on the day-to-day lives of less privileged people living during WWI through WWII. My latest novel, *Deadly Assumption,* concentrates on the lives of those more privileged and spans WW2 through the 1980s.

It is interesting to note how priorities change with the surrounding environment. War-time—a time of extreme suffering, pain and financial hardship for many, yet the never-ending spirit, compassion, comradery for fellow neighbours demonstrated throughout those times is all-encompassing.

The descendants of the wartime generation enjoyed the huge rise in a new period of consumerism. The post-war economic boom saw rapid growth, paving the way for our current society.

Today, we live in an increasingly sterile environment—a time of commercial and technological advancement with waste and excess to the extreme, seriously compromising the very environment within which we live and require for our survival. We are becoming desensitized and alienated from each other in our quest for more—perhaps a little less and a rekindling of the spirit and soul of our predecessors might not be a bad thing?

In fact, to covet the simple things in life, such as opening a new book…

Enjoy!

*Linden Carroll.*

# Introduction

Should a horrifying occurrence be witnessed, such as the retrieval of a woman's dead body from the ocean, any number of assumptions could be made and many questions raised.

Who was she? Where did she come from? How did she come to be there? What circumstances had taken her to that shoreline and her ultimate demise?

And the biggest question of all—was her death accidental or…?

If the imagination is powerful enough, a story can evolve.

# Prologue

When the death of a young man's beloved separates them, he dedicates himself to work and a life of loneliness without her.

Jonathan, the young man, has travelled from England to Canada on business as an international antique dealer. He witnesses the rescue of a woman's body from the ocean and as the authorities draw it nearer to the dock, he is struck by the familiarity of the woman. It is only when they place her on the landing stage that he recognizes the tattoo on her shoulder as belonging to his prospective fiancé, Sarah. Shocked and traumatized he flees the gruesome scene unaware of the ensuing suspected homicide investigation or its findings.

Unable to face returning to an England without his loved one, he relocates to Germany and commits to a life of work without his soulmate. A driven man, he throws himself into the project of setting up a new branch for his company in Germany. Work becomes his driving force as he tries to forget, but Sarah is with him always. Unable to let her go, he is persistently tormented by the circumstances of her death and how her body came to be floating off Vancouver, more than 100 miles from Vancouver Island. He knew she was to have visited friends on the Island and had arranged his business schedule in the hopes of a reconciliation with her following their stupid disagreement before he left England. He had planned on asking her to marry him but their difference of opinion had separated them. Filled with remorse, he now realizes the opportunity is lost to him forever.

The passing years see Jonathan still struggling to forget Sarah and overcome the trauma of witnessing her beautiful body being navigated to shore by the authorities. Homesickness and loneliness finally drive him back to England where he learns the shocking truth of the homicide investigation and the twist of fate which changes his chosen path forever.

*Deadly Assumption* is a generational saga of suspected homicide, never-ending love and emotional trauma, the loss of loved ones, and the fight to recapture those closest to the heart. With a root setting in England, the story is rich in history encompassing Canada, Germany and France, spanning the period prior to World War II into the 1980s. The multicultural characters are figments of the author's imagination and evolved around an idea developed following the retrieval of a body from the ocean.

# Part 1

# Chapter 1
# Deadly Reunion

Jonathan stood at the foot of the main street in the town overlooking the inlet. Mesmerized, he watched as they hauled her body closer to the landing stage. Luxurious black hair flowed around her like a sinister cape, contrasting sharply with her stark white body. He reckoned she must have been in the water for about a week, judging by the state of her swollen corpse, not immediately recognizable, albeit still beautiful.

Floating closer to the dock, she was now in range of a small boat purposefully pushing through the waves to meet her, its crew standing at the ready. The craft came to an abrupt stop upon reaching her. Using rakes, they drew her alongside and then moved slowly towards the shoreline. Upon reaching the dock, her body was angled in parallel with the slimy landing stage, where a stretcher was waiting to receive her. A man moved swiftly forward with an assortment of implements at the ready. He was dressed formally, a medical smock partially covering his business suit, and was very obviously from the coroner's office.

Carefully lifting the body from the water, two men placed her on the stretcher, bringing her closer to Jonathan, affording him a better view. There was no mistaking the woman's uncommon features.

*It can't be her!* his mind screamed, recoiling behind that special carapace within him. *It can't be her!*

Aligning her with the stretcher, they poured some kind of solution over her. Jonathan assumed it was to wash away the accumulation of seaweed and grime covering her clothes and body. He was shocked to see how scantily clad she was—so unlike her, in a bikini brief, her sleeveless blouse waterlogged and diaphanous.

"For God's sake, why doesn't somebody cover her?"

He spoke sharply, more to himself than the world at large, but he was angry. He hated her body being exposed to the looky-loos who were beginning to gather as close to the landing as they could possibly get.

"Morbid buggers," he yelled in their direction. He couldn't help himself. Needless to say, his voice was unheeded, so intent were they on getting a better view.

Fortunately, an official moved forward and started urging the crowd back, further away from the gruesome scene, before Jonathan cracked up completely. "Thank God!" he rasped. "And not a minute too soon."

His eyes searched her left shoulder, which had not been readily visible to him until they repositioned her. There it was! The little butterfly tattoo. The sea water had wreaked havoc, flooding her body and distorting the image inked into her skin. Nevertheless, misshapen as it was, the tattoo was still clearly recognizable. He froze. The outline of the butterfly was indelible in his mind. He remembered, very clearly, every detail of the night Sarah had first shown it to him. How proud she had been of her new acquisition.

"Darling, what do you think of it?" she had asked effusively. Thrusting herself sideways, she had slipped off her shawl, exposing her shoulder, her eyes seeking his approval.

As always, not wishing to disappoint her, he had smiled agreeably and bent to kiss her. He'd thought it vandalism to mar the perfection of her otherwise flawless skin, but as time passed, he had become more accepting.

The business-type moved in and bent over the body like the grim reaper. Unable to bear the sight of the gory scene unfolding before his eyes, Jonathan turned and moved away. Grief and regret ate into his very soul as he stumbled up the hill, towards the town centre.

****

He had loved her completely and unwaveringly all these years. Their stupid difference of opinion had been blown out of all proportion, ultimately separating them. Knowing she had made plans to visit the West Coast of Canada, he had arranged his work schedule accordingly, hoping for a reconciliation.

*Obviously too late for that now,* he thought bitterly.

*How the devil had she wound up in the water at the lower end of the town? Her visit to Vancouver was to have taken her to Vancouver Island to visit friends. Had the currents brought her here? Had she fallen into the water further up the coast? Or worse?* He didn't dare think about that possibility. No doubt they would find out in due course. Either way, he was sick to his stomach.

The full impact of events was beginning to take its toll, making his passage up the hill even more arduous. Overhead, a rainstorm threatened, gathering momentum. Suddenly, it burst into a torrential flood and drenched him to the skin, hindering his progress yet further. Gasping by the time he finally arrived at the top of Granville Street, he leaned gratefully against one of the pillars bordering the steps of a building, valiantly trying to catch his breath. His lungs felt like they were about to collapse.

****

Jonathan and his partner, Mark, ran a very profitable art gallery in London, England, along with an equally profitable antique business. Both operations dealt with high-end merchandise, catering to the needs of the crème de la crème of clients, with the money to match.

The schedule for Jonathan's business in Canada had worked out perfectly, allowing him time to seek out Sarah upon its conclusion. He had travelled to Vancouver to bid upon certain Inuit artefacts which, should he be successful, would be shipped back to England and displayed at a large exhibition set up in the partners' store.

Both partners had a keen interest in acquiring Inuit art, which had gained popularity in Europe since the end of the war. The opening up of the North, and the subsequent disappearance of the whales, had made whalebone carvings scarce, although the use of soapstone as an alternative was making an appearance, affording the Inuit a much better economy. Their art was of a more commercial nature, better suited to meet the needs of their local market.

Several pieces in particular were on the partners' radar. They were to be exhibited for sale at one of Vancouver's oldest and most established auction houses. Founded in the early 1900s in Victoria, on Vancouver Island, the house had subsequently relocated to Vancouver and was the largest of its kind in Canada, specializing in Northwest Coast native and Inuit art.

Prior to the actual auction, Jonathan had some time to kill and visited the venue to preview the items coming up for bid. The auction house had a fine display of indigenous artefacts, and he was soon completely engrossed in the art. Having studied the five evolutionary periods of Inuit culture—Pre-Dorset, Dorset, Thule, Historic, and Contemporary—Jonathan had an intimate knowledge of the exhibits.

Dorset was a more male-dominated art related to weapons and tools, as opposed to Thule, which depicted female forms with their personal effects, such as combs, crafts, and jeweller. The arrival of the white man in the Arctic, along with much colder weather and the loss of the whales, had spelled the demise of Thule art and culture.

Although Jonathan's focus was specifically on soapstone carvings which would show well and be an easy sell, he was also interested in the few very rare female figurines on display from the Thule period. These miniatures were exquisitely decorated, making up for the typical lack of facial features. Depicting swimmers, they showed only the upper parts of their forms. They were delicately fashioned and in later years became the forerunners of gaming pieces.

While business surrounding the auction kept Jonathan on the run, the next few days were a nightmare from hell, with Sarah creeping into his every thought and move. The day of the auction finally arrived, only to find him struggling to get out of bed. He was exhausted—at his lowest ebb ever. But he could not and would not let his partner down, so as always, he forced his mind to concentrate on work. Struggling laboriously to the bathroom and finally getting under the shower, he felt the cascading water warm his bones and revive him. He began mental preparations for the day's business.

\*\*\*\*

The auction was about to commence, and following a last careful scrutiny of the exhibits, Jonathan settled himself down in his seat. He had thought he might have some difficulty concentrating, but he needn't have worried. A lifetime of discipline and training, plus an almost obsessive love of art, soon had him fully ensnared. As always, the excitement took over, and as bidding ensued, he was successful in adding to the collection he and Mark were planning to exhibit in London.

After settling up with the cashier and organizing his shipping details, Jonathan wandered into a cozy bar adjacent to the auction house and ordered himself a stiff Scotch. He was relaxed and contemplative prior to phoning Mark. The whisky calmed and warmed him as he set his plans in place. He would talk to Mark in a few minutes, he decided.

His few minutes stretched to half an hour; looking at his watch, he picked up the phone.

"Hi Mark, Jonathan here; good news and bad, I'm afraid."

Mark was thrilled to hear about the purchases and inevitably gushed about their display layout for the marketing drive, and the presentation they were planning. Finally, after a seemingly endless spell, he paused for breath.

"Jon, you're very quiet. You mentioned bad news. What's up, old chap?"

He was horrified to learn of the previous day's events, and Jonathan thanked the powers that be that he'd ordered a second drink, as he was about to fall apart again.

"I'm going to have to take a bit of a break, Mark. Thought I'd look up some friends in Germany. I need to get myself together. I don't want to return to London for a while. I can work on a plan for our marketing drive and presentation while I'm away. It'll take some weeks to organize anyway, and I can easily pop back to the UK in a few weeks if necessary."

"You take all the time you need, and we'll just stay in touch regularly. If you don't feel able to get patched into the conference call the day after tomorrow, I completely understand. I know I'm putting you over a barrel by even mentioning the call, but I need to cancel it if you can't take part. I'll have to think about another line of action. The stakes are too high, as you know, and it means huge money in the coffers if we pull off the deal. It could pave the way to us expanding our business into Germany. This would definitely be the time to think seriously about the expansion, and I stress this," he added emphatically, "timing is crucial. That being said, even though your input is really needed, I'll make arrangements to meet with the sellers privately if you're not up to it."

Mark was aware of the guilt trip he was laying on his partner; but not only was the deal important—it was doubly important to keep his friend fully occupied at this awful time. Having known the workaholic Jonathan for a good many years, Mark was fully aware of the importance of keeping him gainfully employed. He also knew how deeply his friend had felt about Sarah. The only way to handle his diabolical situation was work and then some.

*Damnation,* Jonathan thought. He had completely forgotten about the call. *Oh yes, here he goes again, all business as usual.*

He was immediately remorseful, and making a supreme effort to shelve his negativity, gave himself a firm dressing down. *Better get more positive, Jonathan lad. You still have a living to earn—and you be thankful for it.*

Mark had been his friend and partner for many years, and Jonathan knew in his heart that he was concerned for his well-being and wanted to keep him on track. They had a business to run—a business very much in the fast lane, thanks to Mark's aggressive response to matters at hand.

"Don't worry about the call. I'm up to it, just need a change of pace for a while. I'll patch everyone into the conference while I'm here in Vancouver for the next few days before going on to Germany. I'll be in touch with the details as soon as I schedule the call. Thanks very much for bearing with me, Mark, and for your understanding. I really appreciate it."

"Good lad; knew you wouldn't let the side down. Just give me a buzz when you're ready, and let me know how you're making out."

Jonathan had been working non-stop for months on the deals he'd just concluded and definitely needed some time to work things out and see what direction he should take to get on with his life. He had no qualms about taking the time off, and as he would be sorting out the marketing for their presentation, it would work well for the business and his personal needs. This was definitely the time to take a much-needed break and regroup. That being said, there was no way he would ever let his friend and business partner down. He'd make that conference call if it killed him.

He ordered a third drink—unusual for him, but if ever a time required it, this was the time. He sat back again and contemplated his abysmal future without Sarah, wondering how he would ever be able to pick up the threads again in England.

Straightening in his chair, the solution suddenly dawned on him as his thoughts cleared.

*Of course, the conference call, that's the answer. If I pull it off, we'll be well positioned to expand into Germany, as Mark said, and I can base myself there. Definitely this is the best option for me at this rotten* time, because I sure as hell can't go back to living in England for a while.

*Actually, it's so transparent. Don't know why I didn't catch on before. Of course, that's what Mark was alluding to when he went on about our expansion into Germany. Probably thought I could scout out possibilities while I'm there—obviously had that card up his sleeve all along, just waiting for the right time to play it.*

By the time he'd finished his drink, Jonathan felt somewhat more optimistic and a little sheepish that he had doubted his friend's intentions. Plans began to percolate in his head.

\*\*\*\*

Jonathan was staying at the Hotel Vancouver on Burrard Street. Built in 1939, its traditional elegance rendered it the most beautiful of all the city's hotels, in his opinion. It was his favourite place to stay when he was in Vancouver. The actual opening of the hotel's doors had not occurred until more than ten years after construction began, when King George VI and Queen Elizabeth visited.

Being completely immersed in the world of antiques and history, he revelled in the hotel's old-world charm, solidity, and luxurious comfort. It was an excellent place for him to stay while he set up the conference call. His suite was well equipped for business, with two rooms and an adjoining bathroom off the main. A beautiful mahogany desk sat in an alcove in the sitting room, accompanied by a chair of rich burgundy leather upholstery, buttoned in the traditional way. Absolutely perfect for his needs.

Throwing his coat over a chair immediately upon arriving in the suite, Jonathan went straight to the phone and booked a flight, departing five days hence.

\*\*\*\*

Reluctantly leaving the hotel's quiet ambience, the day following the conference call, he was soon on a plane headed for Germany. Business had taken him there many times over the years, and the country was completely familiar to him. It would be an ideal opportunity to hide out and rejuvenate. When he felt more like it, he would look up his friends, in particular Helmut and Gertrude. But in the meantime, reclining his seat, he closed his eyes.

*If only I could just sleep, wake up, and find it was all a bad dream.* His mind was besieged with the questions he had been asking himself over and over again.

*How did my sweet Sarah end up in the water like that? It is just too horrible to contemplate. Where did she come from? Was it Vancouver Island? Had she been onboard Luke's cruiser?*

He had heard that Luke was headed to Canada soon to put a new boat through its paces. Trials were to be carried out between Vancouver and Vancouver Island. Jonathan had always distanced himself from the playboy, even though their paths had crossed quite frequently when mingling with the moneyed crowd. He always had the feeling Luke could be ruthless and would stop at nothing to get what he wanted. Luke had been known to have a fetish for Sarah for some time. Although never encouraged, he had still persisted.

*If Sarah was aboard with Luke, did she fall overboard or what?*

The 'what' plagued him.

\*\*\*\*

Jonathan was aware that Jordan, Luke's friend and business partner, ran boating trips from Vancouver to Vancouver Island. He had met both of them at a marketing function some time previously in London. Jordan had been visiting from Canada, and a fellow called Doug was there. Apparently, he was attached to the UK company and worked closely with Luke. They had been quite forthcoming about their business.

Jordan handled excursions up and down the West Coast of Canada, calling in at local ports. Some of the longer trips included night stops and took in Vancouver Island and the surrounding Gulf Islands. It seemed to be a thriving concern all round and was long established in Vancouver's boating community. The steady local clientele, plus innumerable visitors to Vancouver, made the arrangement very profitable. Luke had invested considerable funds into the Canadian side of their business and acted as a silent partner, while Jordan, holding the majority of the shares, ran the company.

Luke apparently would take leave from the London-based business, leaving Doug to handle the day-to-day running of the UK office. He would travel to Vancouver to work with Jordan when he needed a change of pace and to update himself on the business and any emerging issues.

\*\*\*\*

Jonathan dragged himself away from his musings and turned his attention to the present.

Sarah was gone, and he would just have to accept this. It was a bit late in the day to analyse events. She was never coming back, and at that moment he felt as if his whole world had disintegrated. All the plans they had made seemed like figments of his imagination. His thoughts filled with the usual questions people ask when they have suffered the loss of a loved one, particularly if the passing was in bad circumstances.

*Why her? She never hurt a living creature. She was goodness personified.*

He was too sick at heart to even contemplate starting any major investigation. Plenty of time for that once he had got his mind around the whole wretched business. Nevertheless, the same armies of questions marched through his brain.

Brightening momentarily, he thought about the conference call in Vancouver. What a resounding success it had been, and when he'd phoned Mark later, both had been hot to trot to throw some ideas around regarding their new foray into a business in the Rhineland. They were both in agreement that Jonathan would head there from Vancouver and take a much-needed rest.

Nevertheless, while he was there, he would carry out a complete reconnaissance of the area, with a view to either renting or buying premises suitable for their needs.

Sleep eluded him, and when the stewardess asked whether he wanted refreshments, Jonathan ordered a drink and some salted nuts but had no appetite for a meal—perhaps later, when they were further into the flight and his stomach had settled. As he closed his eyes again, her presence once more invaded his senses.

Maybe in years to come, the sharpness of her memory would be softened and blended, as with clouds slowly dissipating throughout the universe. His soul yearned to be with her on one of those clouds, merging as one into eternity, her exquisite image before him forever.

## Chapter 2
## Rose and Stewart

The year was 1941. Rose sat in the bar at the end of the dance hall. Times were about as bad as they could be. The Prime Minister's ultimatum in 1939 to Hitler that Britain would intervene if he didn't cease Germany's invasion of Poland had been ignored, and a state of war had been declared.

Hitler, furious and frustrated by the superiority of the British Royal Air Force, had unleashed a vengeance of enormous magnitude and vowed to annihilate Britain irrevocably with a series of raids, beginning in London. An attack raged over the city, relentlessly killing and injuring civilians. Fighter command regrouped and launched retaliatory attacks. The citizens were not to know at the time that the mayhem would last over eight months and all the major cities in England would be targeted, resulting in over 40,000 dead and injured. This vicious series of attacks devastated the country and would forever be referred to as the Blitz.

Rose shuddered when she thought of the huge loss of life and devastation since the beginning of the war. She had made a special effort with her appearance that night and wanted to look as appealing as she could for the servicemen, who were arriving in droves. The place was packed wall to wall. It was essential that she look her best for them and put on a good show.

Appraising the gathering of the troops, she felt her heart fill with sadness, knowing that many would be shipped out in the morning, and almost certainly only a handful would return to their homes and loved ones. Her discerning gaze fell once again upon the young RAF pilot.

She had seen him once before during a previous performance. How proudly he wore his wings on the shoulder of his leather bomber jacket. Such a good-looking young man. Their eyes had met several times during the half-hour she allowed herself before going on stage. There was no denying the enormous attraction each had for the other. Finishing her soda, she made her way backstage, but not without one last glance over her shoulder. His eyes had not left her—those piercing blue eyes boring into her very soul, as if he were loath to lose sight of her for even a second. Smiling, she turned and floated down the stairs leading to the back of the stage.

\*\*\*\*

Rose's dressing room was a special place for her, a sanctuary where she could have a few minutes away from the exhausting business of performing—a place to regroup and prepare to be her best for her audience. Smiling, she set a slide in place in her hair and cast a final look at her reflection in the mirror; she was pleased with her appearance. Her dress was a pencil-shaped kaleidoscope of varying shades of pink, embossed with a scattering of sequins dancing across the bodice. Although fairly plain, the effect was stunning.

Fabric in the 1940s was scarce, and slinky designs portrayed that fact. Man's ingenuity and designers' forethought and talent to improvise in keeping with the times had initiated tubular dresses, which were becoming extremely popular. Outfits which lacked fabric were more than compensated by an abundance of glitter, usually achieved by excessive jewellery, beads, bangles, brooches, anything that sparkled.

Rose's only jewellery, however, was a simple band in her hair and a single rose brooch, set with rubies and seed pearls, adorning her right shoulder. The brooch had been passed down from her grandmother and was one of the few remaining items of value from her parents' estate. She had always hoped to have a pair of earrings made specially to match the brooch, but these were still on her wish list. Satin strapped shoes with a small cluster of embroidered roses and wedge heels completed her ensemble.

Her tresses of platinum hair were elaborately waved, and Rose held them with the slide and a small glittering headband. Her features were classically beautiful, delicate with a finely chiselled chin and nose. With only a touch of shadow to emphasize the depth of her vivid, violet eyes, and a dash of lip colour, her natural beauty was outstanding. The one item of decadence she allowed herself was a natural beauty spot—a mole on the rise of her cheek bone, which she darkened slightly, as beauty spots were coming back into style.

Stepping out onto the stage once more, she noticed that he was still there, riveted to his original position, his gaze just as intense. She lost her stride momentarily and almost missed her timing but in a trice had deftly repositioned herself. Again, they were drawn to each other for a brief moment reserved just for them. Pulling herself together, she moved gracefully towards the piano, smiled at the pianist, and broke into song. The lyrics were all the old wartime favourites, bringing tears to the eyes of many in the audience who remembered a time that was better, when their loved ones were with them, before war had taken them so mercilessly and without remorse.

The applause was deafening as Rose went through her repertoire of songs, also taking requests. Suddenly, a deep voice echoed across the room: "How about 'We'll Meet Again,' love?"

Rose knew the lyrics by heart. It truly was a beautiful wartime song, originally recorded by Vera Lynn following British Prime Minister Neville Chamberlain's formal declaration of war on 3 September 1939. The famous singer had devoted much of her time singing to the troops, boosting morale before they shipped out. Rose also knew where the voice came from, even though she had never before heard her handsome young pilot speak. How could she refuse his request? The song was one of her favourites also. She had sung it often and poured her whole heart into it on every occasion. This night she would do it especially for him.

As soon as she began her rendition, the young man bowed his head, his emotions getting the better of him. Totally lost, he surrendered himself completely to the beautiful words of hope and promise. When Rose delivered her final closing, he raised his eyes and blew her a kiss, which she felt as strongly as if it had actually brushed her lips. She returned the affection, seducing him outrageously as she left the stage.

Having cleansed her face and tidied her hair, Rose made her way back up the stairs to the dance hall and warmed to see that he was waiting patiently for her to emerge. Her smile was radiant as she moved eagerly towards him. Taking her hand gently, he raised it to his lips and then led her firmly to a table.

How precious was that evening, magical, in fact—as was every minute of their time together, even though their conversation centred on the war. Rose was in awe when he told her he had been part of the biggest dog fight of 1940, between the RAF and the Luftwaffe over the Thames Estuary at the beginning of the Blitz. She was flabbergasted that he had actually survived, when so many had lost their lives. They had all been such young men, still boys, really, sent to war before they had even completed their full education. They were never given a chance to live their lives.

The beginning of 1941 also saw Fighter Command attempting to control air space over France, and Stewart was part of those operations. He declined to go into detail, underplaying his part in the war effort. Nevertheless, she sensed his pride in being part of the RAF.

They were lost to each other, oblivious to the noise of the crowded room, when suddenly all hell broke loose as the sirens sounded. Grabbing her and holding her close, he whispered in her ear, "We'll meet again," and then he was gone.

Rose was devastated, knowing that for a pilot, the odds of him coming back were slim, let alone them ever meeting again. Their paths had crossed in a charmed moment, purely by chance—she likened it to a spin of the roulette wheel, won in a moment and lost in a heartbeat.

****

Stewart did come back to her, though, and that was the beginning of a love affair which neither wanted to end. The weeks following his return were a merry-go-round of snatched time between his missions, every reunion becoming more intense, each of them living every stolen moment, dying every time they parted.

Rose had been staying at the famed London Windmill Club, where she was entertaining the troops. All the girls were holed up in rough sleeping accommodation, bedding down in the same bunks, living on the job and working horrendous hours. One night, whilst standing in her usual place again by the piano as Arnie, the pianist, ran his fingers up and down the keys to warm up before performing, Rose was despondent. The war was ever-worsening, as was her depression. She was beginning to lose hope—unusual for her, because she always tried to be positive.

A movement by the entrance door caught her eye. Raising her head, she saw him, and her heart clenched. Their eyes met, and there was the crooked smile that she loved so much. How tired and worn he looked, and oh, how much weight he had lost, but mercifully he had been returned to her once again.

In spite of loving her work, getting through her performance that night was the hardest and longest time Rose had ever experienced. But once finished, while acknowledging her audience with smiles and waves, she made her way quickly to his table. Following a socially decent interval, they left the club, and she was in his arms again, in the room that Stewart had rented in a small hotel down the street. The roulette wheel spun in her favour at that moment, as she sent up a silent prayer of thanks.

That night, Rose couldn't help but notice that he held her extra firmly and seemed preoccupied.

"Ok, let's have it. Spit it out. No point in torturing both of us," she said as the tension ripped through her.

"Didn't want to ruin the evening, but I only have a couple of days, and we need to make the most of them. I'm going on a mission and not sure how this one will turn out—got to be realistic."

Rose knew it must be very serious because he'd always been so optimistic, but there was no mistaking the utter resignation in his voice.

"Let's make the next two days really count. Rose, will you marry me? You know I adore you. Let's tie the knot. It will give us strength to hang on and something to look forward to when I come back and," looking at her very seriously, "you'll be well taken care of financially if things get balled up."

Struggling to get her breath, she threw her arms around his neck and held onto him for grim death.

"But things aren't going to get balled up, are they? You're coming back to me, and I want you to promise me that." She was striving, without much success, to keep the desperation out of her voice. "You know that once you make a promise, you have to abide by it."

"I promise you, my love, I'll do my best."

"Yes, of course I'll marry you. I'm crazy about you. Don't you know that, my darling?"

Stewart kissed her tenderly.

"You've made my life perfect—well, almost," he added, and both convulsed in laughter, as his words seemed so ludicrous in view of the times they were living in, and the bedlam of sirens going off everywhere around them.

Stewart closed the heavy brocade curtains. The storm raged outside, but a velvet night embraced them in warmth and love, and they were safe within.

Dawn slowly broke, and as they roused themselves, Stewart announced that he was off to get a special license for them to be married.

It was a quiet but rushed ceremony, as was common during those times, but they didn't care. They were joined irrevocably. Stewart had presented Rose with a single silk flower, a rose, which she clasped tightly to her bosom throughout the ceremony, wondering where on earth he had found it. And for a couple of joyous days and nights, past and present merged, and their future was their present.

****

In 1942, the war was as intense as ever, with seemingly no end in sight. Their first-borne, Jane, was sound asleep, having kept her mother up most of the night. Rose was sleep-deprived and, having finished her porridge and tea, was contemplating the apparently hopeless situation of the world at large, and the foolish ignorance of man. Why couldn't the emphasis be on love instead of wanton killing in the quest for personal power? Her appetite had been poor, and she had not felt well for some weeks. She had refused the indulgence of allowing herself to fall victim to her body's whims; nevertheless, she knew she was pregnant with her second child.

A knock at the door brought her abruptly to the present. The day she had dreaded, along with all the other war wives, had arrived. The courier handed her an official envelope and offered a sympathetic smile. Her husband's plane had been shot down over Dieppe, France. The RAF mission had been to protect shipping against attacks by the Luftwaffe. It was a mission of devastating loss, both human and aircraft.

By some miracle, Stewart made it back across the channel to British shores, only to crash in a field outside Newhaven, Sussex. Local farm workers had raced to his aid minutes before his plane burst into flames. The fire reached enormous proportions, with flames licking their way around the cockpit. The men risked their own lives as they dragged him clear minutes before the plane gave itself up to the fire. Stewart was severely injured and unconscious by the time they cut him out. He was immediately transported to the Queen Victoria Hospital; its special burns unit had been developed for the war's aircraft casualties and even incorporated a social club and support group for the many men and their families.

Would she go immediately?

Sitting for a moment to collect herself after the courier had left, she was alerted by another knock at the door. Getting no response, her neighbour Daphne poked her head around. They were the best of friends and, being war brides, had become very close—always there for each other. Fearing the worst as soon as she saw Rose's face, Daphne rushed to comfort her distraught friend. As she listened to the story, she was overcome with sorrow, followed by sheer relief upon hearing that Stewart was still alive—only barely, but nevertheless alive.

"There, there, lovey, you go and have a nice bath. I'll take care of the babe, and you go to him right away. Don't worry about a thing. I'll handle it."

Later on, in the train speeding towards her beloved husband, Rose thanked her lucky stars for a friend such as dear, sweet Daphne, who had never let her down; it felt like they had been friends forever.

Rose never ceased to be amazed at how the best of human nature had come out in these war-ridden times. Everyone pulled together, showing phenomenal qualities of personal strength, comradery, and compassion for their neighbours. Although Daphne was naturally good and always had been, war or no war. She was a true angel in disguise.

****

Dr Saunders met Rose at the hospital ward. Waving her over to his office, he spoke kindly and with compassion.

"Mrs. Buchanan, please take a seat."

Clasping her hands together tightly, Rose braced herself.

"Your husband is very lucky to be alive. The bad news is," he continued sombrely, "his legs are badly burned, with severe muscle loss, and we may have to amputate. We might be able to save his left, but the right one is too far gone. It's highly unlikely we can save it."

Rose sat silently chewing on her lip while he continued speaking.

"Either way, he's going to need months of rehabilitation. Even if by some miracle we save both of his legs, it's doubtful he'll walk again.

I'm so sorry, my dear; don't know any other way to tell you except the way it is. No sense in glossing this over. He's in bad shape. How he survived I can't imagine."

"Please, I must see him. Which room is he in? Can I see him now?"

"Of course you can. He's still in shock, but he needs you now more than ever before. He's in room 210, just up the hall, on the left."

After the doctor had gone, Rose found herself outside of room 210 and took a few moments to get herself in tow and regain her composure. It was essential she put on a cheery front to greet her husband.

****

His face was as white as the pillow he rested upon, strained and hardly recognizable, with multiple cuts and abrasions. He opened his eyes at the sound of her coming in. There it was—that crooked smile, so familiar and so very endearing. Thank God he had not lost that.

After the hugging and the crying, he pulled away, making a supreme effort to hang onto the last shred of vitality he could muster.

"Now, Rose, I'm putting it straight out there. I'm not having any of my legs taken off, and regardless of what they've been alluding to, I'm walking out of here."

He was still sharp in spite of being so ill and drugged to the hilt.

"Let's not talk about it now, sweetheart. But you may have to accept what the doctors say. Let's just wait and see. I'll be with you to help in every way. You know that and I'll love you forever, regardless of how this pans out. I'll take you any way I can get you. We'll get through this together. Now go to sleep. I'll be here when you wake up. Daphne is looking after Jane. What a lovely person she is…"

Off she went again. She was rambling, but she needn't have worried. Stewart had slipped into unconsciousness again, his features relaxed, seemingly at peace for a while. The drugs the nurse had administered were potent and certainly taking effect.

Because of the huge loss of seasoned pilots, the process at that time was to patch up those remaining when they were injured or had been shot down and send them back into battle. The only ghastly glimmer of hope, she thought, was that because her husband's condition was so very serious, he obviously wouldn't be sent back to the hell hole of killing.

They had put a cot in the room so that she could stay with him. There was a mini bathroom adjacent, so she was all set for the long haul. And what a long haul it was.

****

The months that followed were hard to endure for both of them, with Rose going back and forth between baby Jane and the hospital. The unfailingly loyal Daphne brought tears to Rose's eyes whenever she thought about her, with her unselfish kindness and compassion, and how she doted on the infant.

They had managed to save both of Stewart's legs from amputation, but the right one was badly smashed. There was no question of him ever flying again. It had been suggested that partial amputation might be considered; at least he could be fitted with a prosthetic, which would possibly enable him to walk with aid. Stewart steadfastly refused, and on the last occasion the suggestion was put forward by the doctor, he fell into a blind rage.

"Don't bring this up again. As far as I'm concerned, it's not an option. Now please leave, and close the door behind you."

The doctor did as he was told, casting a sympathetic grimace at Rose as he left. Rose simply sat quietly but held her hands together so tightly that the whites of her knuckles were clearly visible. Stewart turned his face to the pillow. Rose had grown inured to his recurring depressions, but just as suddenly, he spun and clung to her as if he were drowning. His arm fell on her expanded midriff, and he became very still.

"My God, Rose, you're not! You can't be. Are you?"

"Yes, I am, five months or so. Didn't want to bother you, as it seems you have a lot on your mind."

And they laughed together so uproariously as to raise practically the entire ward's medical personnel.

"Well, that does it. No more feeling sorry for myself. I'm definitely walking out of here."

Stewart could be very stubborn when he wanted, and Rose thought that anticipating another child might just be the turning of the tide for him.

****

The next period in Rose's life was a lesson of pure endurance, as was her husband's. It was a constant struggle, but he was determined to be a complete man to her, with all his faculties.

*Such a male thing,* she thought. She loved him for what he was, his spirit and soul. The rest was just an added bonus. Nevertheless, Stewart forged on. He was determined to keep both legs, regardless of what they said. And he worked, oh, how he worked with the physiotherapists.

"Pig-headed bugger, aren't you? Talk about staying power." His favourite therapist was always getting him going. "Good on you, mate."

Everybody was in awe at the sheer tenacity of the man.

The weeks thereafter were a torment for both of them. Rose had to reduce her trips to see Stewart because of baby Jane's needs and the expected child. Stewart plugged on alone, in and out of depression but fighting every inch of the way, motivated in no small part by the pending birth of his second child. Reconstructive surgery was performed on both of his legs, with the right one needing the most detailed and complicated work due to the severe muscle loss.

One day, Rose visited and was overjoyed to see him up standing with an arm on each railing of his training equipment. Her emotions were overwhelming, and scalding tears blinded her momentarily as she fought to control the violent attack of the shakes overtaking her. Finally, her brave soldier had won the battle, and there was the crooked grin and thumbs up sign to welcome her. The rest was history.

He was as good as his word. One battle-worn and stormy day, they staggered out of there, him hanging onto the handles of his chair, her in the last stages of pregnancy, and sirens going off everywhere, scaring the bejabbers out of the pair of them.

Baby Sarah was born, but the war continued. Rose and Stewart, filled with the joy of their second child, each thanked God for the umpteenth time that she was able to look into the eyes of her adoring father.

# Chapter 3
# Sarah

Sarah walked slowly down the avenue of trees, which cut through magnificent lawns. Meticulously manicured, the lawns were bordered with perennials, intermingled with brightly coloured impatiens in shady nooks. Huge lace-cap hydrangeas, rhododendrons, and giant molle azaleas formed a backdrop in the slightly sunnier areas of the gardens. Sarah was still heady from her amble through the rose gardens earlier. The glorious peace rose, with its delicate perfume, still occupied her senses, in direct contrast to the heavy scent unmasked by the honeysuckle azalea earlier in the year when she had visited.

The peace rose had always held a special place in her heart, so much so that she had planted one on the patio shortly after moving into her townhouse. The rose was complemented royally by the traditional stonework. Sitting in the place of honour, it was admired by every visitor, as was her home, which was a unique residence. Forming part of a three-unit complex within a Victorian mansion, it was situated in close proximity to the beautiful Regents Park. The designer had done a fabulous job of retaining and enhancing the original features of the property while updating the interior with stellar fixtures and fittings. The mansion was one of many Victorian properties in the area that, following the war, had been updated and the units within them were in very high demand, boasting huge and still-rising prices.

Sarah sat herself down on one of the many benches dispersed throughout the grounds, each cleverly placed to capture the best aspects of the gardens. She was determined that nothing would disturb her equanimity, but today, even the serenity of the gardens failed to embrace in their usual way. The day was ostensibly perfect, warm and balmy, but unable to allay her sadness and depression. She felt wretched. Her elder sister, Jane, had once again been admitted into a rehabilitation centre, having fallen into the hopeless pit of despair through substance abuse.

*What a waste,* Sarah thought. *My beautiful, vibrant sister, succumbing yet again to her needs because she's totally incapable of dealing with day-to-day living. Such a brilliant actress and model when she applies herself to the assignment at hand, but oh how she hates routine of any kind. She has not a shred of discipline to stay with anything for any length of time. Jane's coquettish ways are also bringing a multitude of other problems, and her involvement with her numerous suitors is positively disgusting. Coming in varying ages, shapes, and sizes, they all bring with them the same ridiculous notion that they are the chosen one and will possess her forever.*

Sarah was shocked at her own cynicism, but everybody was fed up with Jane's goings-on.

Jane had shown signs of mental disturbance in their junior school years, even to the point of hearing voices and thinking everyone was against her. Her parents had always made allowances for her behaviour. Eventually, when Jane began exhibiting severe signs of paranoia and grossly obsessive-compulsive behaviour, even Rose and Stewart could no longer ignore it and had finally sought medical help for their daughter.

Jane was officially diagnosed as a paranoid schizophrenic and treated with a variety of prescription medications over the years, all of which seemed to lose their potency. As time passed, her condition rocketed and mental issues escalated, becoming increasingly painful to everybody around her, but not for herself, as she seemed to be on a permanent high. There were times when her erratic conversations were impossible to keep up with, let alone understand. They were always a sure indication of trouble to follow. When her high mood spiked, she would inevitably burn out, and the heavens would close down on her with a vengeance, leaving her helpless, whinging and whining like a small child who had just lost her favourite toy.

Sarah would always try to be there for her sister and on those terrible occasions was invariably reminded of Shakespeare's graphic description of *The Seven Ages of Man,* particularly the initial stage:

*At first the infant, mewling and puking in the nurse's arms.*

And then the final stages:

*Turning again toward childish treble, pipes and whistles in his sound.*

But her sister was an infant no more, she reasoned, her thoughts wrestling to make some sense out of it all. *She's my sister, a grown woman. How can this be happening?* Nevertheless, she would hold her sibling to her and wait patiently for her to return to a reasonable state of balance.

****

The two sisters were very similar in appearance, although Jane's build was slightly heavier, and she had their mother's fair hair, with lighter eyes. Sarah, on the other hand, had a dark, sultry complexion like her father, whose heritage was Spanish. His predecessors had migrated to Britain in the 1500s, intermarried, and settled in Scotland where they had remained for centuries, in later years becoming wealthy landowners. The migrants had also landed on Irish shores. Stewart resembled many Irish with his black hair and blue eyes, instead of the red hair and freckles usually associated with the Scots.

The girls had lacked for nothing as they grew up. Their parents were well placed and spared no effort in trying to help Jane through her numerous crises. Her father had become weary of the whole situation, which was driving a wedge between him and their mother, who could not and would not let go of her daughter. Their love for Jane was obvious, but not enough to dissolve her belief that Sarah was the favourite and she was forever second in line.

Whenever Jane became physically and verbally abusive, driven by jealousy towards her sister, she was admitted for further treatment and a tweaking of medications. The same destructive pattern would always develop, as Jane's hatred for Sarah surfaced more and more frequently. Finally, in desperation, their parents had parted them and educated them in separate schools. Needless to say, Sarah excelled, and without her support, Jane fell by the wayside, playing the recalcitrant truant and getting into a variety of troubles. In recent years, her criminal activities and associates had become 'big league'.

Sarah had always lacked confidence, considering Jane to be the great socialite whose magnetic vitality drew people to her. When things were right in Jane's world, she shone like the brightest star, then dropped so low in between.

Jane was a gifted actress, but this talent was not enough to save her from rapidly earning a reputation as a bad risk in the business, because of her unpredictability and persistent inability to show up consistently at rehearsals or meetings. Her life centred around associating with artificial and affected extremists in the arty set. All those she referred to as her friends had long since lost touch with reality, living merely for the diminishing accolades their audiences had, in bygone days, lavished upon them.

Jane had always grabbed what she wanted. Sarah envied her sister's temerity. Quite the opposite, Sarah was a plodder, much more reserved, the 'smart' one of the two. Her pursuits centred on further education. Over the years, she became quite an authority and was considered an expert in her chosen field of antiquities.

\*\*\*\*

The family still retained a vacation home in Scotland, with a scaled-down wool business, and Sarah's thoughts turned there momentarily, as they always did in times of stress. Years before, the property had been a prosperous sheep farm, until that industry had been virtually closed down. While some of the acreage had been sold off, the property remained a family home for vacationing and included an adjacent small but exclusive wool and tourist business, offering bed and breakfast, riding, and educational tours of the sheep farm and woollen industry.

Sarah missed Mrs. Hobbs, the long-widowed caretaker who lived on-site. Elspeth, as she preferred to be called, maintained the main house with a few staff to assist her in handling the tourist side of the business. These visitors were accommodated on the north side of the house, overlooking the moors.

Tom, the manager, ran the farm, along with his five border collies. They were inseparable and indispensable. The property could not be run without them. Sarah also missed Tom and his clan with all her heart.

Her family home was a wonderful place, holding a plethora of childhood memories and recollections of great family get-togethers. At this moment, she felt the need to return, a need so strong she could smell the sweet, woody perfume of the heath and moors. Her eyes closed against the burning rush of tears as she pictured the rolling, wild landscape with its dark patches of bogs, their acrid odour filling her nostrils, just as if she were actually there.

Giving herself a shake and changing her position, she calculated how long it had been since she'd been home. *It's unbelievable that time has gone so fast. I've been away from home for so long. I'm going to have to force myself to take a break from this ridiculously hectic routine I've made for myself, and get back up there as soon as I can,* she resolved.

The hammering of woodpeckers in a neighbouring tree broke Sarah's train of thought, dragging her back to the present. Suddenly, they appeared, a male and a female. They were known as green woodpeckers, although brilliantly adorned in both green and yellow. Each sported lusty moustaches, the male distinguished by the red splotch in the middle of his. Sarah was familiar with these birds, having read up on them after seeing one on a visit to the Isle of Wight a few months previously. She'd learned that the birds were introduced in the early 1900s, never having been native to the island. It was generally thought they may have had an aversion to crossing water, accounting for their previous absence.

Once again, the problems and issues at hand returned with a mind-numbing vengeance. It was really strange that her sister exhibited such hatred towards her, and yet, when having a bad spell, she would scream bloody murder relentlessly for her sibling. She'd keep it up until Sarah was sent for by the medical staff to calm her.

"How could this trick of fate happen to sisters? One so dynamic but completely mixed up and the other staid to the point of boring."

Sarah realized she was talking to herself, a habit she'd acquired in recent months as she became more stressed out because of the deteriorating family situation. Hurrying to her feet, she started walking again until she reached the regal willow, her favourite tree.

Casting a wary eye around in case she was being watched, she sat herself down on one of the benches under the boughs of the magnificent tree. She'd become aware over the past weeks that she was being followed. Her father had insisted on hiring security for her. He worried constantly about Sarah's safety, in view of her sister's lurid activities and her association with drug dealers and other undesirable elements of the human species. Sarah had more than once been accosted by dealers demanding money, who had mistaken her for her wayward sibling, particularly when her hair had been concealed under a scarf.

Sarah fidgeted on the bench, trying to get more comfortable while agonizing over the family predicament. Her only confidantes were a couple of blue jays who had joined the scene and were listening attentively to her mumblings.

"Oh, I'm at my wits end with all this. Mum and Dad so alienated that Dad's now virtually living in his Ex-Servicemen's Club, and Mum's buried herself in her old profession. How on earth did the family get to this state?"

Her audience danced up and down in agitation on one of the tree's lower branches. Sarah couldn't decide whether they were looking for food or picking up on her deteriorating mood.

Closing her eyes, she recalled Jane's last stage appearance. How magnificent her performance had been. How she had captivated her audience, urging them into her world of make-believe. The roaring applause could have brought the roof down. Jane's whole life was fantasy. She was unable to find a balance.

Their mother Rose had also been on the stage. She too had enormous talent. Her exquisite features and pure, sweet voice had been well known. Her craft had been her world until she married Stewart, who became the love of her life. Theirs had been a fairy-tale romance, as were many during wartime.

Rose had begun her career in the London pubs and clubs. Sarah had been told by her mother that she and Stewart had met when she was performing at the famous Windmill Club. Formerly a poor business venture as a theatre, it had risen to fame when its Windmill Girls were included with their very own and very original show. And 'show' was the operative word, their nudity breaking all the rules of morality then in place. The Windmill and its show continued throughout WWII, in spite of the mayhem surrounding them. The club boasted they were never closed—or never clothed, to the raunchier set. Rose, of course, was a singer in her own right and had always appeared fully and beautifully attired, with a charm and grace which were hers alone.

The two blue jays screeched suddenly on the nearby bough, voicing their demands for Sarah's attention. Their enthusiasm caused her to jump forward on her seat, ripping her back to the present. The birds were in their first year and had not yet acquired their vivid blue adult plumage. Even though a little on the drab side, their inherent beauty was not marred by the brownish cloaks they were showing off. There was no lack of confidence or cheek either, and she laughed at their antics, in spite of the situation. Even their crests seemed to be skew-whiff as they vied for her attention.

Sarah knew she should be getting back to see how her mother was coping. These episodes with Jane always knocked the stuffing out of her. Disagreements between her parents had centred on Jane's behaviour and had become steadily more frequent, exacerbated by the fact that they were now living apart for most of the time. Instinctively drawing her hand to protect her side, Sarah remembered the fateful night as vividly as if it had just happened.

****

The day had been long, with a packed gallery. The volley of questions to field, not to mention the effort in nurturing the many blossoming artists, had proved totally gruelling. She always worked hard at putting on a good front, no matter how she was feeling. That day, however, had been hard going, rendering her totally exhausted. Hurrying home that night, she had relaxed only when she was nursing a special herbal tea on her little patio. It never failed to sooth. The perfume of the peace rose filled the courtyard, and she had paused to marvel again at the utter beauty of the plant. These were invaluable times for her to regroup and organize her thoughts for the next day's business.

Later, the embalming, luxurious fragrance of rosemary permeated her bathroom, as she sank into the foamy water in her soaker tub. *How over-indulgent!* she was thinking but gave herself over to the luxury of it anyway.

She had dived into unconsciousness almost immediately once her head hit the pillow. The warmth of her bed overtook her completely. Then, suddenly awakened, all senses alert, she realized she was not alone. The curtains moved slightly. She must have forgotten to lock the window again. To her horror, she could just make out the figure of somebody lurking inside the room, behind the curtains. Her body froze. Seconds seemed like hours as nobody moved—the silence was suffocating. Suddenly, the hidden person leapt out, and she heard her sister's voice, raised and incoherent: "You have everything you could possibly wish for and still that's not enough for you, is it?"

Her sister was shrieking, her tone malevolent and menacing.

Sarah was frightened, more than she had ever been before. She had never seen Jane so virulent. Obviously, she either had not been taking her medications or desperately needed to have them adjusted.

"Well, you're not taking Luke as well." Jane was screaming again.

There had been a scuffle. Sarah felt the full weight of Jane's sturdy body bearing down on her as she struggled halfway out of the bed. She did manage to grab the lamp as she hit the floor. Fortunately, it was unplugged, as she had planned to take it into the electrical shop for repair the next day.

Jane was lashing out at her. Sarah felt sharp, stabbing pains in her side. Frantically struggling and freeing her arm, she brought the lamp down as hard as she could. It was a heavy, solid brass lamp, and Jane was momentarily stunned, falling into a heap at Sarah's side. Staggering to her feet, Sarah saw blood pouring out of her side, saturating her nightgown. It was then that she saw the letter opener still in Jane's hand and knew she was in real trouble, particularly as nausea and weakness were overcoming her.

"Oh my God, she tried to kill me!" Sarah was shocked, the feeling of faintness closing in on her rapidly. "Must get to the phone before she comes to," she mumbled. "No, no must stay conscious at all costs."

Fighting to stay alert and dragging herself to the phone, she barely managed to make the call before slipping into a pit of darkness.

The medical attendants arrived just as Jane was starting to stir. It was clear to them what had happened and, strapping her to a stretcher, they took her away screaming.

Sarah had drifted in and out of consciousness. Finally opening her eyes, her gaze fell upon her dear parents, their poor faces white and strained as they patiently waited by her hospital bedside for her to show signs of returning to the world.

"Well, hello there, welcome back."

It was a doctor's voice. After a brief introduction, he got down to the business of checking Sarah's vitals.

"You're a lucky young woman. We've stitched up three bad gashes, but you'll make a good recovery. Fortunately, the weapon didn't penetrate too far, which is a miracle, considering the force used."

Rose was crying. Her brave father, always the leader in battle, now seemed a fallen emperor, his spirit defeated as he struggled to keep up a good front. Both hugged their daughter, but delicately so as not to cause her more pain.

Apparently, Jane had been returned to a psychiatric facility. She had not been taking her medication and was deemed a serious threat until stabilized. She was to remain in the medical facility for an indeterminate time and undergo a complete assessment.

****

Reluctant to leave her paradise, which had by that time once again worked its magic in restoring her calm, Sarah pulled herself to her feet, feeling a huge appreciation for the sheer warmth of the day and beauty of her surroundings. The outstanding colour of the trees, the lush green of the lawns, dozens of little birds trilling in the trees, and the slight heady perfume of the flowers all had lifted her mood.

Even though she felt inadequate to deal with her sister's problems and had always lacked confidence, she was finally beginning to fully recognize her own achievements, gaining more self-esteem in the process. How lucky she was in her own world and endeavours, with a beautiful home and a fabulous career which she loved. She was beginning to reap the rewards and enjoying resounding success while building a firm professional reputation.

Her thoughts settled pleasingly on the exclusive little gallery/showroom which she had recently opened to the public. The gallery was the culmination of many months of hard work and planning. While not big and flashy, it reflected the character of the area and was an easy walk from her home. She had a penchant for historical and traditional works of art and capitalized on her training and research, seeking out and purchasing art treasures for subsequent sale in her showroom.

Although travelling abroad on occasion, Sarah was also heavily committed to supporting and promoting local talent in the neighbouring community. Her establishment was fast becoming a much sought-after venue for artists of all types. One section of the gallery catered to the more avant-garde group of newcomers to the area, exhibiting modern and abstract art. Sarah recognized the necessity of diversifying and not falling into a set format in her displays. The public were fickle and required constant stimulation.

Shivering suddenly, she cast one more cursory glance around and moved briskly towards the wrought iron gates forming part of the boundary of the property. Her sleek Jaguar parked at the end of the driveway came into her line of vision, and a smile teased her lips as she admired it. Easing herself in behind the wheel, she felt mildly ashamed of her materialism but was grateful for her possessions anyway.

*Ah yes, the spoils of the trade. I might not be a raving socialite, but I do have a good business head on my shoulders.*

Revelling in the comfort of the luxurious leather upholstery, she urged the engineering miracle into traffic, feeling more at ease upon seeing her security people firmly ensconced in their car, parked a little further up the hill. They were keeping tabs on her every movement.

Sarah was looking forward to the following week's trip to Bonn in West Germany and felt ecstatic when she thought about the hustle and bustle of the auction. The bidding process had originally scared her half to death, but she had grown accustomed to it over the years. The anticipation and general atmosphere were thrilling, almost intoxicating.

"H'm," she mused. "I wonder what fate has in store for me on this trip."

Oh, if only she could have imagined the journey on which she was about to embark.

# Chapter 4
# The Meeting

Shaken to consciousness, Jonathan looked up into the smiling face of the stewardess. Befuddled with sleep from the lulling motion of the plane and sheer exhaustion, he was unable to concentrate on what she was saying as she handed him his drink and salted nuts. She spoke again. Could she get him anything else? No, she could not, perhaps later. Then once again, he was dragged back to 1976, when he'd first seen the picture and looked into Sarah's eyes.

\*\*\*\*

Jonathan had flown to Bonn on business to attend the art auction. Over the years, he'd built up an extensive portfolio of contacts and friends in Germany, in fact internationally, as he travelled seeking out the best in the art world. He seldom failed to scoop the pieces the partners had set their sights upon. Mark was the home base of the business, the spine of the operation—much more involved in the day-to-day affairs of running both establishments, with hand-picked staff for assistance. He did travel occasionally but only on an as-needed basis. The arrangement worked very well for both of them, particularly as Jonathan craved the adrenaline rush of the bid, and they were developing an extremely profitable partnership.

The picture was previewed at the auction, and the enraptured Jonathan knew he had to have it in his private collection. Simply named *Sarah*, it was an exquisite work of art depicting an equally exquisite woman. She captured him completely. Her raven-black hair had caught his eye initially, but it was her smile that really threw him over the edge. It was the purest, sweetest smile that dimpled at the corners with a hint, merely a hint, of compassion and just enough mystery to push a man to insanity—the driving force that ensnared him irrevocably.

Jonathan was surprised at himself for actually feeling jealous of the artist, who must have known her pretty well, as he'd painted her face onto the canvas with such precision. Making a note of the artist's name, he determined to carry out a full investigation of the painting and, in particular, its model, when he arrived back in London.

He knew he would have to pull out all the stops if he was to outbid any interested opponents. Fortunately, Mark was not interested in any of the paintings on offer, as his mind was set on specific pieces on which Jonathan would be bidding. His partner was single-minded, and Jonathan knew there would be no deviation. He also knew exactly where this painting was going to hang. It would be placed above the fireplace in the library, his favourite room, where he gravitated with his tea and newspaper after breakfast. What better way to start the day than with her smiling down at him, and what better setting could there be for her than his beautiful heritage house in Lyndhurst, in Hampshire's New Forest.

****

Jonathan had always been drawn to the village, which was named after the Old English Saxon words lind (lime tree) and hyrst (wooded hill), although the lime trees had long since been lost over succeeding generations. Lyndhurst's history since the 900s was particularly intriguing to Jonathan. He could picture William the Conqueror riding through the streets in the area he had designated as his New Forest and pronouncing it a safe haven for hunted animals.

Lyndhurst appealed to Jonathan for many reasons. Apart from its quaint beauty, it was a thriving antique mecca. He was bent on retiring there and had hopes of opening a little antique shop, possibly another branch of the business he and Mark shared. They had visited the subject and put it on the back burner. The matter would certainly be entertained again once they had set up the branch in Germany. The south of England was an easy rail commute to London via Southampton and ideally suited for him. It would still be a practical proposition for him to retain his London flat for those occasions when he was there on prolonged business visits.

During one of his earlier real estate forays, Jonathan had found the perfect house and had sealed the deal immediately before he lost it. The property was still a work in progress, as he'd been dealing with contractors on an as-needed basis, fitting jobs in with his busy work schedule as and when opportunities presented themselves. The project was expensive. Nevertheless, the extensive renovations were turning the place into a showpiece, even if it was taking much longer than originally anticipated. The location couldn't have been better, as the travel time from London was so short. He would be able to spend odd weekends and days working on the refurbishment.

****

Tearing himself away from Sarah's face with some reluctance, he began wandering around the exhibits, then stopped dead in his tracks. He couldn't believe his eyes. She was actually there in the flesh, directly in his line of vision, approximately one hundred yards away, so inconceivably beautiful he felt light-headed just looking at her. Yes, definitely compassion and enough mystery to turn a man to insanity. And the hair, that gorgeous black hair, likening her to an Egyptian goddess, not dissimilar to his mother, who was of Roma and Italian origin. The painting did not do Sarah justice, nor could any other, for that matter. She was perfection incarnate.

*I have to meet her,* he was thinking, as he frantically tried to dream up some plausible reason for breaking into her world. He moved forward swiftly, only to be thwarted by a group of supporters who descended upon her like a swarm of locusts, surrounding her tiny frame, momentarily blocking her from his view. Breaking away, she moved along the art pieces up for auction, obviously enlightening her audience as to the attributes of each treasure.

There was a call to order, and everybody converged on their seats. Jonathan did the same, annoyed at himself for losing his focus. He was there to purchase art, including some much sought-after miniatures from the Russian village of Mstera. The village was renowned for its porcelain and papier mâché eggs, and the famous Fabergé eggs produced for the Russian royal family between 1800 and 1900. He needed every ounce of concentration if he was to procure his wares at the best possible price—not to mention the picture, which he was hellbent on owning. The young woman was now firmly nestled in between two large businessmen. They appeared to be bodyguards, but Jonathan immediately dismissed the idea. She obviously knew them well, judging by the joviality they all exuded.

*Cut it out, Jonathan. Get on with the job at hand,* he reminded himself. He knew Mark was relying on him. He had to keep his eye on the ball. The pieces up for auction were well known to both men, and Mark would be expecting to end up with at least two of them on show in their gallery. They'd really done their homework, and Mark had released a huge amount of company money for purchases. He would be very disappointed if he didn't get his hands on the pieces they'd both agreed upon.

The auction convened. All eyes fastened on the auctioneer as he proffered his wares. Jonathan sat out from the bidding on the first few pieces up for auction. His eyes searched relentlessly for the woman, who would not leave his mind. He caught a brief glimpse of her when one of the behemoths next to her moved from his seat to speak to another man, of similar proportions, at the end of the row. She met his gaze, and for the briefest moment, he thought he saw fear in her eyes, so fleeting that he assumed it was a figment of his imagination. In a flash, the perception was gone. She appeared to recognize him—probably remembering him wandering around the gallery prior to the auction. He had not even been aware that she'd seen him, but her expression belied that fact now as her eyes widened. She was obviously trying to remember whether she actually knew him, or whether he was just a passing attraction. There was no time to find out, because the big man reappeared, taking up his position and obliterating her again from Jonathan's view.

The bidding started. Sarah was all business. Jonathan had applied the painting's title to her already. She was a woman who knew just what she wanted and, it would seem, didn't care what she paid for it. She entered into some seriously heavy-duty bidding on two art pieces and came up trumps. Jonathan was impressed, particularly when the blonde behemoth bent forward and she managed to fire a wink his way, which he returned wholeheartedly. He was euphoric, his obsession burgeoning by the minute. How could she have this effect on him?

The coveted lot number was called. There she was on canvas. There was no mistaking the black hair and the seductive look in her eyes. He already felt he knew her intimately, and his thoughts were running rampant. Nonetheless, his enthusiasm for the artist's talent waned slightly, as the canvas cheapened the real thing, not giving her the full credit she deserved. In retrospect, however, it was doubtful that any artist, even the most talented, could succeed in capturing that beauty entirely.

Jonathan came in low, delaying his bid by waiting for the third prompt. Some insignificant sod at the back of the room outbid him. Once again taking his time, Jonathan raised the ante slightly as the hammer was about to come down, not wishing to divulge that he would give the coat off his back if necessary. Mr. Insignificant came at him again, and with much annoyance, Jonathan countered. It seemed they were the only two bidders who wanted the picture. By that time, Jonathan was even thinking, *If I have to mortgage the house, so be it.* As it happened, his opponent withdrew.

Jonathan was exultant, and his spirits soared. She was his—well, on canvas anyway, with the added bonus that he got to keep his house. Once again, she leaned back and caught his attention, extending another knowing wink. She knew he was hooked. He smiled gainfully.

*Welcome to my world, Sarah, I'll be seeing you in my library,* he thought triumphantly.

****

It turned out to be an extremely successful day. Jonathan knew Mark would be pleased. He had acquired both of the pieces that his partner had been so set on adding to the firm's inventory, and at very reasonable prices, well within budget.

The crowd was dispersing. What more auspicious time than now to go and introduce himself. Looking across the room, he saw, to his horror, that she was gone. Propelled to his feet, he rushed towards the office. She was just concluding her transactions, and before he could push his way through the throng, the behemoths closed in and hustled her through the swing doors, out the exit, and out of his life. Forcing his way through the hordes of people, hoping to catch her outside, he saw her enter a taxi and be whisked away into the night like the fairy princess she was.

Disconsolate, he went back into the office to claim his prizes and settle up his accounts. At least he would be able to possess her on canvas, if nothing else. No way was he going to lose that as well as the real thing.

After arranging the transfer of his new acquisitions, he turned his attention to personal matters and addressed the clerk.

"Who was the lady bidding on lot numbers 3, 4, and 6?"

Her eyes moved over him, sizing him up in an accusatory manner.

"Oh, that's confidential sir. We don't give out that information. More than my life's worth to divulge the personal facts on our clients."

"That's unfortunate, as I have some other pieces she might be interested in."

"Well, I'm sorry sir, but that's our policy."

Jonathan was deflated. Where would he go from here in his search? What a conundrum.

Suddenly he perked up, an idea percolating in his brain.

"Well, I see no problem in giving me her name. As I said, I have items I'm sure she would like to preview."

The clerk was getting more than a little ruffled at his importunity.

Jonathan had already seen the sales registry sitting on her desk, so he 'accidentally' tripped, knocking almost everything on the desk to the floor.

"That damned carpet is frayed. Someone should report that."

Staggering forward and picking up the odd thing, he scanned the registry. With a practiced eye for detail, he soon picked out her name against the lot numbers. There was only one Sarah on the registry. Sarah Buchanan, recipient of lots 3, 4 and 6. She shouldn't be too hard to trace.

Apologizing profusely to the clerk, he said, "At least tell me, is she British?"

"Oh no mistaking that," she said with exaggerated derision, obviously annoyed at the mess he'd created, "definitely hoity-toity." Immediately abashed at her own lack of tact and downright ignorance, she hastily retracted her comments. "I'm so sorry. I've had a rough day and spoke out of line. Please accept my apologies. And now, do you mind, sir? I have to keep this desk in order, can't have anything go wrong. My boss and I are flying back to London tonight."

"Well, you've done a great job here, and I hope we'll run into each other again at the London auctions. I must say, it's been a pleasure meeting you."

He left her simpering and flushed with pleasure.

# Chapter 5
# Mönchengladbach

When Jonathan was in Germany, he generally stayed with his long-standing friend Helmut, who had a funky little flat off the market square in Mönchengladbach, not far from Bonn.

Strolling down the cobbled streets that night after the auction, Jonathan was exuberant and practically jigging as he passed through the Mönchengladbach Square, working his way slowly towards Helmut's flat. He was over the moon with the day's very successful business dealings and, of course, encountering Sarah.

*I wonder if I'll find her in London,* he thought. *As soon as I get back, I'll look for her. Her name isn't all that common; can't be too many Buchanans in London in the business. According to that clerk, she was obviously British and established in the art world. It has to be London.*

Jonathan was eager to see Helmut again, as it had been quite a while, although they had kept in touch regularly. He could hardly wait to tell him all about the trip. They had met on Jonathan's first school outing to Germany and had remained close friends ever since. Helmut's sincerity was something Jonathan had hung onto since the beginning. Their friendship had been the spine of his existence in the earlier years, strengthened by common educational and career goals—both pursuing degrees with a view to working in the field of antiques in one capacity or another.

Jonathan's life had been up and down. He'd lost his older brother to substance abuse many years prior, and his parents had never recovered. Their lifestyle had become one long social round, their marriage superficial, apparently without true meaning anymore. Extreme wealth enabled them to travel constantly.

A youth robbed of the normal traditional family upbringing, Jonathan was isolated. He felt that he was simply getting in the way of his parents' fanciful plans of the moment. The fact that their lifestyle resulted in him spending a large portion of his earlier years in expensive boarding schools and being shipped out every holiday to some educational camp or other had only served to exacerbate his loneliness. Helmut and his grandparents had been his lifeline, always inviting him for the holidays and such. Fortunately, Jonathan's parents had allowed him to spend time with them over school breaks; hence, Germany had become his second home.

Helmut's parents were casualties of WWII, and his grandparents had taken over his care. They had been very good to Jonathan when he first went to Germany, welcoming him into their household as an integral part of the family. They couldn't speak a word of English, so Jonathan became fluent in the German language very quickly. Helmut had originally introduced them as his Oma and Opa, and that's how Jonathan always addressed them. As Helmut shared them so generously, he regarded them as his own grandparents. They loved him as if he was of their own blood, and he felt the same way.

Meals were always very formal, with Opa taking his place at the head of the table, and Oma inevitably fussing around, discarding her apron, and finally seating herself to her husband's immediate right. Dinner was a well-guarded ritual, a formal occasion at which all family members were present, if possible. The gathering was regarded as a special forum for the family to get together each day and talk, and it usually lasted a good two hours or more, with a number of delectable dishes to sample. Jonathan's favourite foods were the herring salad and calt hund (cold dog)—a chocolate layer cake made of biscuits and ice cream, sliced very thinly and kept in the freezer until ready to be demolished at the table. And demolished it truly was, being absolutely delicious and loved by everybody. His mouth watered just at the thought of it.

Unfortunately, those wonderful old people had passed on, but Helmut and Jonathan's friendship remained constant.

Anxious to share all his news with his friend, Jonathan quickened his step. He'd missed Helmut and was really looking forward to seeing him again. The deep-blue door was a welcome sight as he approached the threshold. Helmut had made a great job of painting it and had influenced the other tenants to do the same with their doors. They had the added inducement of him providing his painting skills to further the project and had been more than happy to chip in on the cost and labour. The choice of colour had worked out well, and the overall uniformity had greatly upgraded the homes. Helmut's apartment was part of a triplex, all the units being placed in a row like miniature houses, except that each was three levels high. Helmut had been lucky to get his hands on a ground-floor unit, having been on the waitlist for some time. He particularly wanted to grow a few herbs for his culinary delights, and there was a sizeable patio area at his disposal, overlooking a green belt.

Jonathan banged on the door, which was immediately flung open. He was enveloped in a suffocating bear hug, leaving him gasping for breath. Helmut was a huge fellow, and an embrace from him was enough to fell any young man.

They spoke in unison.

"Wie geht's, Jonathan?"

"How are you? Long time, no see."

Beaming from ear to ear, Helmut ushered Jonathan inside.

"Come in. Come in, my friend. I have so missed you. Let's eat. I'm starving, seems like I've been waiting for you for hours."

Helmut had consumed copious quantities of food ever since Jonathan had known him. When they were boys, it had been phenomenal, and it seemed that nothing had changed.

Jonathan smiled. "Yes, that's my Helmut, always hungry. No wonder you're so gigantic."

"Solid muscle, old man, solid muscle."

Helmut had laid out a buffet fit for a king, with the usual range of tasty dishes. As a young man, had learned all domestic skills, courtesy of his Oma's dedicated tutoring. The spread was outstanding, with hot and cold plates. Homemade kartoffelsalat and cold cuts of all types were accompanied by a platter of pumpernickel bread and an assortment of liver sausage and pickles. Hot dishes were a selection of butter chicken with herby potatoes, fried to a crisp, roasted vegetables, and a variety of other items, each sitting on their own individual hot plates.

Jonathan's eyes stood out like organ stops as he surveyed the expansive table. "Well, you've done us proud, as usual. The woman that snares you will be a lucky one indeed. Talking of women, how's Gertrude doing?"

Gertrude was Helmut's long-time girlfriend. They had first met in school and had remained together as a couple.

"Isn't it about time you two tied the knot?"

"No. Not right now. We're both still trying to save up for our own place. We want to start off right, and we're just fine at the moment. Gertrude is doing great. She talks about our future wedding all the time. With a bit of luck, we should be in a position next year. In the meantime, she's really excited about seeing you again and will be popping in later to say hello."

"Terrific, I'm really looking forward to seeing her as well. Honestly though, Helmut, don't leave it too late when it comes to setting the date. Gertrude's one of a kind. You always were very cautious and much too practical, and really, Helmut, when you think about it, there's absolutely nothing wrong with this flat. It's certainly big enough for both of you, with loads of storage, and the patio is an absolute bonus. You know, two can live for the price of one, and if you were sharing, you could afford your own place much sooner."

"I suppose we could revisit that; we've talked about it often enough. Maybe I'll bring it up with Gertrude again. Anyway, that's enough about me. What are you up to these days? Are you seeing anybody—seriously, I mean? I know you're always seeing plenty of girls, but is there anyone special?"

Jonathan just sat with a stupid grin fixed on his face and a faraway look in his eyes.

"Come on, man, tell me. You're very obviously up to something."

"Well, today at the auction, I met a goddess. Actually, I didn't exactly meet her. She slipped through my fingers, but I did manage to get her name from the clerk's registry book. She's obviously part of the art scene, and I had a brief interlude with her at the auction. Judging by what the clerk told me, she's right up there on the societal ladder, very British, and certainly seems to know her way around the art world. Paid a pretty penny, too, for the lot numbers she bid on—obviously knows what she wants and goes for it, no holds barred.

"She shouldn't be too hard to trace now that I have her name. I'm surprised I haven't run into her before, though. We're obviously moving in a similar environment. Had our paths crossed, I would have remembered.

"It was a funny thing, Helmut, but before I even set eyes on her, I saw this picture of a gorgeous, black-haired woman previewed at the auction, and I knew I had to possess it. Little did I know that I would be seeing the real thing before the day was out. Anyway, to cut a long story short, I did end up with the picture and, as we speak, it is on its way back to England. I know exactly where it's going to hang. It will have the place of honour, above the fireplace, in my library. I can hardly wait to get it up on the wall.

"Mark is going to be thrilled to bits, as well. He had set his sights on a couple of pieces, and I managed to get them at a good price. You know he's all about money. He's going to be ecstatic when our treasures arrive."

"Won't Mark think the 'goddess' is part of the business collection, as it seems to be so special?"

"No, definitely not. I made sure the picture is clearly labelled 'For Jonathan's personal collection,' and I did leave him a message to that effect. By the way, the picture is titled *Sarah*, just plain *Sarah*, although she's anything but plain. My God, what a vision of loveliness."

"Well, you've certainly got it bad, my friend. I wish you luck in finding her. Hope you're not disappointed. She could be married or something."

"There was no ring on either hand, if that's anything to go by."

"That's my friend Jon, never misses a beat, real eye for detail."

Jonathan was starting to relax and could hardly keep his eyes open, sprawled on the sofa, his empty glass dangling from his fingers; the brandy had just about finished him off after the enormous meal.

"Come on, old chap, let's get you settled down for the night and we'll talk some more tomorrow."

Helmut retrieved the glass from Jonathan's hand, before it dropped to the floor, hauled him to his feet and hustled him towards the bedroom.

"Thanks for a great evening, Helmut. It really is terrific seeing you again, friend. Sleep well."

****

Jonathan stretched languidly. It was 1976 and he was 31 years old, in his prime, successful and feeling the world was his oyster. He'd slept well, very unusual for him, as his brain never seemed to shut down.

*Yes, this is going to be a great year. I just feel it in my bones,* he thought, lazily stretching again.

Helmut had booked a night's stay in the Eifel Mountains. They were spending the following day at the races at Nürburgring. Car racing was the friends' favourite sport. The highlight of their excursions to the track had been the 1968 Grand Prix, where they had witnessed Jackie Stewart win by a four-minute lead. Graham Hill had placed second that year.

Jonathan followed the careers of both of these British drivers religiously. Two years after that victory, a stand was made by the drivers about the unsafe conditions of the track, nicknamed The Green Hell by Jackie Stewart. Major modifications were carried out, but it was still considered the most dangerous of racing circuits.

The two friends were thrilled to be back at their old haunt. Little did they know that the day's race was to be a portentous event—the last to be held on the Nordschleife section of the track.

The heavy smell of motor oil, rubber, and exhaust fumes pervaded the air and their nostrils. It was almost overwhelming, exacerbated by extreme rain and foggy conditions, nurturing a sense of imminent danger. The reigning world champion, Niki Lauda, attempted to have the race stopped because of the extreme conditions and inadequate medical staff for a track of that length. There were also some dangerous areas that hospital personnel could not reach in reasonable time, should an accident occur. The concern was voted down, and the race went ahead as planned.

The accident that burned Niki Lauder so very badly that fateful day would have killed him but for the quick actions of other drivers on the circuit, sadly proving the champion's point. Jonathan and Helmut were privy to a racing horror of such magnitude that it somewhat dampened their enthusiasm for the sport, leaving an indelible memory in both their minds ever after.

# Chapter 6
# Jonathan Reflects

Following the trip to Bonn, Jonathan met up with Mark. After giving him the rundown of the trip and attending to other business, he made his way to Lyndhurst for a few days. He was anxious to see how the contractors had made out on the next phase of the renovations. As always, his house welcomed him. Safety and security dwelt within its walls. He was home.

Later that day, following an invigorating shower, Jonathan sat in his library, quietly studying the beautiful cherry bookshelves running the length of the room. He admired yet again the depth of his favourite wood, so rich, so natural. The shelves were complemented by an enormous range of books, many of which were collectors' items in rich leathers, spines etched in gold. His interest in books and music had escalated from an early age, with an appreciation and insatiable quest for learning and research, which had never diminished. He loved the entire house, but this room in particular was his favourite retreat, imbued with a sense of permanency and warmth, feelings he had lacked in his earlier years.

Leaning back in his chair while revelling in some classical gypsy guitar music, his eye fell on the antique guitar hanging on the wall. The instrument was said to have been played by Django Reinhardt at one time, a statement which Jonathan had always viewed with scepticism. Nevertheless, there was no doubt that the hand-carved piece was a classic and a very fine work of art. The instrument was heavily embellished with intricate designs.

How sad and what a loss that Django's personal guitar had been burnt following his death, along with all his other possessions, in keeping with the customs of his people. Very few of his recordings were left; his legacy remained in the hearts and souls of those who would always remember him. Even though he had never read sheet music—playing by ear and natural instinct—the gypsy guitarist was recognized as the master of improvisation, moving with ease from the 1920s to the '40s, from musette to jazz. Born in Paris in the 1800s, musette, the music of the gypsies, was named after the bagpipes and recognized as a musical genre in its own right. Evolving into Bal-Musette, this gypsy jazz was emanating from practically every club and café in Paris by the 1900s, subsequently becoming Django's major inspiration.

Jonathan's gaze left the guitar as he studied his own hands, the fingers in particular. They were long and slender, of unusual strength because of their familiarity with the piano keys. He was thinking how amazingly gifted the musician had been, even more so considering the life-threatening burns he had sustained as a teen when his caravan caught on fire. He had almost succumbed, and although his life was spared, one hand was severely damaged, robbing him of the use of several fingers.

The culture of the travelling communities had always played a large part in Jonathan's research, an interest shared by his mother. She'd often spoken of her heritage originating from the Gitano in Spain on her mother's side, but an Italian father on the other. She'd talked wistfully of her early years growing up in Provence, her eyes full of sadness every time she spoke of the white horses of Camargue, said to be spiritual.

How she missed the marshland where these magnificent horses roamed freely over 200,000 acres of surreal landscape cascading into a crystalline ocean. The mystical, almost illusory qualities of the terrain provided ample pasture and dunes for the horses, along with their neighbours, the wild cattle and snowy white egrets.

Jonathan had always been close to his mother and loved hearing about her beginnings. He had developed a keen interest in exploring that part of his heritage.

Lost in the quietude of his favourite room, he had, as usual, forgotten the coffee sitting on the little walnut table at his side. *Cold, as always,* he thought as, cup in hand, he studied the surface of the antique table, intricately inlaid with woods of so many shapes and hues. Rising, he made his way reluctantly to the kitchen. He'd been so comfortable and had not wanted to move, but his coffee needed heating up.

Settling back once again in his seat, his mind wandered back to his upbringing.

\*\*\*\*

He knew full well how privileged he was to have been exposed to the two very diverse heritages of his parents, Gina and Ronald. His life had definitely been enriched. The fact that they had always placed so much emphasis on education and his further development had also served him well. A wealthy background hadn't hurt either and enabled him to develop a fine appreciation for the better things in life. Yes, there was no doubt about it, his parents had certainly given him every opportunity, even though their own lives had become so superficial and empty after the loss of their firstborn.

Rehashing circumstances yet again, inevitably his stress level rose, as the brother he had hardly known filled his thoughts.

Nathan was born six years before Jonathan and had been a brilliant young man, full of promise. Jonathan thought about the words "brilliance borders on madness," but his recollections of his brother were not of madness. Nathan had been completely dysfunctional, though, and very highly strung, never really fitting in with the world at large. As he matured, he gave up trying to live up to societal expectations. Seeking what was out of reach to him, he tried anything new that came his way. That had been his downfall, paving the way to his drug use, which became hardcore at an early age.

Jonathan would never forget the events that led up to his brother's death. It was night-time when the phone call had come. The look on his father's face when he took the call was earth-shattering. His son had been found outside a flat suspected of being a haunt for homosexuals. The residence was on the police radar and, up to their usual form, they conducted a surprise raid. Nathan had fled down a back fire escape but had collapsed in the street below, where the paramedics were working on him.

Young men with the same inclinations as Nathan who did not escape the clutches of the police faced the cruel wrath of the judicial system and probable imprisonment. Those years had seen hundreds of such men interned within the penal system because of their sexual orientation.

The message relayed to Ronald was that his son had overdosed and was not expected to survive. He should get to the scene immediately.

Jonathan stood by, hopelessly watching his parents' misery.

Ronald's love for his wife was apparent as he broke the news. Clasping her tightly to him, her muffled sobbing emanating from his chest, they remained for a few moments, sharing their misery, until he firmly broke them apart.

"We have to go straightaway; they're waiting for us."

Catching Gina's hand, he hustled them both out of the room, yelling over his shoulder to the housekeeper as they went down the hall.

"Giselle, come and look after Jonathan."

Jonathan hadn't thought he needed looking after—he was almost a teenager, for cripes' sake.

"Nate's in trouble again. We have to go."

Jonathan was shocked to see his father's eyes filled with tears. He had never seen him cry before. Vision blurred, Ronald struggled to pick up the keys from the hall table and then off the floor where they lay after falling from his trembling fingers. Grabbing hold of Gina to steady himself, he then straightened up and herded her towards the door—and they were gone.

Later that night, his devastated parents had broken the news to Jonathan that he would never see his brother again.

****

Even sitting in the library, this most tranquil of settings, after so many years had passed, he still felt the usual trauma to his system as he recalled every detail of that fateful evening.

He had lost not only a brother that night, but his parents as well. His father handed over his law offices for an associate to run and took a leave of absence. The denigrating press about his son's dissenting activities and implied homosexuality were ruining the family's reputation. Ronald lost himself in travel, virtually living on his yacht. Jonathan's beautiful mother couldn't stand not having her husband by her side, so she accompanied him. She travelled the path of artificial living with artificial people, living on the yacht and doing sailing trips for most of the year, missing her home and beloved horses, everything she treasured with all her heart and soul.

Somehow, Jonathan had been lost in the shuffle. Theirs had always been a close-knit family, but he seemed to have been forgotten. His perception of life sharpened from that time on, when he realized that one's circumstances could change in the blink of an eye. What he had taken for granted as being his due suddenly had been cruelly taken away.

He became withdrawn through the years of his youth, relentlessly pursuing his studies, obsessively striving to achieve excellence in all his endeavours. These traits were carried over into his career in later years.

His father had handled Nathan's death in a similar manner, although sailing and travel had become his obsessive refuges, rather than business. Both were driven men.

****

Ronald had retained his London flat for business purposes. After marrying Gina, he'd set them up in his home in Hertfordshire—a convenient location for his work in London, but also the place of his roots, his birth.

The house had been in his father's family for several generations. A full complement of stables ran along the back of the property, with adjoining pastures stretching over several acres. The stables had housed purebred racehorses in bygone days. Racing had never really been Ronald's scene, although he had always nurtured a great love of riding. His horses were his pride and joy, to be shared with guests, friends, and family who enjoyed riding weekends through the bucolic countryside of that green and pleasant county.

One wall in the house's library displayed nothing but pictures and photographs of the champion horses that had been housed and trained on the property. Even though racing was not to Ronald's taste, he did nurture a huge respect for the property's history and applauded the sheer beauty of the animals.

Nestled amongst the art displays on the library walls was a painting by British artist George Stubbs, famed for his anatomical detailing of animals, particularly the horse. This piece of art from the 1760s had been acquired by one of Ronald's predecessors two generations back. Groups of horses had been favoured during this period, but this particular painting, although small and seemingly insignificant, was of a single, magnificent creature said to have sired one of the original racehorses of the property. The piece was highly valued by the family.

A short distance from the estate was Ashwell, one of the oldest villages in England, dating back to the ninth century. Ronald made a point of visiting the little village with Gina whenever time permitted. He often spoke about the history of the beautiful Saxo-Norman church of St. Mary's that presided over the village. Built in the fourteenth century, it boasted the highest steeple in Hertfordshire. The walls within the church were inscribed with the gut-wrenching words of those dying of the bubonic plague or 'black death' which ravaged the land between the thirteenth and sixteenth centuries. Those poor souls had sought refuge inside the holy place in their last anguished hours on this earth.

When they visited the ancient building, Ronald would offer words of comfort to Gina if they found themselves looking at the engravings on the church walls. He always concluded the horror story on a more positive note by saying that he firmly believed those poor wretches' love of their God gave them strength in their last moments, and they derived some comfort from the sanctuary of the church.

The couple's visits usually coincided with the early spring bulbs welcoming the birth of a new year. Snowdrops and crocuses spread prolifically throughout the ancient graveyard, softening the harshness of the stonework with their simple, natural beauty. If they visited in late spring, Gina and Ronald were privy to thousands of bluebells nestling under massive oak trees. Miracles of nature, the trees were hundreds of years old, their boughs reaching two-and-a-half feet or more in diameter. The vibrancy of the bluebells beneath the branches was breathtaking, enthralling the couple as they wandered down the paths hand in hand throughout the vast property adjoining St. Mary's.

Gina had always shared those visits with her son, a few of which he recalled, as he had accompanied his parents. That was in the earlier years, of course. Climbing the stairs to the belfry always stood out in Jonathan's memory. The images were crystal clear, even with the passing of time—of them all staggering up the dark, narrow stairs of the church, finally reaching the great bells hanging at the very top of the steeple in the belfry. They would pass by narrow cut-outs in the walls, which allowed shards of light to pour through the thin slits, aiding their laborious ascent. Thankfully, coming back down was much easier and faster. Jonathan had always felt weird in that environment; he was definitely not a big fan of climbing the stairs in that eerie place.

****

Time was getting on. Jonathan knew he shouldn't but nevertheless indulged himself by pouring a glass of wine. Lounging back in his roomy chair, he tried to relax, a feeling he had to work really hard to achieve.

In retrospect, he didn't really blame his parents. Their lives had been shattered into thousands of fragments. Those earlier and most precious of shared moments seemed to have been forgotten, and he had inadvertently been set aside amidst the turmoil.

Jonathan's dedication to his work over the years had provided the impetus required to get on with his life, and here he was, about to embark on a new endeavour. His eyes fell on the portrait, and once again, he was hypnotized by her exquisite beauty.

*I have to find her, and I will! There's no doubt about that.*

Picking up his glass, he blew her a kiss. It really seemed that her smile was for him, and him alone—a smile full of promise.

"I'll be seeing you again, and in the not-too-distant future," he said as he raised the crystal goblet to her, studying the bubbles keenly. Their joie de vivre matched the spirit within him.

## Chapter 7
## In Search of Sarah

Jonathan was feeling more than a little despondent. His search for information on the artist who had painted Sarah's portrait had thus far been fruitless.

He had travelled to England's beautiful west coast to attend an auction, which was to be held on a private estate outside of Lamorna Cove. This cove had become famous since the establishment of the first art colonies in the area in the early 1900s. Artists had come from all over the world to capture and immortalize the magnificent panorama spread before them. The dramatic granite cliffs along the Cornish coast, defaced by numerous storms and the lashing of raging waves with every passing year, proved an irresistible lure to painters and writers of every description.

Following the auction, Jonathan spent a few days schmoozing with the locals. Much to his delight, he discovered that some of them were actually descended from the original settlers in the colonies. He had hoped to pick up some information on the elusive artist he was seeking but drew a blank. His visit to the auction had not met expectations either, although he was able to acquire some very well-preserved earlier examples of Wedgewood pottery, as well as carvings by one of the original artists to live in the area. He had also managed to bid successfully on two exquisite miniature paintings. All things considered, he was reasonably pleased with his business dealings, although bitterly disappointed at not finding some history on his painting.

****

A couple of months later, in spite of enjoying his cup of coffee in a funky little café in St. John's Wood, Jonathan's thoughts were gloomy. *It looks like it just wasn't meant to be. I've come up with nothing on her. I may as well forget the whole thing.* He had just about given up on ever finding Sarah.

The café was one of a few that Jonathan regularly frequented. The proprietor was an avid supporter of arts and artists of every genre, with local art events and news articles spread about like confetti on tables and bulletin boards. Jonathan was one of the die-hard supporters of the café, as establishments such as this were becoming a thing of the past. During the 1950s and 1960s, coffee shops had sprung up all over and were a major venue for the artsy crowd, would-be writers, actors, and activists. They were meeting places, providing forums for discussion and knowledge sharing. Unfortunately, the recession in the '70s was causing services of this nature to disappear from the scene—a new crowd of pub-goers were arriving with gusto, all anxious to enjoy a lower-priced classic pub menu of burgers, fish and chips, and such.

He was browsing through the local rag when an art exhibition caught his full attention. His mouth creased into a fatuous grin. There she was, staring up at him. She had been photographed standing outside her art gallery, marketing her upcoming event. Her gallery had only recently opened, and he wondered how he could have missed the promotion. No doubt she had been boosting her stock levels when he saw her in Bonn, in readiness for a major publicity splash at her opening.

She'd obviously sunk a sizeable sum into the marketing, judging by the eye-catching advertisement for the gallery opening, as it impressively covered most of the page, listing the date, location, and ticket availability.

"Sarah, my goddess, finally the hunt comes to fruition." He almost shrieked in delight.

The waiter raised his eyebrows as he refilled Jonathan's coffee cup.

*Hmm, another fruit loop invades the establishment,* he was thinking. *If they're not wailing and weeping over somebody's creativity, they're talking to pictures.*

He was new to the job, and in fact the whole area, and had no idea how his prosaic personality was about to undergo a major change, as he was introduced to the chiaroscuro of a new and colourful life in the neighbourhood.

The coffee shop proprietor was one of the distributors of the costly tickets. Their high price helped to offset the costs of the afternoon catering and festivities to be included in the exhibition. Gulping back the last of his coffee, Jonathan wasted no time in rushing over to the counter to pay for his ticket, actually snatching it feverishly from the man's hand as it was handed to him. About to leave the café, he was hauled up sharply at the sound of the waiter's irate voice.

"Hang on there a minute. Aren't we forgetting something? What about the coffee?"

"Sincere apologies, I completely forgot in my haste to get the ticket."

Covered with embarrassment, Jonathan paid the waiter, pacifying him with a generous tip, and made a speedy exit out of the door.

\*\*\*\*

The day of the exhibition finally dawned. The month of waiting had passed slowly and Jonathan, almost sick with anticipation, had a hard time downing his breakfast. This was unusual for him, considering that his first meal of the day was generally his favourite and quite the ritual, to be eaten slowly and leisurely.

Following a long shower, he surveyed his wardrobe. What would he wear? Eventually, mind made up, he settled on a fine wool blazer, his favourite Italian silk tie and shirt, with pure wool flannel slacks, the crease of which would have cut a man's finger. Finally, dressed to his satisfaction, he made his way out and, after a cursory glance at himself in the hall mirror, took off before his nerves got the better of him.

The little gallery was crowded when he arrived, even though he had allowed copious amounts of time. Once again, Sarah was surrounded by avid admirers, their interest focused as much on her as on the art she was introducing.

She looked up, and her eyes met his, this time with not a hint of alarm, only keen interest, much to Jonathan's delight.

*I can't let her slip through my fingers this time,* he thought, moving swiftly in her direction.

He was within a stone's throw when she was besieged by another group.

"This calls for extreme measures," he said under his breath as he propelled himself forward. "Sarah, darling, you look ravishing, sweetheart."

Pushing his way through the throng, he threw his arms around her and, bending to her upturned face, kissed her passionately—a kiss neither seemed disposed to break off.

"Don't forget our luncheon at The Black Bear," he said, catching his breath as he came up for air. "1:00 sharp! I'll be waiting for you."

He then breezed out of the gallery without even pausing to look at the art on display, in case she saw how ruffled he was and that his nerve was about to escape him.

****

The Black Bear pub was just a few minutes from the gallery. He'd chosen it specially, thinking she would be pressed for time, as it was the grand opening of the gallery. He knew he'd dropped the luncheon on her unexpectedly but was hoping she could spare some time with him—she did have to eat, after all.

It was already ten minutes past one, although to an extremely agitated Jonathan, the time seemed longer than it actually was. He sat, swirling his glass of whisky on the rocks, anguishing that she was not going to show.

Just when he was hoping an earthquake or something similar would swallow him up, he was rewarded with her enigmatic presence. A light touch on his arm urged him to look up into her face, so full of warmth, and there was the mystery again. Leaping to his feet, he grabbed her hand, not knowing quite what else to do, and definitely not wishing to push his luck with another passionate kiss now that she was actually here with him.

"You startled me," he said, pulling her chair out to seat her. "Caught me at a disadvantage, sneaking up behind me like that."

Laughing, she tossed her cascading hair over her shoulder. How intoxicating she was!

"Well, just thought I'd return the Favor. Best not to meet your opponent head on, don't you think?"

"Opponent, no, just your devoted servant, madam, to do with what you wish."

Jonathan had noticed earlier that refreshments in the gallery included champagne. He had seen Sarah mingling with her guests with a glass in her hand. Of course, that had been before he'd created such a rumpus and the glass had been almost torn from her grasp when he engulfed her in a passionate embrace. Needless to say, he reckoned champagne was a safe bet and had taken the liberty of having a bottle of the best put on ice for them, to soften the proceedings at the day's lunch.

As he had suspected, she was short on time, so they ordered a large salad and a chicken pie, which they halved, as the portions were enormous.

During lunch, his gaze periodically strayed surreptitiously in the direction of her two behemoths, who were standing across the street.

*If I'm lucky enough to get the chance to know her better, maybe she'll divulge why she has bodyguards on her everywhere she goes,* he thought.

Jonathan had already decided that the two men had to be bodyguards. He actually felt a little uncomfortable at their forbidding presence but was not going to be put off completely—not this early in the game, anyway.

"So, tell me a little about yourself," he said as he poured them both another glass of champagne.

"Well, our family home is in Scotland. It is quite beautiful, really—if you can stand the cold, of course. The lakes never warm up, even in the summer, so you can't swim, and the winters are long, cold, and rainy, but the days in between would take your breath away. The heath is mind-boggling, with miles and miles of purple and white heather. You can see massive salmon leaping in the streams crisscrossing the moors. Then the miracle of dozens of full-antlered stags suddenly appearing in procession, crossing the tip of a mountain ridge, silhouetted against an angry sky of raging clouds. Yes," she sighed, "it's a wonderful place; it grabs hold of you and refuses to let you go completely. Scotland will always be my roots. We always spend Christmas there; it's very special. Somehow, the family always manages to be together at that time."

She seemed to be lost, deep in thought, taking her trip down memory lane.

Jonathan nudged her. "I'm still here and all ears."

"Oops, I'm so sorry! How very rude of me. I just get so completely carried away when I think of home. Of course, one always remembers the good things. The winters are evil, as I said; months and months of freezing rain and drizzle, not to mention the snow. The frailties of the human body certainly become apparent when doing battle with the snow. And no matter how warmly dressed you are, the damp cold seems to penetrate every layer of clothing. Mind you, having said all that, the sheer beauty of the place cleanses and energizes your whole spirit and soul."

Jonathan was hanging onto every word. "Wow! That's quite a commendation."

"I know. I'm like a homing pigeon, always trying to go back. I usually aim for the warmest time of year." Her face was flushed with happiness. "Maybe you'll get up there sometime. In fact, maybe I'll take you up there myself, if only to see how hardy you are." She was laughing at him as he screwed up his face with an exaggerated shudder.

Their luncheon was a huge success. By the time they got through the pie and salad, along with the champagne, they found they had so much in common. It was as if they'd known each other forever. They devoured the apple crumble and vanilla ice cream when it arrived shortly after, and were deep into planning their next outing when the coffee was served with a flourish.

Jonathan was hoping at that moment that Sarah wouldn't be suggesting a trip to Scotland for their next get together. He was feeling the effects of the cold ice cream on a tooth which had been acting up and grimaced. His mind had been wandering through the highlands as Sarah was speaking. He'd been imagining himself plunging into one of those icy lakes that apparently never warmed up. *Ah well, perhaps down the road, maybe a mid-summer trip might be nice.*

Taking her arm outside the café, Jonathan looked down at her. "May I walk you back to the gallery, my lady?" he asked with some reluctance, wishing he could spend the rest of the day with her, even though he knew their luncheon had run longer than either of them had expected.

"Of course. It's a nice walk. But we do have to step lively." And laying her hand on his arm a trifle primly, she continued, "We can go through the park."

Once outside the gallery, he bent and planted an innocent kiss on her cheek, resisting the urge to grab and devour her on the spot. He was determined not to rush things and perhaps scare her off. Prudence ruling, he reached into his inside pocket, dragged out his wallet and produced his business card.

"Oh, I almost forgot, you can always reach me on one or the other of these numbers."

Stuffing it into her hand, he was about to turn away when she touched his arm lightly whilst groping in her handbag.

"And here's mine. This will alleviate the necessity for any gate crashing that you might be tempted to try. Of course," she added mischievously, "we needn't exclude the hugs, need we?"

"Darn right, my own sentiments exactly," and he swept her up into his arms again, holding her as long as was decently possible before setting her carefully back on her feet again.

Walking away, he cast a backward glance over his shoulder and was gratified to see she hadn't moved—still standing by the door, obviously wishing to see him off properly until he had disappeared into the trees in the park.

The two behemoths also had not moved. They stood close together across the street, making a feeble attempt at conversation but very obviously not missing a beat.

*Hmm,* he pondered, *what on earth could be so bad that she has to be guarded and protected? There's more to her than meets the eye.*

# Chapter 8
# The Exuberance of Youth

Following their first date, Sarah and Jonathan got together whenever the opportunity presented itself, bonding ever closer with each meeting, both impatient for the next time they would see each other again.

They eventually managed to plan the long-awaited trip to Sarah's family home in Scotland, although it had proved challenging. Both were working on extremely tight schedules, but finally, they were able to coordinate business and set the dates.

Excitement was mounting as they boarded the train. The trip was long overdue—life had kept getting in the way every time they tried to plan a break. Sarah was really looking forward to showing Jonathan around her home and introducing him to her family and friends. They had originally planned to travel in the early summer but had been forced to reschedule to early September. This had actually worked out for the best, as not only was the weather a little warmer but they also had the opportunity of seeing the heather in its prime. The moors were a shimmering carpet of varying shades of purple as far as the eye could see.

Sarah was telling Jonathan all about her northern home as they sat in the dining car of the train, each caressing their glasses of wine, drinking slowly and savouring every moment. Jonathan watched her intently. Business forgotten for a time, her face softened and glowed when she talked about her birthplace and the beauty of the area.

"Scotland is really quite beautiful you know, Jon, quite a different beauty from your parent's place in Hertfordshire. It's a wild land, raw and natural, a mystical place where the land and sea meld into a huge sky stretching into infinity. The controversy that pits sheep farming, with its clearing of forested areas, against the reforestation needed to support deer has been going on for centuries. But even with man's interference, it's still relatively wild and for the most part still untouched in some parts, in the same way that the true voice of a Gaelic singer is untouched before losing its purity to overtraining in readiness for acceptance into the opera hall."

"Yes, I know exactly what you mean—unspoilt and pure. But do go on, Sarah, sorry to interrupt. I want to hear all about it and can hardly wait to see some of this." And this was sincere. Jonathan was eager to see everything, although he was harbouring some anxiety at the prospect of meeting Sarah's parents.

"Our property still maintains a small flock of sheep, consisting of mixed Cheviots and Merinos bred for both fine and coarser wools. The adjacent mill was converted to a much smaller building in recent years, with all the mod cons. We now produce a small, but very exclusive, range of specialized wool in many dyes and shades, reminiscent of the beautiful colours we see throughout the Scottish countryside. It's quite a tourist pull to the area. We offer a full overview and pamphlets, on the rearing of the sheep, through the wool processes, up to and including the wearing of the woollen articles of clothing.

"The cloth industry is still around, although not what it was some years ago, and our business still utilizes individual small cloth companies in the towns. We also employ personal weavers from the smaller villages. These people produce handmade sweaters, scarves, hats, and the like. Because those items are not mass produced, they're classed as luxury goods, hence the very high price. The finer wools can be mixed with cashmere, producing fabulous cardigans and sweaters. All of our items can also be purchased by special order from a catalogue which generates a large percentage of our business. That being said, the operation is really more of an educational hobby-farm to give tourists an idea of the dyeing business, if you'll pardon the pun."

She laughed at her own wit, in spite of the industry's serious decline.

"That being said, our business ventures do pay their way, with a very modest profit margin, which makes them a viable proposition. We also provide employment for quite a number of people. A small section of the house has been turned over to bed and breakfast, and parts of the out-buildings have been converted to stables housing a few horses for guests' riding pleasure. That's about it, really."

"Your family certainly seems to have thought of everything. Who on earth manages that lot?"

"Tom, our resident manager, supervises all the staff, including a couple of shepherds who are employed by the estate and work under the estate manager's supervision. Tom lives in an adjacent cottage, along with a clan of border collies who, if the truth were known, are the ones that actually manage the sheep. As with the sheep, for the most part these dogs are hand-picked for their barking and focusing abilities. Did you know that most border collies rarely bark at the sheep they focus? One look from one of them is all it takes to weaken the toughest sheep's argument. Some dogs will bark if necessary, and between them, they can take on the most ornery and formidable group of woollies. They're a force to be reckoned with and really take some handling, but they certainly know how to keep the flock in line.

"It may all sound very grand, but as I say, it's actually a hobby business more than anything, just to keep the industry alive. It's not on the scale that sheep farming used to be by any means. While the estate is much smaller now, it's still a huge running expenditure, what with taxes etcetera, so it really has to be self-sustaining. Our main living accommodation in the house is maintained by Elspeth; she's the housekeeper. That area is used by the family as a retreat for vacations. Anyway, you'll see all that during our visit. Are you excited? I know I am to actually be going home again. It's been a while."

"Yes, it really is exciting. I've been up to Scotland a few times, but never by train and never for a prolonged stay. This trip is quite an adventure for me. Isn't it gorgeous, absolutely superb?"

Jonathan and his lovely companion fell silent, lulled by the comfort of the train as they gazed out of the window. Jonathan suddenly broke their contemplative silence with an enthusiastic yelp, as he leaned forward in his seat to get a better view out of the window.

"It's exactly as you said, Sarah! What an absolute delight—miles and miles of purple heather."

And it was. Stretching into the horizon, the glorious display was broken only by the numerous rivers, streams, and large dark patches of bog chiselling lines across the moors, defining even further the backcloth of magnificent hills. Jonathan was enthralled.

Rose and Stewart were at the station to meet them. Sarah was thrilled to see her parents smiling broadly. Their faces lit up the minute they caught sight of the pair clambering down onto the platform. They'd obviously made the effort to be a complete family when greeting their daughter's new man friend for the first time. Sarah had known they'd rise to the occasion, in spite of their separation.

She could see immediately how impressed they were with Jonathan, and why wouldn't they be? He was gorgeous, the typical tall, dark, handsome prince every girl dreams of. His manners were impeccable. He was charming, and of course, Rose was absolutely bowled over.

Sarah squeezed Jonathan's hand and whispered in his ear, as they followed her parents to the car, "Well, it looks like you've made quite a hit with Mum."

"It's your dad I'm worried about. He looks like he's reserving judgement. Jury's definitely out."

Jonathan loved the little he had seen of the property as they entered through wrought iron gates. Once inside, they were met by Elspeth. The huge hall, even though a little intimidating, exuded warmth and welcome, with flowers everywhere, obviously Rose's contribution. He was filled with admiration for this beautiful, gracious lady who welcomed him into their family as if he'd been around forever.

Jonathan was not aware of the full details of Rose and Stewart's separation, only that they were living apart. Seeing them together arm in arm, it was apparent to him that they still adored each other, their eyes meeting at regular intervals, never really leaving each other, it seemed. He was not to know that Rose and Stewart had united temporarily in the home that they both loved to distraction. Everything else bearing down on them was irrelevant at this moment, as they led the young people into the house.

Their daughter, who had always been so hell-bent on the pursuit of her career, had actually brought a man home to meet them. This was a man she obviously thought highly of, and Sarah was anxiously looking from one to the other, willing their approval—which, of course, they extended.

That night, everybody gathered in the dining room. Tom had been invited, and of course, his border collies were not excluded from the invitation, particularly as they had just come through a few hectically busy months.

Tom's pride in his clan was obvious as he explained how the year had begun with their work during lambing season. This had been a particularly perilous time, with several pregnant ewes getting stuck in snow banks or lost in the inevitable blizzards. The dogs had put in fifteen hours a day, on occasion, searching out the ewes and herding them to safer ground. They had worked to the point of exhaustion. Shearing of the sheep had come at the end of June, once again with no respite for them, as they played a major role in the operation—really earning their keep by herding and nipping the flanks of the more obstinate sheep to get them into their respective pens.

"What have they been up to during the last two months then?" said Jonathan, bending to pet them as they leaned against his legs. "Or have they been able to rest a bit?"

"These dogs never rest." Tom cast an appraising glance over them. "They've been assisting me with training some new pups. We generally start the pups off with the older, more seasoned sheep, who are used to working with the dogs. You'd be amazed at how quickly the pups learn—the herding instinct comes out almost immediately they get through the gate into the fields, and if they get too rambunctious, they find themselves also being herded. They catch on right away. We even managed to attend a couple of local sheep dog trials and, I'm proud to say, picked up a ribbon or two."

After the last course had been served, and eaten with gusto, everyone adjourned to the library. What a prodigious gathering it had been. For the first time in years, Jonathan had the feeling of belonging, as if he were actually part of a genuine family. He was beginning to realize just how truly alone he had been over the years. There was no substitute for a warm house with loving people and hordes of dogs lounging on your feet in front of a roaring fire. Not to mention the wee dram of Drambuie. What bliss!

The next morning, Jonathan stretched languidly in his four-poster bed. The warmth of the sun penetrated the lace curtains in his bedroom, welcoming him with the promise of a fantastic day. Following an invigorating shower, he dressed and made his way downstairs.

The house was shrouded in silence, like being cocooned after a heavy snowstorm. Jonathan absorbed the quiet atmosphere. He was calm and completely rested after a really good night's sleep. He'd even placed a quick call to Mark to settle a matter they had been pondering.

*Yes, this is definitely a soothing environment.*

Making his way to the kitchen, he noticed that cups were set up at the ready, and a big urn of tea sat on the hob. What a welcome sight.

Elspeth suddenly made an appearance.

"Good morning, sir," she said, positively bowing. "Did you sleep well?"

"I most certainly did. What a wonderful old house this is, so inviting."

"Well, it's the people, that what I say. I've worked on this estate practically all my life, and my family before that. The Buchanans are good people, the best, and you can feel it as soon as you step through the front door."

"I know exactly what you mean. I felt it too when I arrived yesterday."

It was true. He had experienced the warmth of the people as soon as he walked through the door into the great hallway. He felt he was welcome in this house, with this family, a family he was just beginning to discover.

Elspeth ushered him into the library with tea, homemade crumpets, and jam to hold him until breakfast was formally served. He hesitated as he entered the library, his eyes falling upon Stewart, who was standing over by the fireplace with his tea. Jonathan needn't have been apprehensive. Stewart's smile was spontaneous, his expression open, as it had been the night before. That was the beginning of a strong, father-type relationship, which had been sorely lacking up to that point in Jonathan's life.

That day was just for lounging about and having a short tour of the property. Jonathan was fascinated with the whole operation and getting along famously with Tom, who took him through the processes of running the operation. While both men were occupied, Sarah took the opportunity to go in and make a few business calls that couldn't wait for her return to London the following week. Sitting at the desk by her bedroom window, she was idly turning the pages of her calendar when there was a knock at the door. It was her mother, and she was absolutely full of it as she sat on the end of the bed, gushing.

"Where on earth did you find him? He's absolutely perfect."

Putting her pen down, Sarah smiled coyly. "Yes, he is, isn't he? Actually, he found me," she added. "He literally swept me off my feet."

Her mother was all ears, hanging on every word as Sarah relayed the story of Jonathan grabbing her in a passionate embrace the first time he had come into the gallery.

"Thank God he took the initiative. You certainly never would have." Rose was grinning knowingly.

"And you'll never believe it; he tracked me down after that auction, you know, the one I attended in Bonn. It was quite a few months ago now. Anyway, he was bidding like crazy on the painting that François did for me. He was determined to have it. And," with an impish grin at her mother, "he paid a pretty penny for it, too. In fact, it's hanging in his library as we speak."

"Well, it's just as well I didn't get a chance to buy the portrait before you auctioned it. I loved that picture and was really peeved when I missed the boat. But I suppose it all works out in the end. We probably wouldn't be seeing the two of you together this way and so deliriously happy if Jonathan hadn't bought the picture and gone searching for you."

"Oh, stop it, Mum. He's just a really good friend."

"I think he's more than that, sweetheart."

"Anyway, just to continue with the story," Sarah blundered on, "as I was having my gallery promotion, he suddenly appeared. Of course, I was surrounded by people, and he literally barged through and swept me off my feet and into his arms, telling me not to forget about our luncheon later that day at The Black Bear. After kissing me passionately, he breezed out. I didn't even have a chance to refuse or anything. You remember that little pub near the gallery, don't you? You know, the one with the lovely brocade upholstery on the seats. We had lunch in there that day."

"Yes, of course I know the one. Stewart and I have had lunch there several times also." Rose's face clouded momentarily, but she forged on. "And come off it, Sarah. It's highly unlikely you would have refused lunch after an entrance like that by Jonathan."

"Well, I suppose you're right. He's really something, isn't he? I can't believe we found each other."

Neither realized how quickly the time flew by, as it always did when they got talking. They had remained very close and never ran out of things to talk about.

Rose glanced down at her watch.

"Oh my goodness, we'd better break this up. There's a load to be done before dinner and our get-together this evening." Leaping to her feet, Rose hugged her daughter. "I love you, sweetheart."

"And I do too. I mean, I love you as well."

Both were laughing as they went downstairs to check on the eating arrangements and set the plans for the evening's entertainment.

# Chapter 9
# Memories for the Treasure Chest

The next day dawned. Peering over the satin edge of the blanket, Jonathan surveyed his surroundings and stretched expansively. What a splendid morning, promising another great day.

*Hmm, two amazing days in a row; this is too good to last.*

And it was. At that very moment of bliss, Sarah began banging on his door, begging him to get a move on. Jonathan had thought they were going riding a little later in the day, perhaps after mid-morning coffee. Alas, not to be.

*Sparrow fart—it's barely sun-up.* Mildly irritated, he turned over again and pulled the blanket over his head. *What on earth is she thinking?*

He'd always had a hard time getting the day underway, preferring to feed into it gently. He had been up and about before anyone else the preceding day, as it was the beginning of his holiday, but this morning, he'd been planning on a later start.

What a struggle to get himself organized. Finally, he made it downstairs, to be greeted in the kitchen once again with a huge pot of tea and some warm crumpets to sustain him for a while, as a breakfast/lunch picnic had been planned for the day's outing. There was no holding him. Determined to make sure he was well and truly fortified, he grabbed a plate and got stuck in. After all, there could be some delays before they finally got their picnic organized.

Once outside, Jonathan took a moment to gaze about him. The horses were already harnessed, saddled, and ready to go. Sarah grinned at him as she hauled herself up into the saddle.

"Are you still in shock? You look absolutely befuddled. I told you, didn't I? It grabs hold of you, doesn't it? You may arrive as a stranger, but when you leave, a tiny part of your heart lingers in your wake, and you take a little of the country when you go, wherever you go."

"What's really grabbing hold of me right now is this unearthly hour. I had thought a leisurely breakfast, followed by coffee on the veranda a little later, and then a gentle ride across the heath."

"Well, the sheer wild beauty will certainly capture you during our ride, and you'll be glad we made the effort to leave early to get the most out of the day."

"I'll take your word for it," he grumbled, savouring the taste of the crumpet still on his tongue.

"Elspeth has packed us a wonderful picnic hamper. See over there? It's strapped on Humphrey's back." Sarah pointed to the bigger of the two horses. "He's the one you'll be riding."

Completely enamoured with the thought of the day ahead, Sarah was not to be put off, and rambled on in spite of Jonathan's ill humour.

"It's a really old wicker hamper that has passed through several generations. Just think of all the people who have enjoyed a ride and picnic before us. Isn't it something?"

"Yes, it certainly is," said Jonathan as he climbed up into Humphrey's saddle. "Mind you, I'm a little more interested in what's inside the hamper rather than its history, after the ungainly rush this morning."

Sarah mounted Primrose, and they were off.

They had been ambling along for an hour or so when, following an easy trek up one of the gentler hills, they arrived at the summit. Pausing to scan the spell-binding view, both deeply inhaled the good, clean air into their lungs. The sun had climbed higher and was now peeping above the neighbouring mountains, casting a soft glow over the landscape.

Jonathan was utterly entranced. It was indeed a cathartic moment, absolutely breathtaking.

Dismounting, they turned the horses loose to graze, and after arranging their tartan blanket on an even piece of ground, sat scanning the horizon as the early morning mist slowly cleared.

"You are absolutely right about getting off smartly this morning. Now we have the whole day before us. This is euphoric."

"Yes, I told you, and so is the spread," said Sarah as she began rifling through the chequered cloths, finally managing to retrieve the bottle of wine as a starter.

"You're as bad as Helmut when it comes to food, always hungry," Jonathan said. "And look at the size of you. Such a tiny little thing; can't imagine where you put it."

"Well, you didn't do so badly earlier in the kitchen either. Don't think I didn't notice you hawking back those crumpets. How many did you have, anyway?"

Without waiting for a response, she moved towards a little mountain stream close to their picnic spot and, smiling back at him, placed the wine bottle carefully on some white pebbles just below the clear surface of the water.

"That'll keep it extra cold until we're ready," she said, eagerly, laying out their lunch on a well-worn chequered tablecloth.

What a picnic hamper that was, seemingly endless, filled with all sorts of goodies to tempt them. Good old Elspeth.

Then the deer appeared—the icing on the cake—making their way slowly over the top of the neighbouring mountain. They wore their new, fully grown antlers proudly, having shed the old ones in spring. What a sight. The couple were in awe of the regal animals as they cruised across the horizon—a silent procession of incredible grace in spite of their size.

"It's like watching a mute slide show in full motion, isn't it?"

Sarah smiled and even stopped fiddling with the hamper while both avidly watched the magnificent procession.

Once the animals had passed from sight, Jonathan retrieved the wine from the spring. The air was filled with their squeals of delight as they pounced on the hamper and arranged the food on the blanket. Then silence ensued, as both quietly munched their way through lunch.

Appetite finally appeased; Jonathan stretched his lean frame on the blanket.

"What a smart decision to take this time out to be together and do a few things. We've both been going flat out, pushing our work to the hilt and need this down time."

"I should say. It really is lovely here and I'm so looking forward to our visit to Germany after this. Finally, I'll get to meet your friends Helmut and Gertrude. You've talked so much about them; I feel as if I know them myself."

"Yes, I'm looking forward to that as well; haven't seen them for quite a while. I can't wait to catch up on all the news and introduce you. I know they're going to just love you. What a gathering it will be."

Jonathan was aware that he had not seen any behemoths on this trip and Sarah appeared completely relaxed. He eased himself up on his elbow.

"Sarah, forgive me for asking, and just say the word if I'm out of line, but I haven't seen any of the 'big boys' on this trip. Why do you have bodyguards around you? Or are they security?"

Sarah paled under Jonathan's scrutiny.

"I'm not sure if I should tell you or not, but I suppose if we're to move on, we need to drag it all out of the cupboard and get it on the table."

And so Sarah relayed the sad tale of her sister's turmoil and the toll it was taking on all of their lives.

"My sister has also involved herself with drug pushers and the more unsavoury element of the human species. A couple of times, thugs have been thwarted in their attempts to grab me because of Jane's drug-dealing business with them. Things can get pretty ugly when people of this calibre are owed money. My father has been very concerned for my safety and has insisted on hiring some security people to keep an eye on me. They are ex-police and dad's friends. I've known them for years, as they've visited the house quite regularly. Must say, I'm relieved they are around. I've had more frights than I want. The lowlifes that Jane is messing around with can be dangerous and have to be taken seriously."

Sarah was quiet for a few moments, her thoughts wandering. "Mum and Dad have called a truce on their separation while you're here, but their marriage is all but destroyed because of Jane's history."

"Well, they're putting up a really good front; they're obviously still very much in love—anyone can see that."

"Yes, and I'm glad that you're here, because they both gravitate to this place. This is their real home, and it's here where everything comes together for them. This get-together just might rekindle old and good memories. So let's be positive. I still believe there's hope for them getting back as they were."

"I feel the same way about my parents, but my brother Nate really did a number on us and left us with a pile of issues to sort out."

Sarah stretched out on the blanket, causing her sweater to ride up exposing the outline of the scars on her side.

Jonathan diverted his gaze but not before he'd seen the vivid red gashes on her skin. He was aghast. He could see that the scars were angry and obviously fairly recent.

"What in God's name happened to you?"

"Oh, that's just another example of Jane's problem. She hadn't taken her medication, and that brings out the worst in her. She's being held indefinitely in rehab under psychiatric care until she's been stabilized."

Jonathan frowned. "Well, those wounds are fairly recent. This must have happened just before we met. I remember you had said you were out of commission for a while? It was all very secretive."

"Well, I couldn't really get into the fact that my sister tried to kill me, now, could I?"

On the spur of the moment, Jonathan reached out and grabbed her, holding her close, his mind reeling at the thought of her beautiful body being hacked into with such ferocity. Shaken to the core, he was thinking that with all he had suffered, physical violence had not been part of it. He abhorred the very thought of Sarah being subjected to such trauma.

"I had no idea you were in hospital and for such a vile reason. Any hospital visit is foul, but that is unspeakable. I'm so sorry I was not there. I wish I'd been in your life at that time. I would have taken care of you, and that's a given. What a rotten experience for you."

Sarah put her arms around him and felt a shudder pass through his body. She thought again what a very caring man he was. He had a calming protectiveness about him that she found very endearing.

"Now that's out in the open, thank goodness. Let's move on. What about your family, Jon?"

"Aha, the moment of reckoning is here. I suppose I should fess up about my own situation and you can see what a lash-up my family's lives have been."

Sarah raised an eyebrow. "I'm all ears." And then, upon hearing the story, became deadly serious. "Oh Jon, how sad. I'm so sorry, you poor thing. What a pair we are. We've both had such horrors to overcome. Isn't it strange that we've walked parallel paths through our lives?"

Drugged by the earthy smell of the heath, the heavy lunch, wine, emotional upheaval, followed by perfect relaxation, both were overtaken by sleep, tightly enveloped in each other's arms. Warm, secure, at peace with the world and each other.

Sarah was the first to awaken. "Oh my goodness, look at the time. We've slept almost two hours."

Jonathan sat up with a start. "What about the horses? Are they still around?"

"Of course they are, silly. They're quite used to this. A picnic usually ends in a little doze, although, I must admit, it was more than a little doze. We really gave into it, didn't we? Everything's so perfect, though a little nap just rounds it off, don't you think?"

They glanced around and sure enough, Humphrey and Primrose were a short distance away, quietly munching on the verdure. Rising quickly to their feet, they gathered up the remains of the picnic. Sarah reached into the hamper and pulled out two carrots. The horses trotted forward eagerly for their treats and munched away happily as the young couple folded the blanket, placed it back in the hamper, and closed the lid.

As they were about to leave, Jonathan took Sarah in his arms. "This has been so great, Sarah. I'll always remember this terrific day. Being here with you has been so special, and there's more to come. It's going to be fabulous taking you around and showing you all my stomping grounds and favourite haunts in Germany. Not to mention showing you off to all my friends there."

Well, he wouldn't have to wait too long. Following a brief stopover in London to attend to business, soon enough they were boarding their flight to Germany.

# Chapter 10
## Germany, Here We Come

The door was flung open in welcome as Helmut met them with joyous greetings.

"Wie get's, Bär?" Jonathan squeaked as he struggled for breath while trying to hug his friend—an almost impossible feat, as his arms would barely reach around Helmut's midriff.

Sarah howled with laughter because even with her limited German, she recognized the word bear and how fitting it was for Helmut. What an enormous man and what a welcome he extended to her. In no time at all, she slotted into the group as if she'd always been an integral part.

The two women took to each other right away and were soon deeply entrenched in some serious talk. Helmut nudged Jonathan as they joined the girls in the lounge.

"Just look at them. It's as if they've known each other all their lives."

"Yes, it's terrific, really great! There's usually one person who doesn't fit in, but it looks like we're all a perfect match for each other."

Quite some time later, Gertrude leapt to her feet and literally shoved Helmut towards the kitchen.

"Dinner, Liebchen! If we don't get dinner underway soon, our friends are going to desert us in search of sustenance elsewhere."

Helmut laughed. He loved it when she bossed him around. He very obviously adored her and, sweeping her off her feet, he propelled her into the kitchen, kicking the door shut behind him. Gertrude's shrieks of laughter echoed from behind the closed door.

When they were alone, Jonathan lowered his voice as he took Sarah's hand. "Well, what do you think of them then?" he said softly.

"I just love them, simply love them. What a super couple they are."

They were both grinning broadly at each other as they listened to the chatter and clatter emanating from the kitchen. What a joy to have such friends, and how decadent was the pampering Helmut and Gertrude were extending to them.

After a dinner fit for the gentry, Helmut carried a tray of coffee into the lounge. The enticing aroma of freshly ground beans spread throughout the little apartment. Gertrude brought up the rear, carefully balancing a tray of liqueurs to go with it. She cast a concerned glance at Sarah.

"Hope you like this one, Sarah, but have a small taste first. It's really strong, and if you aren't used to it, it could have a bad effect on you. It's called 'traffic lights' to the locals and is a mix of Jägermeister, Eierlikör, and Killepitsch, a local liqueur originating in Düsseldorf. You'll notice the colours stay in place in the glass, red, yellow and green, hence 'traffic lights'. As I said, you have to be careful with this stuff. It'll knock the socks off you if you're not used to it. Don't feel bad if you can't handle it. I can take it off your hands."

Sarah practically went into convulsions after taking her first sip, gasping as the warmth flooded throughout her body, while Gertrude stood patiently, awaiting her approval or otherwise. As soon as Sarah was able to regain her breath, she looked up at her new-found friend, grinning sheepishly.

"Delicious, absolutely delicious, and yes, I can certainly finish my glass. No need to take it off my hands. I can handle it."

"Well, I'll have my eye on you in case there are any repercussions. We're used to it, aren't we Jon?" and with a knowing wink, she added, "I can see this girl of yours has led a very sheltered life."

"Yep, we'll have to break her in gently, won't we, sweetie?"

He was looking fondly at Sarah, who was so relaxed that she was practically falling off the sofa. Needless to say, she wasn't the brightest star in the sky when Helmut's favourite game, Monopoly, got underway later.

When sleep finally overcame Sarah, the party left her snuggled up and dozing at the end of the sofa. Jonathan played her round, as his had lost abysmally and he'd ended up rotting in the Monopoly jail after losing all of his property and going bankrupt.

Gertrude looked across at Sarah. "Just as well I made sure she only had a taste. Dread to think what would have happened if she'd had a regular tot."

****

The next day, after a short drive to the station, all four piled onto the Schwebebahn, Wuppertal's unique train, which ran suspended from tracks over the Wupper River. Opening in 1901, it was the oldest overhead railway in the world and considered the most efficient of its kind.

They were going to have an easy day of sightseeing in the town, hopping off and on the train at various ports of call. What a shopping spree they had, ending up later in a little hofbräu, eating seafood and drinking lager.

"Anyone for dessert?" Helmut said expansively.

Jonathan leaned back in his chair, feeling more than a little stuffed. "Boy oh boy, you've eaten enough already to feed an army, and I'm absolutely bloated. What about you two?" He looked across at Sarah and Gertrude.

Helmut conceded. "Tell you what, why don't we have gelato for dessert a little later when we get back to Mönchengladbach? There's a terrific gelateria just down the street from our place. They've been springing up everywhere over the last few years. Of course, we're all getting a bit on the mature side," he added soberly. "Some of these cafes still have the old jukebox in the corner. They used to be a major attraction for the young crowd, so we may feel a bit out of place."

"I for one don't care about the age thing, and I don't mind a trip down memory lane with Elvis later," Sarah said. "An ice cream just to cool me down would round the day off. I think it's a great idea, and I think I'm justified in having dessert, as I didn't make a pig of myself like the rest of you. We can discuss and plan our trip down the Rhine tomorrow, which I'm so looking forward to doing."

"It's a done deal," said Helmut, smacking his lips and rolling his eyes. "Mm, gelato, my favorite treat."

Sarah gave him a playful shove. "Come off it, Helmut. From what I hear, everything edible is your favourite treat."

****

They had scheduled a trip down the Rhine to "castle hop," tasting the delights of the wine cellars in the old castles scattered on the way. Helmut had booked them all into a hotel for the night, and they had plans to continue on to the famous Lorelei the following morning.

That evening was very special for the friends, as they sat around the huge stone fireplace running the width of the lounge in the ancient heritage hotel. They were sipping huge mugs of hot chocolate smothered in cream and chocolate sprinkles before going to bed, and not one of them was anxious to break it up. They were all enjoying each other's company so much, and the hotel staff had spared no effort to ensure their visit was everything it should be and more.

"What an excellent dinner, and what better ending to the perfect evening than a warming mug of cocoa in front of the fire," Helmut purred, stretching like an old cat as he warmed his feet on the hearth.

Sarah wrinkled her nose. "You'll get chilblains if you continue to fry your toes like that."

"What on earth are chilblains?" Helmut spluttered, drawing his feet under his chair. "Let's have it, Sarah. I'm on the edge of my seat."

"Chilblains are nasty, itchy red patches that can develop on your feet, or hands, for that matter. It happens when your extremities have been really cold and then are warmed up too quickly—by sticking them practically in the fire, for example. The small blood vessels get inflamed by the sudden change in temperature. The Brits are very familiar with chilblains, as half the time there's no heating, because of strikes or lack of money to keep their fires going. They're a tough nation—they just grit their teeth and put on another jumper and extra socks."

By now, Sarah was laughing as an increasingly uncomfortable Helmut moved his chair back from the hearth.

"Of course, the brick and stone houses in England don't hold much heat, so if your heating system packs up, it can get pretty cold, but if you're lucky enough to have a fire, everybody huddles around it for warmth. Then you're in for a really uncomfortable time of it if you stick your feet too near the flames."

As Sarah finished her spiel, Jonathan grabbed her hands and hauled her to her feet.

"And that's telling you," he said, shaking his head at Helmut. "Come on, we'd better make tracks, or we'll never get to bed."

They left, smiling over their shoulders at Helmut, who was avidly examining his toes, trying to ignore the peals of laughter emanating from Gertrude in the far corner of the room.

The next morning, Gertrude was getting a little impatient. Helmut knew it never paid to keep her waiting. She was a bundle of energy and couldn't stand hanging about. It was particularly bad now, as she was excited about the trip and couldn't wait to get going. They had been standing outside by the car, waiting for Sarah and Jonathan, for quite a few minutes.

"They're certainly taking their time, aren't they?" Gertrude was now stomping from one foot to the other dangling the car keys.

"Ah, here comes the lovely couple now, and they really do make a lovely pair, don't they Gertrude? They're made for each other."

Helmut was relieved to see Jonathan and Sarah and was making light of the situation, as he expected Gertrude to self-combust at any moment.

Sarah and Jonathan were strolling nonchalantly towards them, arm in arm, faces wreathed in smiles, apparently unaware that they were holding up the party.

"It's hard to stay annoyed with them for being late," Gertrude conceded. "I absolutely agree with you Helmut. Look at their faces, just radiating happiness."

Gertrude was the designated driver and had already made it very plain she wouldn't be touching any drink. Nothing was going to spoil their time together. There was no argument from the rest of them, as all three were relishing the prospect of the wine tasting during their foray into the castles and their cellars. They had planned a night stop in St. Goarshausen so that they could have a fresh start the following day to explore the area.

Helmut certainly knew his stuff when it came to organizing a trip. His choice of hotel was a lovely old traditional building constructed in pink bricks and sporting loads of turrets and tiny windows overlooking the Rhine.

Jonathan raised his glass that evening when the four gathered around the table for dinner.

"To my friends and my soul mate," he added, his gaze settling on Sarah. "What a truly wonderful day."

Sarah smiled. She was beginning to love this man so deeply; it was a little unnerving. She had never felt this way about any man before. Jonathan, enthusiastic and handsome, was looking at her with such love in his eyes, simply exuding warmth and charm. He offered everything her heart could possibly desire.

Lost in his gaze, her thoughts running astray, she had to give herself a shake, suddenly becoming aware that she was the centre of attention. Helmut and Gertrude were nudging each other, grinning from ear to ear.

Sarah began prattling. "Well, I'm fascinated by this beautiful woman of the Lorelei that people talk about. Imagine having the ability to cause captains to lose their ships against the rocks because of her sheer beauty and allure. The stories and legends seem to have immortalized her forever."

"Funnily enough," said Jonathan, "I've thought the same thing every time I've looked at your picture in my library. I marvel at the sheer beauty of the woman who has, most definitely, the ability to bring a man to his ruin. There's no doubt about it, she's certainly been immortalized forever on canvas." He fixed his eyes steadily on her.

"Oh, stop it, for heaven's sake, you're embarrassing our friends."

"Let me tell you a story of that lovely legendary lady on the rock," Helmut interrupted, diving in lest his tale should remain untold. "The Lorelei cliff is surrounded by the most dangerous waters of the Rhine, as evidenced by the number of shipwrecks lurking in its murky depths."

Being a true raconteur, Helmut made the most of the stage and enjoyed every minute of it, words rolling off his tongue and drifting on the winds of drama.

"There are many legends and stories surrounding the whole area, tales told to this day of a beautiful woman who used to sit and sunbathe and lure the ships' captains and sailors to their deaths by mesmerizing them with her sheer beauty. Of course, it's debatable as to whether it was her sunbathing or her wonderful hair that did them in. Nevertheless, there are very strong beliefs and myths surrounding her, and they've been around for several centuries."

Helmut would have carried on all night if Gertrude hadn't broken up the gathering.

"Raus! Everyone out. If we don't break this up, we'll never make it in the morning. We have another early start."

None of them had any trouble sleeping that night. Waking up refreshed the next morning, they were all eager and ready to see the area. Towering more than 400 feet above St. Goarshausen was the rock of Lorelei—an impressive sight. They had decided to walk to the outskirts of the town, where it met up with the rocky headland jutting out at its furthest point into the river. Their one-mile jaunt from the town became increasingly exhausting and treacherous, especially for Helmut, who was really beginning to suffer. Several times, they almost decided to turn back but were suddenly rewarded with another spectacular view, whether of the widest sweep of the Rhine or the 14th-century castles Katz and Maus, a little further north. Affectionately known as Cat and Mouse, the larger and more impressive of the two was Katz, which had been built to outshine Maus during the many territorial rivalries in that century.

From this viewpoint, it was easy to imagine the woman of legend sitting out on the peninsula, complacently confident that her beauty had the ability to sap a man's will and judgement.

The entire area had been so alluring that they hated to leave the next day, but a tight schedule had to be kept. They knew Helmut had gone to a great deal of trouble to make their trip to Germany as memorable as possible and was really packing in all the must-dos and must-sees during their stay, although the general consensus was that because he was wiped out from the hike, Helmut would be cutting a few items from their agenda over the next few days.

They made good time on their trip back to Mönchengladbach, as they weren't making any stopovers. Helmut briefly outlined the itinerary he'd planned for the visit over the upcoming days, and it was, as they had suspected, reduced somewhat to more realistic proportions. Nevertheless, if they were to keep to it, they had to stay on the move for the rest of their vacation.

Their car ride home was exhilarating, with non-stop talk of the fabulous sights, food, and wine, and it was agreed unanimously that resting up the next day was a good idea, because the morning following would see them setting out for Holland—specifically, Amsterdam.

****

Sarah and Jonathan were outside of Helmut's and Gertrude's residence punctually, bright-eyed and bushy-tailed. They had been determined not to risk Gertrude's wrath by being late this time.

Jonathan, as always, had business on his mind and had arranged a meeting with Hans, a long-standing friend and contact in the antique dealing business. He was going to preview some Delftware, as well as an engagement ring Hans had acquired from an estate sale. Jonathan knew Sarah was the only one for him and had been thinking about asking her to marry him for some time, so Hans's call was fortuitous. Realizing how serious his friend was about Sarah, Hans had earmarked the ring. He knew it would grab Jonathan's interest as soon as he saw it—a rare piece indeed.

As it happened, like two peas in a pod, Sarah was also interested in taking the opportunity to hook up with one of her business contacts in the antique world. He was holding a couple of Dutch oils they had previously discussed and agreed would be of interest to her.

After a mouth-watering lunch at one of the more sought-out pannekoek restaurants in Amsterdam, Helmut grabbed Gertrude's arm.

"Ok, people," he said, "we'll all meet up at 5:00 sharp at the Windmill Restaurant, by the sea. See you then." They were also set on their own pursuits and didn't want to waste a minute.

"And don't be late, do you hear me?" Gertrude was laughing and pointing a finger at Sarah and Jonathan, but they knew she was deadly serious.

The two couples split up after exchanging the address of the restaurant where they would meet later. There would be no mistaking the building. It was an actual windmill, set back from the sea in Harderwijk, a clean little seaside town, with soft, sandy beaches bordered by such shallow water that one could wade for hours and never get wet above the waist.

The restaurant portion of the windmill was in the lower level. Very small and intimate, it was known for its great menu and vast number of different foods on offer. True to form, Helmut, knowing where every fine eatery was to be had, came up trumps yet again.

Jonathan's focus had been diverted periodically as he dressed for dinner that night, pleasurable thoughts settling on the earlier business of the day and the ring. Hans had been right. Jonathan was smitten the moment he set eyes upon it: a beautiful Edwardian engagement ring set in platinum, with a large diamond in the centre, surrounded by detailed filigree work typical of the period. Jonathan could picture it on Sarah's tiny hand and knew she would be enraptured. It was just her style.

What a great dinner they enjoyed that evening. And what a wonderful view of the ocean through the restaurant's circular windows they all had, as they exchanged details of their day's events. Not all of the events, of course; Jonathan, wanted to save his special gift for the right moment in the future, when both Sarah and he were back home.

*Hmm,* he mused, *possibly while toasting each other under her picture in my library.*

He could never in a million years have guessed how his plans were to be thwarted.

## Chapter 11
## France and the White Horses

Jonathan shifted his position. The flight from Canada to Germany seemed long, even though he had been sleeping off and on. The stewardess tapped his arm again. It had only been a few days since he'd witnessed the body being retrieved from the ocean. Shock and trauma still tormented him, and the second offer of a drink was this time duly accepted. Nevertheless, he still didn't feel like eating.

His thoughts were full of past days with Sarah—days filled with laughter and joy. The magazine in front of him contained an article on Camargue. As his eye fastened on a picture of a beautiful white stallion, he was drawn back to the summer of 1978, a summer he would never forget.

\*\*\*\*

Throwing the last of his toiletries into his suitcase, Jonathan paused for a charmed moment as he contemplated the days ahead with enormous enthusiasm—three whole weeks alone with Sarah. They were about to embark on a trip to Camargue in the south of France. Since their first meeting three years previously, he had come to worship Sarah. He knew she must feel the same way about him, because she indulged him utterly, sparing no effort. He was outrageously spoilt.

The weather had been foul when they left England, pouring rain and with a nasty damp chill, even though it was May. The flight had been equally uncomfortable, with severe turbulence. They had been glad to drag their weary bodies down the steps from the plane upon arrival. What a contrast in such a short time: blistering heat.

The drive to the hotel was comfortable, positively hedonistic, in fact, with the air conditioning going at full throttle. Nevertheless, the minute they'd arrived at their hotel, Sarah scurried up the stairs to their suite to bag the shower.

"Jon, come here, you must see this!"

Jonathan dropped the bag he was carrying, rushed into the bathroom, and did a double take at the sheer beauty of the décor. The shower room, annexed off the main bathroom, incorporated a glass partition patterned discreetly with fish and waves. The walls of both sections were tiled completely. Beautifully crafted seahorses were etched into the tiles and scattered across the walls. The floor was a gorgeous coordinating sand colour, the entire theme being that of a visit to the sea.

"Wow! They certainly have some special craftsmanship here, don't they? Can't wait for you to get out of there so that I can try the shower. Must say, you didn't waste any time grabbing it, did you?"

"Hold your horses. I'll only be a jiffy."

"There'll be plenty of time to hold the horses when we ride through the Camargue wetlands. In the meantime, I'm dying here. Must get out of these clothes."

Sarah couldn't hear him, though, because the water was rippling over her behind the enclosure.

Jonathan was seriously thinking about going in there and literally dragging her out if she didn't get a move on, so that he could get some relief himself.

"If you don't get out of there within the next few minutes, I'm coming in after you."

****

"Well, this is more like it," Jonathan said, lounging back in his chair, completely relaxed. He was finally showered, shaved, and refreshed and was definitely getting drawn into the holiday mode, as the couple basked in the warmth of Provence and the sun-drenched courtyard of a little bistro. Both were thanking their lucky stars for at last being warm after the miserable weather of England. Lost in thought, they surrendered themselves completely to the moment.

The waiter bustled up to take their orders. Ordering lunch presented no problem, as both were completely at home with the language and its colloquialisms.

As the beverages arrived, Jonathan broke the comfortable silence both had fallen into.

"These two years or so have been wonderful with you. I'm so grateful for each and every day we've had. The memories that we've made together are to be cherished for the rest of our lives. It's like you and I have been given a second chance. We've both grown up living through the similar issues our parents have faced, yet here we are, so very happy, and they seem unable to lay the past to rest and grab hold of each and every precious moment they share together. They've moved so far from the things that always meant so much to them. Even though our families lack for nothing financially, they've certainly had their emotional mountains to climb.

"I've always found it very coincidental that you're named Sarah. My mother has always had a special place in her heart for Saint Sarah, who plays such an enormous part in gypsy culture, as we've already seen on this trip. Ever since I can remember, I've heard my mother talking about her. Mum's always had such faith in the strength of the saint's powers to heal and to grant wishes, and yet she herself has been so lost these past years.

"Do you remember the first time I introduced you to my mother and how she fastened on your name like a dog with a bone? She's saturated in folklore and the spiritualistic stuff—she's always considered you special."

"Yes, I do remember. I was flattered and always have been. Gina has held me in such high regard. Although I must confess that I've always felt more than a little overwhelmed, as I have a saint's name and have to live up to expectations."

Sarah's eyes sparkled as she viewed Jonathan over her glass.

"It's a bit late in the day to ask, but do you have anything else you want to mention about your family before we pass the point of no return?"

"No, I don't think so. And anyway, I believe we've long since passed the point of no return.

"By the way, you really look at home with the horses at my parents' place. I don't know why, but I originally assumed you hadn't had much exposure to riding—I was quite surprised when we visited your home in Scotland the first time. What an eye-opener that was. Your riding skills really are exceptional."

"Thank you. And yes, I have felt comfortable on our visits to your family home in Hertfordshire, both with the horses and with your parents. Gina and Ronald are really great—just like my mum and dad when it comes to entertaining guests. It's such a pity that neither of our parents have been able to get themselves sorted out, even after all this time. We'll just have to hope that one day, things will improve."

Jonathan raised his glass. "Cheers and here's to a wonderful holiday. Now, let's talk about us. You and I have had some lovely sorties over the months, haven't we?"

"We certainly have. Getting back to your horses, though, they really have taken to me, haven't they, just as I have to them? What lovely creatures, so intelligent, with such beauty and grace, considering they're so huge. You're a pretty accomplished rider yourself, Jon. I've often thought I must seem really clumsy to you."

"Not at all; as I say, you look as if you belong with them, and Martello just loves it when you kiss his nose. No doubt about it, those horses think you're the bee's knees—but of course, you know that. You're so completely in tune with them."

She laughed. "Haven't heard that expression in a long time."

Sarah paused to reflect on how far she had moved from her own horses and the natural environment. Her life was now centred in London and, although wonderfully successful, she desperately missed the Scottish Highlands. She'd grown up on the moors, and oh, how far she'd travelled away from the basic lifestyle her family had enjoyed in the early years. They may have been well placed, but they'd still maintained the traditional qualities of everyday family life. The smell of homemade bread came to mind. It had always been wafting out of the kitchen, where her mother puttered around, preparing food for the family—she had loved baking. While Sarah was successful in her career, and her life was pleasantly filled with business and a city lifestyle, she still hankered after her home periodically.

Hunger quelled for the moment, Jonathan topped up their glasses as they sat back, avidly following the activity around them, soaking up the atmosphere.

"Are you looking forward to our trip to the ranch tomorrow and taking a horse ride through the marshlands?"

"Oh, I am, I am, and look, the travellers have started to arrive."

Both gazed up the street, and sure enough, brightly clothed people were appearing at the entrance to the town.

\*\*\*\*

After the last drop of wine was downed, they drifted along with the crowd, mingling for a while, hand in hand. There was an air of excitement and anticipation as the sun gilded the rooftops with the approaching dusk. The town became alive to the sounds of the Flamenco guitarists from the gypsy settlement, and the culinary delights tantalized their nostrils and teased their stomachs into feeling half-starved again.

At the first whiff, Jonathan jumped head in. "Don't know about you, but I'm ravenous. Let's go and grab some more of the local nosh."

"You'll get no argument on that score. We only had lunch a short while ago, and yet here we are, famished again. I can hardly believe how much food we're consuming. It must be all this fresh air after sucking back London fog for weeks, not to mention the stimulating activity everywhere."

Sarah had already picked up her step and was heading in the direction of the wonderful aromas wafting up the street when a little Romany girl broke away from her mother and grabbed her hand. Sarah found herself looking down into the face of an angel, with the darkest, most piercing eyes she had ever seen. The child pressed two adjoining bangles of brightly coloured beads into her hand, bringing tears of delight to the young woman's eyes. The little girl was fiercely determined that Sarah should keep the bracelets.

"These are for you, beautiful lady. They're mine, but I want you to have them as a present from me," all the while pushing Sarah's hand away from her purse as she reached into it. The little girl became indignant. "Don't want no money from you neither."

Sarah was moved to tears. Grappling in her handbag for something to mop her eyes, she retrieved a small lace handkerchief, brand new and still in its tissue wrap. Returning the favour, she pressed it firmly into the little girl's outstretched hand.

"And this is for you, little angel; a gift from me especially for you."

The child's face was wreathed in smiles as she ran back to her mother, who was by then halfway across the street and coming to get her. A backward look over her shoulder, with a smile and a wave, and the little girl was enshrouded in the long, coloured skirts of the women as they moved on down the street.

Jonathan was enchanted. "You really scored a hit there, didn't you?"

"Yes, and wasn't she just adorable and so astute? Did you hear that about not wanting to take any money for the bangles?"

"Yes, I did. They certainly learn young, don't they? Business is business and affairs of the heart are simply another matter. Judging from her accent, her people could have come from England, probably Kent, as it's always been a major base for the Roma, or maybe even further south, possibly in the New Forest area."

****

The next day saw them hurrying through their delicious breakfast of butter croissants served with black fig jam from Provence. What a crime it was to rush, it was so scrumptious, but both were too excited about their upcoming day's events and didn't want to be late.

"Come on. Let's get a move on. I'll meet you out front with the car."

Jonathan was impatient to get going.

Their first sight of the ranch was stunning, as they parked the car and stood studying the building. They had learned from their travel brochures that ranches of this size were generally known in the Camargue area as 'manades' and were built for breeding bulls and horses.

Pierre, the ranch owner, was hurrying to meet them just as another group of tourists was arriving. When all were gathered together, he took them on a tour of the outside areas.

"You will notice," he said in his soft, heavily accented voice, "the fascinating collection of stucco and stone finishes that have been used to build this structure. Although constructed in recent years, it was built to resemble the ancient buildings found in the Dordogne region or Périgord Noir of France. This type of vernacular architecture is common to those areas, with its varying shades and textures. A variety of masonry materials were imported to produce the same weathered effect of the buildings of bygone days. Don't you think the terracotta roof tiles set off the soft tones of the masonry?"

There were numerous 'oohs' and 'ahs' and nodding of heads in agreement as Pierre, obviously filled with pride, led them through the tree-shaded integral courtyards overlooked by numerous shuttered windows. Tall, thin Italian cypress trees had been planted strategically, adding to the overall effect of stately opulence.

As they all headed through the massive front door, they stopped to admire it, with its heavy embellishment of carved horses and bulls' heads. Several staff members then guided them all to their rooms prior to light refreshments being served. Beautiful rooms, open plan with gothic-style arches spread out before them. Walls slightly tinted, contrasting with white masonry, added a cooling effect after the heat of the sun outside, which was already stoking up relentlessly.

After a light but sustaining lunch with cool beverages, everybody retired for the afternoon's siesta. They were all, without exception, utterly fatigued by the day's travel and the heat.

As the air cooled later, shrieks of delight echoed around the courtyard, filling the air with laughter as the guests made merry, finding themselves in the cool waters of the pool and the shaded picnic areas before dinner.

The following day started early and, cognizant of the heat already growing intense from the rapidly rising sun, everyone made ready in earnest, determined to take full advantage of the early departure. Pierre showed them to the horses and, with a practiced eye, instructed each on choosing a suitable one. Riders and mounts properly matched, they saddled up and were off.

Riding through the marshes and the wetlands of the Rhone delta was a mind-blowing experience. Pausing at one of the many lakes, they were rewarded by several sightings of beavers gathering reeds and sticks. But most fascinating were the beautiful flamingos. Their plumage, a vivid pink, was quite stunning and apparently, the colour was caused by the plankton they filtered out from the water with their specialized beaks. So exquisite were the birds that it was no wonder their species had been designated Camargue's emblem.

The trail master held his hand up for them all to stop at one point.

They heard them first—the sound of many hooves galloping towards them. Raising his hand again, the trail master pointed to the east. Suddenly, they came into view. Beautiful white horses with flowing manes and tails, muscles rippling and their coats shimmering like the leaves of a silver birch cascading through the air after the wind had torn them from their branches in autumn.

Sarah and Jonathan were awe-struck. Watching their faces, their guide smiled effusively.

"Magnifique, non? I never tire of watching them."

"Difficult to imagine that they started life with grey hair; doesn't turn white until they've reached adulthood," Jonathan mused, staring at the passing herd. "Although they're small and stocky, the Camargue horse is extremely strong and thought to be the most ancient horse on earth, going back 17,000 years. It's associated esoterically and mystically with Pegasus, the magnificent winged stallion depicted in Greek mythology."

Sarah was impressed. "You certainly harbour a font of information in that handsome head of yours."

"Yes, I do, don't I?"

Their day concluded with the entire group gathering around a huge table, tucking into a wonderful dinner with local wine and the decadence of a dessert guaranteed to expand the waistline.

Bidding farewell to all the staff and their host the following day was an emotional time for Sarah and Jonathan. They had been treated with a kindness and professionalism that would have been hard to beat anywhere. All the ranch personnel had lined up formally outside and with much handshaking and smiles, gave their visitors a really good send-off. Jonathan gave one final wave to Pierre and his staff as they drove away.

"Wow, what a fantastic visit that was."

"Sarah hugged his arm, her face flushed with excitement."

"Yes, it was simply incredible. I'll never forget it. I believe there's a ranch in the UK that breeds descendants of the Camargue horses. We'll have to look it up sometime. I should imagine it would make for a really interesting trip."

****

A more leisurely start was the order of the next day, and after a good breakfast, they ambled slowly towards a little church perched on the edge of the Gulf of Lion. Jonathan, of course, took the opportunity once again to air his knowledge, and Sarah was a willing audience.

"Saint Sarah is known by the gypsies as Sara-la-Kali, which means black. She lives in the little church. There are so many different stories and legends about Sarah, but the one I like best is when she welcomed the mothers of the disciples of Christ to the Provençal shore. They'd been set afloat after being thrown out of Palestine. The commune's name Saintes-Maries-de-la-Mer originated after the arrival of the mothers of the apostles to the shore. Whatever legend one chooses to believe, it seems that Sarah has been around since the 15$^{th}$ century, her origins unsure.

"The gypsies travel annually to Camargue, from different parts of the globe, to pay homage to their saint. Their procession takes them to the little church, where they collect a richly adorned statue of Sarah and carry it through the town and down to the sea and their God, symbolizing the welcome of the saints, who are carried in a likewise manner the following day, also to receive their welcome.

"History states that the Marquis de Baroncelli was instrumental in bringing the parade into being, having sought and gained approval from the archbishop for Saint Sarah's statue to be carried to the sea. The marquis and his fellow Camargue guardians wanted the gypsies to have a place they could call home. Since the parade's inception, the travellers have been welcomed by the Camargue residents, who have opened their hearts and homes to the colourful people ever since."

Sarah was all ears. She loved it when Jonathan became so animated, bursting with enthusiasm. He certainly knew his subject. What a font of information he was, although she was always ribbing him when he climbed up on his soapbox.

"So, what are the guardians and who were they?"

"Well, the guardians of Camargue were the cowboys who herded the black bulls for bullfighting in the ring. The 1920s saw a parade opposing the ban on bullfighting proposed by the Animal Protection Society.

Unfortunately, the cruel and vicious sport still continues for human gratification."

There was a sombre moment, each contemplating the horror of the bull ring, so alien to both, such an effrontery to them as animal advocates. Jonathan broke the mood, as he always did.

"So, sweet Sarah, what did you think of the history lesson today? As you know, I was brought up with this stuff from my mum, since she idolizes Sarah, along with the horses, of course."

"You're in the wrong profession, you know that, don't you? Bet you if you applied for a job as a tour guide for the Camargue, they'd snap you up. Mind you, thank God we were warned about the mosquitoes; weren't they something? Lucky we smothered ourselves in that awful-smelling stuff, otherwise we would have been eaten alive. That was the only negative, though."

Saintes-Maries-de-la-Mer was coming alive again when the couple arrived back at their hotel. Sitting on their little balcony overlooking the streets, which were literally buzzing with excitement in preparation for festivities, their mood was high, in no small part due to the delicious wine they were once again sampling.

"You know, Jon this has been one of the most amazing times of my life, and tomorrow is the official day of the parade, isn't it? All the gypsies will have arrived by then, won't they?"

"They sure will. Something over 8,000 travellers are welcomed here every year, and you can bet your bottom dollar that's when Mum arrives. They promised to meet us here, and this is one occasion when I'm sure they won't let us down. My mother definitely isn't going to miss the festivities, we can be certain of that. It's her roots and distant culture. She's very superstitious, and her beliefs are deeply engrained. You know, she truly believes you and I are meant to be together, and I have to say," Jonathan chuckled, "you look like you fit right in at this moment, so vibrant and gorgeous."

Grabbing a blood-red hibiscus from the tree bordering their balcony, he gently placed it in her hair.

"And now, you're truly part of the Sarah and gypsy cult. Welcome, my darling. Tell me you'll never get on your beautiful white horse and ride out of my life."

Sarah was laughing now, full-bodied, helpless laughter, hanging onto his arm. Jonathan laughed with her. She was magnetic, her joy infectious.

"Honestly, Jon, you're such an idiot, you really are."

Jonathan looked at her with an intensity that caused her to blush.

"I have loved you, Sarah, from the moment I first looked on your face in the picture, and then doubly when I saw you in the flesh."

He knew beyond a shadow of a doubt that this woman had ruined him for any other and that he would love her till the end of time, and then some.

****

He awoke with a start. The stewardess was gently shaking him. "Sir, please put on your safety belt. The pilot has begun our descent."

Leaning forward, Jonathan returned the magazine to the rack in front of him and fastened his seatbelt. He was grimly wondering, once again, whether he could ever pick up the pieces of his life, and in fact, whether he could ever go back to an England without Sarah.

*Right now, I can't see myself ever going back there to live, and that's a fact.*

His thoughts drifted to the recent, very successful conference call in Vancouver. The two partners had been unanimous about opening a new branch in Germany. They'd talked about it for so long, and now was the opportunity for Jonathan to break new ground, both for the company and for himself.

Setting up the branch would be a huge challenge, but Jonathan welcomed the diversion. He was also looking forward to spending some time with dear Helmut, who had made life seem so much brighter somehow. Although Jonathan knew he was never going to recover from his loss, he would be getting away from all the associations, which would be the best move for him. This was the perfect time to do just that.

He might never set foot on English soil again.

# Chapter 12
# The Aftermath

Jonathan had been in Germany for some days, struggling to get on top of his despondency, striving valiantly to get back to a reasonable state of normality.

*It's time to get going,* he told himself repeatedly, *time to give myself a shake and go and see Helmut.*

Without thinking too much more about it, he picked up the phone and called his friend. Having made the arrangements, he felt much better about things. He'd even managed not to discuss what had occurred in Vancouver. *Plenty of time for that later,* he thought and gave himself a pat on the back for managing to keep the conversation on an even keel and not falling to pieces. Of course, the hardest part would be when he was actually face to face later with Helmut.

He spent time wandering around the cathedral while in Cologne. Simply being around the ancient walls always had a wonderful effect on him, giving him spiritual strength to overcome whatever was bothering him. He remembered wandering through the cathedral during his school breaks, particularly after he had lost his brother. It always had the spiritualistic ability to grant him strength, and connection with his inner self. The restorative ambience the ancient building bestowed set him to rights.

Having leased a car, it was about time to get on his way to Mönchengladbach and his close friends. Seeing them both would be completely uplifting. There was also the added bonus that it was an exceptionally beautiful drive. The journey would be enjoyable and would get him back on track.

****

It felt good to be back in Mönchengladbach. After dispensing with the preliminaries, he settled himself into the hotel rooms he'd reserved. He was looking forward to just zoning out for the next couple of days. He still needed some time to himself and resolved to contact Helmut when the timing felt exactly right, which inevitably it was very shortly thereafter. After all, Helmut was his stabilizer and dearest friend, and Jonathan was eager to see him again. It wasn't long before they were face to face.

"How's Sarah?"

Jonathan averted his gaze and said nothing. Helmut grew serious.

"I knew there was something wrong when we spoke on the phone. You didn't sound yourself. Either you're sick or something's very much amiss. Tell me what the problem is."

Jonathan forced himself to remain calm as he relayed events since his arrival in Canada.

"So you see, Sarah is gone. After we had the break-up, I heard that she was going on a trip to Vancouver Island to stay with friends, who were mutual acquaintances. I scheduled my business for a stay in Vancouver, hoping I'd get a chance to see her. Well, I got to see her, alright, drowned and being dragged out of the ocean. I don't even know if she made it to the island or not. I still can't believe my Sarah's gone. I was so determined to get back together with her, and now it's too late."

His voice broke as he struggled to get himself together.

"Helmut, I'm so sorry. Can you give me a minute, please? I still haven't wrapped my brain around this disaster. We'd talked about getting married and spending the rest of our lives together."

Helmut remembered well the trip to Amsterdam. Jonathan had shown him the ring he'd bought for Sarah. He lay his hand on his friend's arm in comfort, but Jonathan continued to stress.

"I was actually going to ask her to marry me, and then we had a stupid misunderstanding, which put the kybosh on that. So stupid, such a silly row, but at what huge cost, and now I've lost her forever."

Jonathan desperately needed to be on his own for a few minutes. He was always so in control, and the last thing he wanted was to cause his friend embarrassment. *And it is a damned embarrassment to see a grown man cry,* he thought, his anger at himself all-consuming. He felt as if he was suffocating. He had to get outside for some air and dived for the door.

Helmut was shocked speechless as he watched his friend disappear, so saddened was he at the loss of Sarah, for whom he'd always felt a deep affection. He couldn't stand seeing his friend looking so gaunt and beside himself with grief. It was unbearable. He went to the bar and poured them both a stiff drink. He simply couldn't digest what he'd just heard. He'd always had a lot of time for Sarah. Handing a glass to Jonathan as soon as he reappeared minutes later, he was shaking so much himself, he could hardly speak.

"Oh God, Jon, I'm so sorry, my dear friend, so pained by your news. It's going to take a very long time to recover from this ghastliness. Get that drink down you; it'll do you good."

Jonathan knocked it back post-haste, feeling the benefit of comfort and warmth almost immediately spreading through his body.

Helmut took the opportunity to pop into the bedroom and put in a quick call to Gertrude, to bring her up to date and forewarn her. They were on their second drink when Gertrude's appearance was a welcome distraction.

She flew into the room and enveloped Jonathan with her ample body.

"Jon, I'm so sorry, my heart goes out to you."

Gertrude had a tight rein on her emotions. It was imperative that she not add to the misery. There would be no dramatics.

Jonathan didn't have to utter another word about the disaster. He was amongst friends, and they loved and comforted him. He'd always liked Gertrude; she was a fun person, and sure enough, as always, she soon had him uplifted and even managing the odd half-hearted laugh. For a while, he was able to forget the horrific sight of Sarah's body being dragged out of the sea.

****

Using their bathroom a while later, Jonathan noticed Gertrude's personal items there and concluded that she'd moved in with Helmut. He recalled making that suggestion a long time ago and wondered now what had happened to their plans to buy their own place. They must have been in a strong financial position by this time, what with sharing costs.

They were all sat enjoying a last coffee and liqueur before Jonathan left for his hotel. He was feeling much better when he suddenly noticed for the first time an element of strain on Helmut's face.

"We've talked enough about me and my troubles tonight, wrung it dry, in fact. So what about you two? How's the job going, Helmut?"

"Well, it's not looking too rosy at the moment," Helmut said pensively.

He had worked in an antique store for a number of years while he continued his studies on ancient civilizations and antiquities. In fact, that's where he and Jonathan had really cemented their long-standing relationship as friends. They had shared a common interest, and while they had been through the same curriculum, it was taking Helmut double the time to qualify, because he had left university before getting his degree in order to assist Oma and Opa prior to their eventual passing. Even though he had not been physically attending school full-time during that period, he still managed to get in several hours of study each day—a major trial, as being a caregiver took an enormous toll on his system. Nevertheless, he had endured, determined to build his credits.

"My boss, Herr Basner—or Dieter, as he is known—is the owner of the store and is thinking about retiring and selling the business. It's only something he's mentioned in passing, but it's come up a couple of times lately. If he does make the move, I'm not sure where that's going to leave me. That's one reason Gertrude and I decided that she should move in here, instead of us waiting. We'd talked about it long enough, and it was the most practical solution for us. We've already established that we love each other and knew years ago that we would be staying together. We'll save much more for our future by pooling expenses, at least until I get myself sorted out."

"We're pretty busy people, aren't we Gertie? What with my studies and you taking some marketing courses and trying to earn a living at the same time, it gets pretty hectic, doesn't it? I should get my degree this year, actually, and had hoped I would have more time and possibly one day be in a position to invest in the shop when Dieter decided to take a bit of a rest. I'd never thought he would be closing up, lock, stock, and barrel, so soon. I'd always imagined him just taking things slower for a number of years, maybe just overseeing the business and looking in from time to time, but it looks like that is not written in the stars. Also, I believe his family is pressuring him to sell, as he's getting old."

"Yes, they're probably hoping to clean up when the shop is sold. His daughter has been taking an avid interest in the business for the first time ever in all these years." Gertrude's disparaging tone was unlike her, and Jonathan could see they were both troubled by the subject. "Don't you worry about it, Liebchen. And anyway," she added, "should it happen, we'll get through it together. We'll certainly be more than qualified between us to come up with something—hopefully something we can do together."

The next few days were a round of visiting old haunts. Jonathan forced himself to do a little shopping one day and, as always when he was in the area, found himself back in the Alte Markt, an old marketplace he knew so well. His feet automatically led him down the cobbled street to the familiar door of the tailor he had frequented for so many years.

*Oh, what the hell*, he thought, *I need to give myself a bit of a lift. I'll say hi to old Mani and have a business suit made. I need to smarten myself up a bit.*

Stumbling over the worn and uneven stone step that had borne the weight of hundreds of eager patrons over the years, he entered the tiny shop. Mani appeared from the back regions, as usual with a swatch of fabric hung over his arm. His face lit up when he saw Jonathan. Following hugs and grins all round, Mani led him to the little kitchenette at the back of the shop. Pouring some tea that had been steeping on the blackened hob, he smiled secretively as he handed a cup to Jonathan.

Jonathan tried not to wince at the first mouthful, but old Mani winked, as always not missing a beat.

"The second gulp is usually the best," he said knowingly.

"It's the second one that's really bothering me."

Jonathan had his eyes fastened on the long, slimy-looking green roots at the bottom of his cup. They were reminiscent of green slugs—even had the dark speckles on their backs.

"I'll have you know this is the best kosher tea, fully certified by the rabbi, and kosher in Hebrew means proper. So you won't get a purer tea than this."

"Well, I'll have to take your word for it, I suppose, but you won't mind if I pass on another cup, will you?" Jonathan fixed him with a cheeky grin.

Mani had been part of a Jewish community of approximately 3,000 residing throughout the Wuppertal-Elberfeld region. He'd run a very small, localized tailoring business for many years after completing his apprenticeship. The little operation attracted long-standing customers through word of mouth, and drop-ins at regular intervals. Mani's needs were small, and he was able to make a simple living out of the shop.

Following 1933 and growing unrest, then the onset of war, more and more of Mani's countrymen had been persecuted, and those with stores watched in horror as their livelihoods were confiscated and destroyed. Fortunately, Mani had had the foresight to leave Wuppertal before it was too late. Shutting down his store, he'd joined his brother in England, who was well established in his community. Mani had narrowly escaped being sent to Dachau concentration camp, where he would have met certain death had he remained in the town. Less than 200 of the original 3,000 or so would ever to return to their homes. The rest had been annihilated before the fighting was over.

Mani and his brother joined the British Armed Forces, along with thousands of other Jews, to do their bit, but Mani returned alone and bearing more grief on his shoulders with the loss of his brother. That he would never see his sibling again weighed heavily upon him, but being a stalwart soul, he forced himself to get on with his life and accept things for what they were. Jonathan had known Mani forever, it seemed, and had the greatest respect for the sheer endurance of the man. That he could still spare compassion for his fellow beings, in spite of the wretchedness of his earlier life, was a pure miracle.

"Gott im Himmel," Mani kept saying, throwing in a splattering of Yiddish occasionally whilst wringing his hands in grief, upon hearing the devastating news from Jonathan.

"Well, God certainly wasn't up in the sky looking after my Sarah, was he?"

The acrimony of Jonathan's remark was surprising even to himself.

Taking a tight hold of both his friend's hands, Mani looked at him intently. "Just give yourself time, Jonathan. It's natural to feel lost and bitter, with so much anger; just give yourself more time, my boy."

"I suppose you're right. I just feel so shattered. Anyway," Jonathan shrugged, "let's talk about the new business suit you're going to make for me."

Mani's face was wreathed in even more wrinkles as, with a broad smile, he ushered Jonathan into the farthest reaches of the shop to look at the latest fabrics, recently arrived from Italy. Mani smoothed an imaginary crease from the swatch, as a mother would smooth her baby's blankie. A look of pure ecstasy swept over his face.

"I do believe your eyes have glazed over, my friend. One would think you had a beautiful woman on your arm."

Mani smiled. "You know, Jon, it's a pity Wuppertal never really got into the suiting industry and lost its footing in textiles. Wouldn't it have been great if you could have considered some locally woven fabric? Wuppertal, as you already know, was the heart of textiles in the Rhineland. In fact, when they first started opening their plants…" his voice trailed off. "Human greed again, my boy, human greed." He paused to reflect.

"Of course, they're building a great tourist industry now, exhibiting all the old plants and machinery as historical draws, and it's nice to know some of the old looms are still being used to produce a limited supply of braiding and bindings and so forth."

Jonathan could see his old friend was getting smothered under a blanket of nostalgia and hastily attempted to drag him back to the present. But old Mani was on a roll and wouldn't be waylaid.

"The '60s really seemed to put the kybosh on the textile industry. When you think that the Wupper had the best water for processing yarns, what with all the bleaching applications involved. Of course, everything comes at a cost. The river soon became so depleted, what with industrialization and the inevitable increase in chemical dyeing plants, that it was just a matter of time. Demand grew so great, and there was a need for more and more textile equipment, resulting in more and more manufacturing plants. And so it goes on."

The old man suddenly left the past, focusing on the present matter at hand—Jonathan's new suit. "Here now, what do you think of these?"

Jonathan was very enthusiastic about the samples, but before he had a chance to comment, Mani was off again on his trip down memory lane.

"You know," he added a trifle wistfully, "I settled very well in Mönchengladbach after arriving back here from England. I didn't have the heart to remain there after losing my brother. I was so lost, you see. Now, I've made a new life for myself, it's not so bad. I have my friends, some of them long-standing from Wuppertal and before. So I can't complain and," he added with enthusiasm, "business is good, I make a reasonable living, enough to get by. I could never live in Wuppertal again, knowing what happened there all that time ago. The memories go deep, my boy. Yes indeed…" He was wandering again.

Jonathan hurriedly began leafing through the swatches to distract his old friend before he completely disappeared again. He was immediately impressed with the samples Mani sectioned off for his inspection and consideration. It was just like old times. They spent the next couple of hours poring over different fabrics. Jonathan felt the soothing balm of healing as he listened to his old friend muttering away in Jewish, eyes glazed as if in heaven as he lovingly fingered the various lengths of cloth.

Their harmony was broken by a knocking on the door. It was Mani's old friend Stanislaw. The room was filled with his presence, one so riveting that Jonathan knew instinctively this man was someone special. He had an indefinable aura about him, slightly intimidating, in fact. His gaze through slate-grey eyes was unwavering.

Mani introduced the newcomer. "Jonathan, I would like you to meet my dear and long-standing friend Stanislaw, originally from Poland."

As their conversation progressed, Jon learned that Stanislaw, being a Jew, had been expropriated to work for a German officer. He became sick and needed to go to the hospital, but the German officer had grown fond of him and was, as it turned out, a compassionate man.

"Stanislaus," he said, calling him by the German equivalent of his name, "if you go to the hospital, they will kill you, or take you to Dachau first and kill you there with their terrible experiments. Or you might be lucky and they'll throw you into another concentration camp, where they'll starve you to death. They won't starve you quickly, but over a period of time so that you really know what's happening to you."

Jonathan had already been undermined and was becoming nauseous as the details were unfolded.

"No, no, boy, don't give up, this is a good story," Mani rushed on, seeing the younger man paling.

"Anyway, the German officer personally cared for Stanislaw and brought him back to health. It just goes to show you that there's good in everybody. And," he added emphatically, "even with the awful time that it was. Stanislaw is living proof of that. Isn't that right, my friend?"

Stanislaw smiled gainfully in an attempt to lighten the proceedings. He'd lost his entire family and was heartily grateful that Mani didn't go into that matter.

After an introduction like that, Jonathan held his trembling hand forward to shake Stanislaw's, humbled that his generation had never been put to the test of a world war and genocide.

"Thank God for good people retaining their compassion and humanity in spite of cruel, mind-numbing, and foul leadership, that's all I can say." The magnitude of the story impacted him dramatically; he felt his comments to be inadequate but had no idea how he could express his sentiments appropriately. "What a blessing you were spared from being taken away. The gods were certainly with you, my friend."

Stanislaw gripped his hand firmly. "It's alright, young man. It's all in the past. Every morning when I wake up, I count my blessings and inhale another day of freedom from oppression."

Later, having said goodbye to Stanislaw, Mani locked up, then he and Jonathan ambled down the cobbled street to the little tavern that Sarah had always loved so much when they had made a foursome with Helmut and Gertrude. Even when Mani herded them to the window seat, Jonathan was able to handle it, as all the old memories rose up to slam him in the face. He was calm, in fact, even comforted to be in this place, so familiar to him and holding so many good times within its walls, still decorated with beer mats from all over Germany.

\*\*\*\*

Thus were Jonathan's days filled, and although his spirit began to renew, he still couldn't face the prospect of returning to England anytime soon.

When he arrived back at his hotel one night, he phoned Mark on an impulse and revisited the subject of opening up a new branch for them in the Rhineland.

"Mark!" he urged, "our call went so well, it looks like it's in the bag, and we've obviously grabbed the business. I've been doing a bit of thinking about our gallery here, and it's opportune for us to get on with it. In view of what has happened to my life, I feel this is a good time for a change and would love to get this going here. It would be an ideal setup for us to move our stock around between London and Germany for showing and buying purposes. I'd really like to take this time and get into this project and run the show, at least until its underway and a viable proposition. We can see what's down the road as we go along."

Mark was ecstatic, seizing upon the opportunity immediately to further their project. He had hoped that Jonathan would come around and be willing to relocate, at least for a while, to get things set up and stay in Germany for a while. With some time to recover from the hell he'd been living through, it looked as if Jonathan's practical side was kicking in.

****

The day had been exhausting, and Jonathan felt drained as he left the building—although, as he walked down the path behind the building and meandered along the river in Bonn, he was proud of himself, his spirits uplifted. The property was perfect, and he had leapt at the rent-to-buy option available as part of their contract. This would give the partners more time to see how the branch worked out as it was developed. He also signed a 'first option to buy' agreement because he wanted to get Helmut and Gertrude to Bonn to see how they liked it—he was pretty sure they would be in raptures. A fully fitted flat occupied the top level, and there was loads of room down stairs for a small showroom and sales office, plus an undeveloped annex, so they could start with a clean slate. He couldn't believe his luck and was quite sure that his friends would feel the same way about the place.

That night, following his hectic day, a cool lager and lime went down well. He sat again on the deck of a little hofbräu overlooking the Rhine River, watching the sunset. This particular tavern had been another of their favourite haunts. Sarah would hold his arm and sit close by him, revelling in the warmth of his body as they gazed at the setting sun. He had not been sure earlier whether he should retrace his steps but had been inexplicably drawn there. The sun would be dropping into the ocean in a few minutes.

The sunset was his parent's favourite time, when they too had relished holding hands whilst watching the day come to an end. Now, that fervent love, shared so possessively, seemed to have also set on the horizon, out of reach to them, so estranged were they in recent years. His mother had even written a poem especially for his father.

**SUNSET SHARED**
*The sunset, always a special time for you,*
*With skies rich in colour of every hue.*
*Your words often spoken of the sight*
*Of the setting sun heralding the night.*
*The red ball of fire is on its downhill slide*
*And images of you on the red beams ride,*
*And as the sun's rays fan out in every direction,*
*I think of you with love and affection.*
*As I watch the sunset yet again*
*Those memories of you invade my brain.*
*My last look as the sun sets out of view,*
*Never to watch again without sweet thoughts of you.*

Oh, how ironic that he should think of that now, of all times, when the image of Sarah and himself was before his eyes—of them also enjoying the view, sitting on this very deck, enthralled by the luminosity of the skies reflecting off the waters of the Rhine. So close had they been as they sat and gazed at the blood-red horizon. Little had they known what would come to pass.

His eyes, blinded by overflowing tears, obscured his lager from view. Rising suddenly, he knocked the remains of the drink to the ground. He had to get away from the river. It was as if she were reaching out to him from the depths of the waves and, God forgive him, he actually considered joining her in the icy waters.

Jonathan was to remain based in Germany and would not return to live in his homeland for several years.

# Chapter 13
# Gina and Ronald

The sleek lines of the yacht were reflected in an unruffled ocean. Anchored a short way off the Italian coast, the vessel was resplendent as it bobbed gently on the rippling water. Gina languished in her favourite spot on the upper deck. She had everything in the world materially, and yet that which she needed and craved most was lost to her.

Her son Jonathan was a prominent international antique dealer, in partnership with an old friend. Between them, they ran two exclusive establishments, an antique gallery and a store in Chelsea. Gina was proud of her son. He had been knowledgeable when choosing his career path and had positioned himself well in the business world of antiques, particularly with the advent of full-blown consumerism in the 1970s in England.

The domination of two world wars during the first half of the 20$^{th}$ century and the subsequent desecration of London had seen many of the well-to-do moving out to their more spacious residences in the suburbs. The demand for antiques had grown steadily in the post-war years, fed by middle-class people who were filling their homes with such treasures. The easing of international travel also brought many more visitors, earning London recognition as the global centre for antiques.

Jonathan and Mark's timing couldn't have been better; business was booming. Gina always enjoyed a browse through the antique store when she was back in London. It was invariably such a treat, especially if Jonathan was in town and they could have lunch together.

Yes, Gina's pride in her son was boundless. He had done well in his career, and his home was magnificent, the envy of many of his guests and friends. She and Ron had met his beautiful lady friend, Sarah. They were both in the same line of work, and it was assumed they would eventually marry. Gina thought it unlikely they would have children, both being firmly entrenched in their careers, but who could tell? After all, she would never have believed she would produce another child after Nate, as so many years had passed since his birth. But she had!

Children or not, there was no doubt about it, Sarah and Jonathan were completely enthralled with each other, obviously very much in love, true soul mates. Sarah was very dark, just like Jonathan. Gina had always thought that Sarah could have the same Romany ancestry as herself on her mother's side. The British were, after all, also a mixture of many nationalities, with an enormous complement of Spanish descendants.

Gina's mother had been part of the Gitano population of Saintes-Maries-de-la-Mer. She had been raised in southern France, although her ancestors had originated in Spain. She had been whisked away by Gina's Italian father, who had been absolutely determined to marry her mother. Together, they had taken up ranching—hence Gina's love of horses, which were an integral part of her heritage.

Gina's father was easy-going and not as highly strung as Italians tended to be. He had loved her mother to the exclusion of all other women before and after she passed away. He steadfastly continued to live in their home, which was later run by Gina's elder brother and nephew. Her father's happiest memories were there at the ranch, deeply imbedded within the walls and the surrounding land. Nothing would be moving him, not even when he died. He was going to be placed at rest next to his dear wife on the property they had built up together throughout their lifetime. Theirs was a never-ending love affair.

****

Raised on the family horse ranch on the outskirts of Provence, Gina had developed a great affinity with horses. It had been her dream to own her own ranch, and when she met Ronald, who shared her love of these beautiful creatures, she thought she was about to have all her dreams fulfilled.

Ronald had taken a break prior to becoming a fully-fledged lawyer in his own right. He had plans to open his own law office a few years down the road. They met by chance in Provence before war broke out and fell hopelessly in love, even though they knew their alliance would be frowned upon by some members of Gina's family, as had the union of her mother and father many years before. Traditional ways were still deeply imbedded.

Ronald adored Gina and, like her father, was not to be thwarted either. Her father could see immediately that the young British army officer loved his daughter to distraction in the same way he had loved her mother, and still did. Following his blessing, the young couple were married quietly in a tiny church steeped in history, where the Rhone River meets the Mediterranean Sea.

\*\*\*\*

It was May 1937, a time when the gypsies would parade through the streets of Saintes-Maries-de-la-Mer in honour of their patron saint, Sarah. The travellers arrived from all over the world to take part in the parade, which had only been instigated a couple of years before.

The warm sun caressed the newlyweds as they sat, arms entwined, each revelling in the sheer joy of being young and in love. Even the fabulous procession oozing slowly down the street could not distract them from each other.

After a whirlwind honeymoon in Provence, they travelled back to England to begin a new life in the large country house in Hertfordshire. The property had been in Ronald's family for several generations. He had been born there, and it was also an easy commute to the city for his work.

When their first child, Nathan, arrived, he became the apple of his parents' eyes. They absolutely doted on him, constantly showing him off to their friends. Their days were filled with the joy of their son. Talk of pending war was pushed firmly to the back of their minds. Sadly and inevitably, predictions came to fruition, and war was declared.

The onslaught of the dreaded conflict had brought their new and idyllic life to an abrupt end, and Ronald was sent into training.

\*\*\*\*

Gina shifted her position in the deck chair and picked up her writing folder from the coffee table. She had always kept a diary, and writing had become a major mainstay for her over the years. She was finding it difficult to concentrate, which was unusual for her, as she always found putting pen to paper so therapeutic. She had been dabbling with combining a series of poems and rhymes, but today, her mood was restless and not conducive to creativity. Her mind insisted on drifting back to the way they had been so many years ago, or so it seemed.

\*\*\*\*

It was a warm July day in 1943. Ronald had been deployed to take part in the Allied invasion across Italy. Head in hands, she had cried and then, clutching a little medallion of Saint Sarah given to her mother by Gina's grandmother so long ago, she prayed. Holding it close to her heart, she prayed throughout the night that her beloved Saint Sarah would protect the father of her child and bring him home safely to her and his son. Throughout the war, she had lived with constant fear that she would not see her husband again.

Her second son, Jonathan, was born prior to the war's end, at the most anxious time of all for Gina, as her husband was firmly entrenched in active duty. Although in a good financial situation, she was, like many new mothers in wartime, chastising herself for the imprudence of producing another child. The nagging fear that her sons would be without a father was always to the fore.

Her own family came to mind, and her heart went out to those of them still in France. Her father refused to leave the ranch but had insisted his son go to Italy to be with family and escape persecution. Other French people of gypsy lineage did not fare so well. Following the 1940 enemy invasion of France, 1941 and 1942 had seen police interning thousands of Roma in both occupied and unoccupied France, some being shipped to Germany for incarceration in camps such as Buchenwald, Dachau, and Ravensbrück, and almost certain death. Hitler's obsession with annihilating them began even before he focused on Jews.

Finally, the allies had invaded Normandy and the mayhem was over. A high-ranking German delegation surrendered their forces, and the final documentation of unconditional surrender was signed at the beginning of May 1945. The 8$^{th}$ of May was a momentous occasion and signified Victory in Europe.

Those valiant saviours who had been spared so mercifully came back to their homes to pick up the remnants of their shattered lives. Gina's prayers were answered, and her husband was returned to her.

Ronald was one of the lucky ones able to resume his career, and with the passage of time he became a very successful lawyer, as evidenced by their lifestyle and palatial country house, with its stables and horses to keep Gina happy. The price of such opulence was that Ronald spent more and more time working and involved in his numerous business affairs. As Nathan grew, his parents over-indulged him in every way, and that was just how he liked it.

The marriage had taken a definite upswing when Jonathan was born. He was a major surprise, and Gina's life was filled with her children and her horses. She never felt entirely comfortable with her husband's friends, and their weekend stays were becoming more and more irksome to her, although she was regarded as a great socialite and wonderful hostess. So life went on until that dreadful night, of which she still had nightmares.

\*\*\*\*

They were enjoying a rare few moments together, finishing off a bottle of wine that their pampered guests had overlooked at the earlier cocktail gathering. Gina couldn't help but notice the strain and fatigue on Ron's face. A hectic lifestyle both professionally and socially was beginning to tell. He always maintained the lifestyle was necessary to further enhance his career, one he was valiantly trying to protect from the derogatory speculations about his elder son's antics. Word was beginning to seep through, and Ronald's business reputation was becoming tarnished. It took a further dive following a few incidents that were picked up by the press, and rather intimate pictures of his son leaving artsy bars known to be frequented by homosexuals. He had been firmly attached to the arm of a blonde man. There was no mistaking the intimacy of the gesture. The situation was becoming too much to bear.

The phone startled them, and Ronald took the call that was to change the course of their lives and cause him to blame himself with every passing hour thenceforth. Nathan and he had so many differences that the last time he had bailed his son out of trouble, he had also bailed him out of their lives, telling him not to come back home until he had straightened himself out.

Ronald's face was drained of colour as he spoke. "Ok, I'll be there shortly; it's not far from our flat." He'd grabbed Gina as if his very life depended upon it. "Nathan has been found on the street in a bad way. The medics are trying to save him."

They arrived at the gruesome scene to find the ambulance crew still working on their son, with all sorts of apparatus attached to him.

Gina's grief knew no bounds. She held her son's hand while his father knelt by his side, firmly hanging onto the other limp hand, his tears falling freely onto his son's cheeks. As Nathan gazed up into his father's face, he cried, and then a small smile played on his lips for the last time.

When Ronald wrapped their son's body in the medic's blanket that night, he wrapped up all the good memories in his life and mummified his very spirit and soul at the same time, shutting out anything remotely resembling emotion.

The press releases and subsequent investigations over the following months were overwhelming. It seemed clear that their son had been heavily involved in the homosexual scene, which had eventually led to drugs and abuse, partly because of societal pressures bestowed upon different lifestyles.

Ronald had virtually given up his career, although he still retained an interest in the company and took the occasional case if it held some level of appeal for him. The remainder of his time was spent travelling on the family yacht. Gina, devoted wife that she was, accompanied him, reluctantly embracing their lifestyle change to that of empty socialites who had long since lost touch with or run away from reality.

\*\*\*\*

Gina reflected on the horrific situation for homosexuals in the 1950s and 1960. Her son had been such a young man. Homosexuals had been pursued and persecuted unmercifully during those years, rounded up like sheep at regular intervals and put on trial. The *Sexual Offenses Act*, decriminalizing homosexuality, had not been put into effect until 1967, and although it was a step forward, there was still a great deal of ground to cover.

*Anyway, it was too late, all too late. My son is dead.*

Gina was aware of a salty taste on her lips and realized, with a jolt, that she was crying, her sadness all consuming. Grief for her dead son had remained buried deep within her, and she was without comfort or solace from her husband. She missed the excitement and vitality of the man she had married and the attention he had previously lavished upon her. She missed her horses, home, and most of all her younger son, who had spent many of his growing years without his parents. And she sobbed as if her heart would break.

*This has to stop now.* Gina's thoughts were racing, but she wasn't sure how to rectify matters. She couldn't bear it. Her husband was lost to her, it seemed, as was her younger son. Jonathan had become so distant over the years, through no fault of his own, and had suddenly gone to live in Germany, leaving his home in the hands of a caretaker.

*I've lost one son, and now I'm losing the other.* She was torn between the needs of her husband and her child.

Jonathan had been in Germany for a long time, making brief visits to London only on business matters. She was confused as to why he had virtually abandoned his home and gone to live on the continent. Even more disturbing was that his move appeared to be permanent. Was he ever coming back? And what had happened to his relationship with that beautiful girlfriend? It had all looked so promising. They had been so much in love. It was all very strange.

The sun washed over her, and closing her eyes, she allowed the warmth to heal, and to lessen some of her restlessness.

# Part 2

# Chapter 14
# Luke

Luke was hosing down the deck of his cruiser. The vessel was the love of his life, and he spent endless hours keeping it in pristine condition. His fascination with boats and being on the water had begun at an early age, growing into an obsession as he matured. He'd worked very hard at becoming a firmly entrenched member of the boating community. His efforts had paid off, and as his contacts grew, so did his job opportunities.

Luke was very industrious and never turned down a position, always making himself available. Working his way up, he'd been willing to pilot anything and everything that would float on water. Finally, he was able to get his first little cabin cruiser. It had been difficult for him to fit in the necessary navigation courses while earning a living, not to mention cultivating the more affluent boating crowd at the same time. He eventually reached his goal, though, and was successful in building a good cruise business of his own, with a vessel that accommodated up to eight passengers in addition to two crew members. Nevertheless, it had taken years of perseverance and hard work.

He paused to take a break and took out his thermos—he always made a good, strong flask of coffee for a little later in the day. Luke was an early riser, and breakfast was generally at dawn, so he felt the need for caffeine and something sweet a little later. Taking a sip of his coffee, he took out his Danish pastry. As he munched his way through it, he contemplated his life in general, particularly the good fortune of having Doug as his business associate here in England. He thought back to how good it had been to see his old friend again last year, after a few years' absence.

****

The year had started off well for Luke. He had been mindlessly gazing at the Thames from his usual window seat in his favourite haunt, a little café sitting by the river. Suddenly, some jovial being slapped him on the shoulder.

"How are you doing, me ol' codger?" a friendly voice boomed from behind Luke. "I thought that was you, sitting there so quietly, and for once, minding your own business."

Luke was amazed to be looking up into the smiling face of his old mate from the past. They had been through school together. Luke had considered Doug his best friend through their youth. Unfortunately, he'd lost his buddy when Doug had moved away from the area and gone to work on the boats up north. Doug had kept in touch off and on over the years, even though he'd been quite the traveller and always on the move. After leaving the north of England, he worked in Canada for a number of years whilst staying with family. Luke hadn't really had much of an update from Doug since he'd been back in England, except that he was based in Southampton.

"Well, I'll be blowed, the renegade finally returns. When did you get back into town?" Luke enquired as he pulled back a chair from the table. It really bucked him up to see his old friend smiling down at him. "Here, take a pew. I'll treat you to lunch."

Doug smiled broadly as he heaved himself into the chair.

"Thanks mate, great to see you again." Grabbing a menu, he fastened on it. "There's quite a range of good stuff here, isn't there. And you don't have to get mine; I'm so hungry, I'll bankrupt you."

Once his friend had placed an order, Luke, said, "Right then, now food's sorted out, let's have it. What have you been up to?" He was anxious to find out what Doug had been doing in Southampton.

"As you know, I did that stint on the fishing boats for a while up north and then went to The Maritime Provinces in Canada. I made some decent money on the boats but it was so bloody wretched, what with the foul weather all the time, talk about brass monkeys, that I couldn't take any more of it. Anyway, I got back from Canada a few months ago and have been working in Southampton for a rich bod who owns a yacht. It's a great job, but the boss can be a bit of a challenge. I've learnt a lot, though, and have worked through all the marine courses, the same as you did. I really want to do something for myself, eventually."

He was watching Luke's grin spread from ear to ear.

"What's so funny, then?" he enquired.

"Well, it's strange you should be talking about doing something for yourself. I've got myself organized with my business since getting hold of the cruiser, and I've been doing quite well, taking small tour groups on trips, just poodling around, nothing screamingly ambitious at the moment, just taking it slow and really starting to feel comfortable with some pretty good regular trips. I plan on getting another cruiser down the road and expanding a bit more here in England.

"Of course, that means getting a partner who wants to invest. That might be something you and I could talk about when the time comes, if it's something that makes your big toe tap, of course."

"You're darn right I'm interested. Let's keep in touch. Always wanted to branch out a bit. Although the pay is pretty good in the job I have, the boss is a difficult old codger. I'm at his beck and call pretty much constantly and don't get much spare time. And there's nothing like working for something you have a vested interest in. Maybe I'll have a chance to see your set-up while I'm in London."

"Sure, why don't we take some time out this week? I'm not doing too much, just getting the boat ready for the next trip. As regards work, at this time I can't pay full-time, but I find myself in need of a back-up person and have been thinking seriously about making a move on that. Jordan is my long-standing friend and partner in Vancouver, and we run a cruiser much the same as here, with eight passengers plus crew. Once again, it's a fairly modest operation. I pop over there from time to time, and it's always a real trial getting things set up here before I leave. I have to shut down when I go anywhere or do anything, whether it's personal stuff or business. I need someone to work with me occasionally, taking over the trips, keeping the continuity, and helping with the backbone of the business.

"If Jordan and I get another cruiser for Vancouver, which we've been considering, we'll definitely need to increase our crew out there as well. Jordan works with a really good guy in Canada, a long-standing contact. Jordan had met him when he worked for a boat manufacturing company, before we set up together.

"Tell you what, why don't we kick a few ideas around and have a few jars at my place, if you have time this week before you go south again. We may be able to do something together before we actually purchase another cruiser. God knows I'm busy enough. And don't laugh when I tell you I live on a houseboat. It's moored a little further up the Thames. I'll also show you the cruiser I have at the same time. She's called Pretty Susan."

Doug raised an eyebrow.

"Well, we won't go into why you picked that name, will we?"

"No, better not. Although, I still think about her from time to time. Anyway, moving on," he shrugged, "this week is good for me if you want to give me a call. Here's my card." Luke dug into his wallet and handed one over to Doug.

Doug wrote his phone number on a napkin and handed it to Luke as he cast an approving eye over the card. "Hmm, pretty fancy, eh?"

Lunch was a pleasant interlude. Both men had always been comfortable with each other. They talked about the business. Doug was anxious to learn all about the workings of the two branches. After they'd settled their bills, Doug took another look at the dinner menu on their way towards the door. *Must pop in here for dinner before I leave,* he was thinking, *the food's excellent.*

Luke extended his hand to his friend as they left the café. "Let's just get this show on the road and meet the day after tomorrow, if that works for you."

"That would be terrific. I don't go back south for another week."

\*\*\*\*

Since their meeting, Doug had spent a few days working closely with Luke to get a feel for the business. He was very impressed with everything and particularly liked the cruiser. Working together, the two men complemented each other. An added bonus was that they enjoyed each other's company, simply picking up where they had left off years before. They met up at the café one night and firmed up on Doug coming in with Luke. He would go back south, work out his notice, and then move back to London. Although they were a bit pressed for time, as Doug's departure for Southampton was imminent, they were able to get some sort of a plan worked out. Doug also looked up some of his contacts and offered to do work for them on their boats in the slack time. But business was brisk, their prospects good, and it wasn't long before Luke took Doug on full-time.

His association with Doug had worked well, and things were looking rosy. *But it hadn't always been like that, had it?* Luke thought.

\*\*\*\*

He'd experienced more than his fair share, a lifetime bereft of all the finer things and filled with hardship and misery. He'd made a superhuman effort to survive against all odds and had taken what he wanted, when he wanted it, clawing his way up the financial ladder. No job had been too small for him. He would transport anyone anywhere, no questions asked, for a very high price. He was proud of his success. Yes, he'd done well. His mother would have been proud of him as well. He could almost hear her now. "Luke, boy, you've made your ol' mam very proud. Any smokes in that backpack of yours, son? Any spare cash for your ol' mam?"

Luke always knew she would be taking it straight down to the pub, but what the hell. If she had a few minutes away from past misery and memories, who gave a damn? He would never say no to her. She was his mum, and she was ok in his book. She'd done her duty in the early years, but no money, an abusive husband, and wretched living conditions had taken their toll. He had known, deep down, that she loved her son more than life itself, and when she was still alive, he had always been there to pick her up, no matter what.

Even so, he'd become embittered and defensive because of the cards he'd been dealt, and when he lost Susan, it was the bitter end. She had meant the world to him, and her loss just served to exacerbate his defensiveness. He had always thought they would get married eventually. Losing her devastated him utterly.

*Look at me,* he thought. *I used to be a really nice bloke once, but that's what life does to you.*

Luke had known true love only once. When he thought of Susan, he felt huge sadness and frustration. He had loved so her deeply and completely, but she hadn't waited for him to make something of himself. Simply wouldn't give him time to crawl out of the cess pit he was living in. She'd gone off and married that Tommy Brown. Common as his name, Luke had always thought, but in retrospect, she did get a home and two nice kids. *Kids that should have been mine,* he thought savagely.

He'd heard that Tommy had died suddenly in an accident and had left Susan well taken care of. She was not rich by any manner of means, but in a good financial position and certainly had enough to bring up the kids properly and look after herself. Luke was glad and had thought of looking her up but somehow never got around to it—his pride getting in the way and all that.

Anyway, too late for that now. There was no going back.

****

The sounds of the water gently swishing to and fro against the boat, and the ropes grinding and rasping against the pilings in the quiet harbour, worked their magic on him, as always, chasing away his negativity. He'd been lucky, he knew that. It wasn't always enough to work hard; it was all about luck and making the right contacts at the right time. So many of his mates were smart, worked their arses off, but what did it get them? Diddly-squat. They were still where they had been when they left school and started working. It was the same for many with their background—never managed to get out of the mire.

*God, how I love being on the water, and everything about it,* he thought for the thousandth time.

The water was so much a part of his life that he made his home on a houseboat moored further up the Thames. It was quite a luxurious home, with every modern convenience. He'd been happier there than anywhere else he'd ever known. He even had a couple of planter boxes attached to the railing and filled with flowers to simulate normal living.

That day, Luke was getting the cruiser ready to take out a small group of would-be adventurers with very specific tastes. He wanted everything to be in order and shipshape. He was taking them on a dinner cruise down the Thames the next day. This trip would be a really good money spinner for him, and for a change of pace he'd lined up a mariachi band and a Mexican menu. His long-time friend was also an excellent cook and was busy preparing one of his extravaganzas for Luke's guests—hot and spicy to promote thirst and the consumption of mammoth quantities of expensive liquor, with dancing and lovely hostesses for dessert.

Good old Doug was a veritable jack of all trades. He'd even taken some of the more advanced chef training courses, and his extensive knowledge and expertise in the kitchen earned him the opportunity to oversee the kitchen and staff. He had planned menus and supervised operations at sea on his previous boss's yacht.

*Ah yes, another successful sortie,* Luke was thinking as he mentally went over the planning of every detail once again, to make absolutely sure he hadn't missed anything. *If this keeps up, I'll be able to add another tour boat soon, probably another motor cruiser, a little more flexibility than a yacht and certainly a longer touring span through the year. Yes, Mum would have been proud.*

A sense of sadness prevailed when he thought of his mum and his last visit to the hospital, two weeks earlier. It was about a month since she had become really sick and he had rushed her to the A&E.

She had died in his arms and saying, "Sweetie, don't blame your da. He wasn't a bad man, just weak. You know we both always loved you, don't you?"

He'd never had a chance to answer. She was gone, irrevocably, and that's the way it was.

Nevertheless, he did blame his dad, and he always would. That no-good had all but destroyed his life.

Brushing these thoughts aside, he simply shrugged his shoulders, as he'd always done when, as a snotty-nosed kid with no hanky, he'd wiped his perpetually runny nose on his sleeve. There was always some kind of solution to any problem if you attacked it in the right way. Just get on with it!

His thoughts turned to the girls he was hiring for the trip the next day. *They're some lookers alright. They'll certainly fit the bill.*

*She's not hard on the eyes either,* he thought as his glance fell on Sarah, further up the towpath and making her way leisurely along. She was obviously deep in thought, totally preoccupied.

*She's always in such a rush. Maybe, just maybe she's taking a break for once,* he surmised.

As it happened, Sarah was taking a much-needed break and had brought her lunch to eat on one of the many benches bordering the Thames.

"Oh my goodness, if it isn't the lovely Lady Sarah." Luke hung over the side of the boat. "And looking as gorgeous as always, I might say."

"Oh Luke, knock it off, for heaven's sake." Sarah was annoyed at herself for forgetting that this was his hangout. She knew he had a thing for her and had been pursuing her for months. Another aggravation to deal with, and she really didn't need it at this moment. She and Jonathan had parted company and gone their separate ways after a bitter difference of opinion that had escalated out of control. She was shattered by the whole incident and wanted to be alone, although she had thought of visiting friends on Vancouver Island for a few days. She needed to get away, clear her head, and knew the trip would do her good. Business had slowed for a while, and she could fit in a few days for a change of pace.

When she got back to the UK, she would try to make it up with Jonathan and apologize to him for overreacting. In retrospect, her behaviour was way out of line. Unfortunately, he could be a little dictatorial and quite dominating at times, and on that particular day, her tolerance had been low. How sorry she was for the way she had spoken to him, when she had a chance to really think about things. How very, very sorry!

Courteous as always, she said, "How's business, Luke? Good, I hope."

"Can't complain, running a Mexican soirée tomorrow night, and then headed to Canada in the next few weeks to meet my partner there. Doug, my friend and business associate, will take care of things here while I'm away. Jordan and I will be taking the cruiser on a trip over to Vancouver Island to test out a new boat. We've had high hopes of expanding the business out there, and now it looks as if we're actually under way. I'm really looking forward to it. Jordan and I have planned this for some time. He has a great contact from the old boating company where he once worked. They've stayed in touch and are now working together. They make a great team. Mike's another great guy, and he's dead keen to do something for himself, just like Doug, so it looks as if we'll all be in clover in the future."

Luke started making his way down the gangplank. "Wouldn't want to impose on you and your busy schedule, but is the trip something you might fancy?" he added as an afterthought.

Against her better judgement and on the spur of the moment, Sarah made a snap decision.

"How strange you should mention that, Luke; I was going to book a flight to Vancouver in the next week or so and go over to Vancouver Island. I thought I would look up a couple of friends. Maybe we could work something out. Your partner Jordan is a terrific guy."

"Ah yes, I forgot you've met him already. Wasn't it at the RV exhibition some months ago?"

Sarah had attended the huge Home and Recreation Exhibition in London held a few months previously, and she'd run into Luke and Jordan, who was visiting from Canada.

"Yes, that's right, I did meet him, and what a nice chap he is. You know, Luke, I'd really like that. The idea of a trip right now really fits the bill. When exactly were you thinking of taking off?"

Luke could hardly believe his luck. He'd been eyeing Sarah for months, and here she was, just dropping into his lap, it seemed.

"I'm flexible. Just give me a call in a few days and let me know what arrangements you've made for the flight. I'll meet you in Vancouver, and we can go to Vancouver Island together."

He gave her one of his newly reprinted business cards. A beautiful picture of a yacht was on one side, with an outline of his company's services inscribed in old English script on the back.

"This is an impressive card," she said, giving it her full attention before putting it in her bag.

Sensing his mounting interest, she was beginning to wonder whether she'd been a little too hasty in accepting the invitation. *This whole idea could be a really big mistake.*

Oh, if only she had known just how big a mistake!

"Don't see many as showy as this," she continued. "Love the graphics."

"Yes, I have a great graphics design person. He's doing all the promotional material. Really has an eye for it, don't you think?"

A couple of weeks later, still against her better judgement, Sarah found herself confirming her schedule with Luke and arranging to meet him two days after her arrival in Vancouver, in the Coal Harbor Yacht Club at the foot of the City of Vancouver, bordering Stanley Park.

Luke sat back in his office, grinning like a well-fed Cheshire cat. He was over the moon. Sarah had never shown a lot of interest in him before. Of course, she'd been so tied up with that fancy antique dealer. *Oh well,* he thought, *let's not be negative. Be thankful and just accept what the powers that be dish out, and see which way the cards fall.*

\*\*\*\*

Later that day, he thought he'd take a stroll along the dock to check out the cabin cruiser. To his delight, there she was again, only this time wearing a very saucy hat with a rosette on the side.

"Hi Sarah, how are you doing?" He stopped mid-ships. "Sarah?"

"No, idiot, it's me, Jane."

"Oh God, you two are so much alike. It's the hat that threw me off. Thought you were Sarah."

Jane dismissed the comment in her usual offhand way. "Got time for a drink, sailor?"

Luke didn't want to get involved with her that day, as he had to attend to business, but she was relentless, and he gave in to her whim.

"Why the hell not? Come aboard, my lady."

And so he escorted her up the gangplank. *How ravishing she looks today; moody so-and-so, though,* he thought. *I'll play it cool; this one proves hard to handle at times.*

# Chapter 15
## A Major Predicament

The cabin cruiser was mid-way between Vancouver and Vancouver Island. Luke sat on one of the benches, head in hands, numb with shock. She was gone. It had all happened so quickly. He had heard her scream, just the once, as she went overboard. She disappeared almost immediately, the waves engulfing her as if she had never been. He had walked every section of the deck, peering down into the churning waves as they broke against the sides of the vessel. Pausing periodically to stare at anything remotely unusual, he waited for her to reappear but there was no sign of her resurfacing. It was all so final.

Finally going below deck, he picked up the phone and called the RCMP and the Coast Guard, reporting a passenger overboard. After giving them his bearings, he awaited their arrival and took the opportunity to phone Jordan to let him know what had happened.

Jordan would have been on the boat but had had to attend to some urgent business. He would instead take the ferry to Vancouver Island later and meet Luke there. He went cold when he heard the story. He allowed Luke to finish his tirade and then got straight to the point, his questions crisp and precise. He was boiling over with rage and frustration. Luke's problems over the years were beginning to get more than a little tiresome, but he'd topped the list with this latest development. It was monumental. That Luke had felt the need to complicate things by getting involved with a woman when they were right in the middle of negotiating the purchase of a new cabin cruiser was mind-boggling. The purchase was a goal they had worked towards for years and was part of their anticipated expansion. The timing couldn't have been worse. Now, it looked as if everything was swirling around the bowl.

"I'll get in touch with Gary. He'll know what to do, being our firm's lawyer here. He has all the right contacts."

Jordan then ended the call abruptly. He needed to get his head around the situation. He wasn't sure whether he even believed it had been an accident. He knew how volatile Luke could be with his rotten temper when he was riled up. He'd always had trouble with women, one way or the other. Damnation, Jordan didn't know what to believe, and he certainly wasn't going to waste time placating Luke—not right then, anyway.

****

Luke didn't have to wait long for the authorities to start appearing. The heavy search and rescue team, complete with helicopters, arrived simultaneously. The RCMP boarded the vessel, and after Luke had shown them into the lounge, they listened to his version of the events leading up to his passenger going overboard.

The search continued until nightfall. Hours stretched into an interminable hell for Luke, with the questioning and the expectation that at any moment, she could be found. The police completed their preliminary report but were non-committal. Luke had a strong feeling his story may have appeared disoriented and weak. In retrospect, maybe he shouldn't have mentioned the argument they'd had before she went overboard.

Finally, rescue operations ceased, and all persons made their way back to Vancouver. Luke was advised not to leave the city without consulting the police, as they might well wish to question him further.

As he headed back to Vancouver, completely wrung out and fraught with anxiety, he phoned Jordan again, saying he was on his way back to Coal Harbour and giving an approximate arrival time.

Jordan had definite misgivings when he heard the police didn't want Luke to go too far. Of course, there would have to be an investigation, he reasoned. Luke would obviously be the prime suspect if foul play was indeed suspected, and even if it wasn't, until the investigation was closed, he would have to stay close. Needless to say, having recovered from the shock of hearing the news initially, he was feeling better disposed towards Luke and able to put up a good front. No need to spook him further, as he was already hanging by a thread. They were sunk if he fell apart this early in the game.

"Don't worry, I've got your back," he said encouragingly. "I did touch base with Gary after you called me initially, and he's referred us to a friend of his who is also a top-notch criminal lawyer—may as well be prepared, just in case this develops badly. Just get back to Vancouver and give me a buzz when you get in.

"Oh, and about our prospective purchase: I think we should put a hold on that until we see which way things are going. I'm going to phone the owner tomorrow. Why don't you spend the night on the boat? Just rest up when you dock, but don't forget to confirm your hotel suite for an earlier arrival date. Mike and I should start getting the cruiser ready later tomorrow for the upcoming trips that are on the stocks, so you need to be settled in accommodation."

"I'll make this up to you, Jordan, I promise. I'm sorry, mate. I've given you a real headache."

"That's putting it mildly, friend. But let's just leave it for now. What's done is done. I just want to keep business going as smoothly as possible in the meantime. I'm also giving Mike the heads-up that he may be putting in extra time until we get through this, although he works pretty much the same hours as me already. Have to say, he's a major asset to the business."

****

After docking in Coal Harbour, the first thing Luke did was to gather a few personal items together in a holdall to have at the ready, in case he was called back while the investigation was ongoing. They would almost certainly take him in for questioning again, and having no idea how long they would detain him, he thought he'd better be prepared.

He was having trouble coordinating his trembling hands as he tried to pack neatly. Once the task had been completed, he ran a really hot bath and revisited his options and possible outcomes. His eyes were closing, but resisting the lure of the bedroom, he made a pot of strong coffee and sat down, attempting to relax.

He was just thinking about phoning Jordan when the phone went. It was Jordan, and very pleased with himself he was, too.

"Well, the gods are with us. Gary and I had a conference call with Sean Blackwell; he's the criminal lawyer, and he's in the picture. He knows you were advised not to leave town because the cops will have further questions for you. In the meantime, he's really putting himself out and is prepared to meet with us in his office tomorrow. So, guy, I'll pick you up at 11:00. We can think ourselves very fortunate that Sean is standing by and will be available, should you need him. Now go and get a good night's sleep. There's nothing anybody can do about it at the moment."

Luke readied himself for an early night, and after selecting a good paperback from the bookshelf, he set his water on the night table and climbed into bed. The gentle rocking of the vessel lulled him…

\*\*\*\*

There was that little boy again, struggling to keep up with his mam. It seemed as if they had been running forever. She held his hand tightly as they entered the woods bordering the Thames.

"Run. Run, Luke my lad. Let's get into the woods and see the wee folk."

They were running as if their lives depended on it, zigzagging through the last of the buildings and down the trail—the magical trail that led them through the woods and to the river.

What an adventure. Luke remembered how he'd revelled in the sheer excitement of conjuring up all sorts of mysterious possibilities of what they could encounter around the next bend in the trail. Pausing, they would rest on a huge rock covered with deep green lichen and soft, cushiony moss for a seat.

Those had been good times, and being such a young child, Luke had looked forward to the outings with childish glee, but as time went by, he began to associate them with danger at the house, when his father's voice grew ever louder. His mam would grab him at the onset of violence, and away they'd run towards their beloved river. And how they ran. The wee folk jumped back under the big swamp cabbage leaves by the ponds, darted under rocks and mossy banks and disappeared from view. He likened them to a beautiful rainbow breaking up and being blown away after a storm, flying in all directions, like his feet trying to keep up with his mother.

Sometimes, they were too late in getting out of the door, and his mam was grabbed roughly by his father. She always started shrieking at Luke: "Lukey boy, run to your room, there's a good lad."

He was a good lad and always did as she told him, but as he ran to his room, he couldn't block out the noise of the beating being inflicted upon her.

Running, running! He was always running. Running, it would appear, had been a pattern for him throughout his life—initially from his drunken father, then from trouble at school. Work or play, it didn't make a lot of difference. Either he went looking for trouble or it found him. And as he grew into manhood, the pattern continued.

****

Awakening suddenly, he realized he was drenched, and beads of perspiration were pooling on his face. His paperback had fallen, unread, to the floor at the side of the bed. *Here I go again, running, only this time, there's no escape and I'm right in the dirt. Right up to the eyeballs,* he thought, ripping the blanket back and throwing himself out of the bed.

Diving into the shower, he stuck his head under the cool water, gulping back a few mouthfuls before heading back to his bed. Boy, that felt good! He began to feel calmer as soon as he lay his head on the pillow. Very soon, his eyes were closing again, and old dreams and memories were once more engulfing him.

\*\*\*\*

What a day it had been at work. Luke was exhausted and fell into the little café, hardly able to coordinate his legs, he was so tired and hungry. The café was busy, but as he made his way to his usual table by the window, he was gratified to see a reserved sign placed strategically in the centre.

*She's looking after me again, bless her little heart.*

He cast around, seeking the angel dressed neatly in her navy dress and crisp white apron. This was his safe haven and she made it so, sparing no effort to see that he enjoyed his food. And what food it was. She always gave him an extra helping and little doggy bags. "To take home to your little doggy," she would say with a sly smile and wink.

How he loved this little foodery overlooking the Thames down on the wharf, and how much he was beginning to love her.

*Wonder if she'd consider going out with a bloke like me?* This was a question he'd been asking himself for weeks, but he hadn't managed to pluck up the courage. *Maybe she'd like to go to the pictures and a bite to eat afterwards.*

He'd been stunned into silence after he had finally blurted out the words. He couldn't believe she had accepted his offer.

Their relationship blossomed. He forced himself to work harder, pushing himself to the limit of endurance with overtime and extra jobs. He needed to make more money so that he would have something to offer her. He planned to ask her to be his wife and was determined to be worthy of her and better himself in every way.

They were both hard workers, leaving little time to get together, but when they did, they made their time special with outings to the park or the zoo. Their best times were walking along the banks of the Thames, on the reedy trails leading to the surrounding woods. Their picnic, the simplest of fare, would be spread out on a blanket beside the river. It may have been modest food, but how good it was. He could still taste it when he thought back to those days.

Images of his impoverished background floated around in his head. He had always known Susan deserved better than the likes of him—deserved more than he could give her. But he couldn't help himself. He had fallen totally and irrevocably in love with her. He was under her spell, and there was no going back for him.

He loved her so much; he hadn't even argued with her when she told him she needed more than he could offer. He'd put up no fight, just let her slip away. He knew in his heart that it was the thing to do.

Once again, Luke awoke and this time didn't bother trying to sleep again. What was the point? He felt desolate. Making himself another cup of coffee and plonking himself in any easy chair in the lounge, he thought about the night Susan had said goodbye. Funny how the direction of fate can be changed for the better. Although his heart had been ripped right out of him when she had left, what a blessing she'd made the decision to go, because he would never have given her up voluntarily. She now had all the security she needed and deserved. She definitely didn't need this latest development in her life, and it just proved once again how totally incapable he was of looking after her. Hell, he couldn't even look after himself.

\*\*\*\*

Over the following weeks, Luke was summoned to the station on several occasions for further questioning. They'd always say it was just to clear up a few points, but Luke knew they were cross-checking every word he said. Fortunately, Sean was right on it, and nothing slipped past him.

"Luke, keep a firm hold on yourself. Until the body surfaces, they don't have too much to go on. They're just going through the routine, making sure they have all the facts from you."

Nevertheless, following each meeting with the police, Sean grilled Luke again. It appeared that even he had his doubts as to Luke's innocence in the matter.

# Chapter 16
# Luke's Best Friends

Jordan was on his way to the airport to pick up Susan. Much to his relief, as soon as she'd received his call, she had agreed to come once she could make the necessary arrangements. He sped through the Vancouver traffic, most of which, he noted to his disgust, seemed to be going his way, to the airport. Jordan stretched his long legs. His pale face reflected the long, arduous hours of work he had put in while attempting to safeguard the business affairs in both England and Canada. Naturally, Luke was not functioning efficiently, so the load had fallen on Jordan's shoulders. Fatigue from sleepless nights and sheer exhaustion were beginning to tell on him, his thoughts running amok, churning like water hurtling through a waterwheel.

He revisited the initial call from Luke and the disastrous events that had occurred on the boat. What a pity he hadn't been on board, as they had originally planned. He may have averted the disaster. Jordan had been angry and frustrated. His friend's vile temper had gotten the better of him again. He'd always courted trouble, and now their business could be in jeopardy.

*Oh God, Luke, why you, of all people, why you? Fought all your life to make something of yourself, and now look at you; one stupid error in judgement, and all your dreams disappearing down the tubes. Why did you get involved with that Buchanan family, and worse, why did you have to make a move on their daughter? You might have known she was out of your league, and yet you persisted; just had to make a point. Will you never learn? Well, too late to go down that path again. Looks like not only are you well and truly messed up, but so is our business. Obviously a lot of reshuffling needed there if we're to keep the thing going.*

Following Luke's second call, Jordan had contacted a couple of people and cancelled the trip to Vancouver Island instead of delaying it. He wanted to see which way things were going. The owner of the cabin cruiser they had been going to take on marine trials was very sympathetic, although disappointed, and they agreed to keep in touch.

Jordan had been aware of Luke's arrangements to transport Sarah to Vancouver Island. He had thought at the time that it was not in the best interests of the company to get involved in personal stuff while dealing with business matters and obviously should have put his foot down right away.

Luke had hardly been recognizable during that second call. His voice was raised; he was hysterical and almost beside himself with grief and frustration. The search had come up empty-handed and they were all on their way back to Vancouver, but obviously there would be further interviews, as Luke had been told not to leave town.

"If only I'd stayed with Susan. Jordan, you know how I loved that woman. She was everything to me. I know that now, and I knew it then. She just wouldn't wait a bit longer for me to make something of myself. Simply wouldn't wait. If I'd been with her, none of this would have happened. There is no God." Luke ranted on. "Why would he want to put me through this hell? My life is ruined. As it if hasn't been tough enough already, and now this."

Jordan was still not feeling well disposed towards Luke and was having trouble keeping himself under control. As soon as there had been a break in the frenzied volleys of self-pitying nonsense, he made an attempt to calm his partner.

"Luke! Wrap it up, for pity's sake. You knew when Susan left that it was for the best. You said it yourself at the time. You couldn't take care of her, certainly not in the way she deserved. Would have! Could have! Should have! Luke, the bottom line is that you've got to get a grip on yourself. It's a done deal. As soon as we're finished, or rather, *you're* finished, I'm calling Gary again. I did get in touch with him after we first spoke. He's in the picture, but I'll call him in a minute and bring him up to date. I think we should establish contact with the lawyer Gary is recommending to us. I'll get on it."

Jordan had not been sure whether Luke was even following what was being said, but made an attempt to pacify him by saying that Gary would get them the right man to build a defence, should it be needed. He thought Luke had hung up because of the deadly silence emanating through the line.

"Luke, are you still there? Answer me."

"'Course I am, and taking in every word. And yes, you're right, I have to get a grip on myself, and I will. Don't worry about me. Just get hold of this lawyer for me so that we can reach out if and when the time comes. And Jordan, one more thing: thanks for standing by me and for being the best friend a man could have. You've always had my back, particularly now with all this crap hitting the fan. I'm sorry for everything and particularly for causing you all the extra work you'll be saddled with, not to mention the worry. If I ever get out of this mess, I swear I'll make it up to you."

"The support goes without saying, Luke. You know I've got your back. Just stay positive, for God's sake, and keep a tight rein on yourself—and your tongue, for that matter. And just remember, at this point, nobody's accusing you of anything. You simply had a passenger go overboard. And I sincerely hope for your sake that it's as simple as you say, and happened exactly as you say."

Jordan had been besieged with doubt as to Luke's innocence.

As soon as he'd hung up the phone, Jordan had called Gary. They'd been friends and business associates ever since Luke and Jordan had set up their business in Vancouver. He controlled all the company's corporate affairs and had a good handle on things. Gary was a yachting man also and knew everything there was to know about the boating and sailing industry. It was good to hear his voice.

Gary listened attentively while Jordan filled him in on all the details of his discussion with Luke. Jordan knew his friend would be pacing back and forth, following the trail he'd worn in his office carpet over the years. He moved constantly when he was on the phone. It always helped him to focus on the business at hand.

"I'll phone Sean. He's the best criminal lawyer I know and also a close friend. In fact, I'll do it right now. If I can get him, I'll pin him down on a time for a meeting. Stay by the phone, Jordan; I'll call you right back."

Gary was as good as his word, and as luck would have it, was able to get hold of Sean. They even managed to have a quick conference call. Their luck was holding, and they were able to schedule a brief meeting for the next day in Sean's downtown office for an update and proper introduction.

"I'll get hold of Luke and bring him to your office tomorrow," Jordan said. His skin was on fire, he was so tense. "Thanks to the saints that this guy is so accommodating. Let's hope Luke knows how lucky he is."

Gary had introduced the two men the next day in Sean's office. Jordan could see immediately that this was a lawyer in a profitable business, obviously oodles of cases coming his way. The opulence of his suite of rooms bore witness to a healthy income. Once they'd settled themselves, Jordan sat back while Luke told his story, actually managing to keep it together and relay events in a relatively calm manner.

Sean listened quietly, his face noncommittal, merely nodding his head from time to time, making copious notes.

"As you probably know from Gary, it's fortunate that I was taking a break between cases, and I'd be happy to take this one, should it develop. At this point, though, they're only pursuing their investigation, and nobody's accusing anybody of anything. I'll stand by, and we'll see how things pan out."

Jordan had made a quiet meal that night, throwing a few bits and pieces together on a platter. He watched a little TV afterwards, dozed off on the couch. Then he took a leisurely shower before phoning Susan, dragging out the time before placing the call because of the eight-hour difference in time between the UK and Canada. When it was opportune, he turned off the late-night movie, thinking it wasn't worth watching anyway, and reached for the phone.

They had always kept in touch, and as with Luke, his friendship with Susan had remained constant through the years. Susan and Luke's break-up over the money situation, or lack thereof, had been a distressing business for Jordan because they were both close friends of his and had been for years. The couple had suffered major after-shocks at the break-up. They had been an item for so long that it was inconceivable they should separate. They were made for each other, except for the lack of money, which was at the top of Susan's must-have list.

Jordan was forever propping Luke up when he fell into his recurring depressions and required rescue from his black moods. The separation had diminished his spirit, and the passing of time had seen him becoming even more embittered and defensive—a true cynic.

*No point in lashing myself about this.* Jordan took another gulp of his water and dialled Susan's number.

She had been horrified when she heard the story. Jordan's news completely derailed her.

"Jordan, you know how I felt about Luke," she had said, "and those feelings are unchanged, but you know he was no good for me back then. I wanted a home and a family, and I couldn't see it happening with him. Times were so desperate. There was no chance of us making a go of it. Marrying Tommy was the best thing I could do for myself. He was a kind man and good to me and the kids, and I did my best by him, always looked after him royally. He never went without a good meal on the table when he came home and was always well cared for. I was so grateful, you see. My own circumstances weren't that great, and Tommy took good care of me. Now he's gone, and I'm alone again. I'll go to Luke, and I'll support him."

She was getting very agitated. "Will you help me Jordan, please? Will you meet me at the airport? I'll get a flight to Vancouver as soon as I can make the arrangements for my mum to stay at my place while I'm away."

Jordan had been thrilled to hear that she intended to stand by Luke and would give him the support he desperately needed at this time. He just hoped that Luke would have the sense to keep his mouth buttoned up when Susan visited him and wouldn't send her away with a flea in her ear.

"Thank God you're on board with this," he'd said. "Your caring will go a long way to helping Luke through this misery. He still holds a torch for you, Susan; he never closed the door. You know that, don't you? It's always been you and only you for him. He never stopped talking about you. Made comparisons with every woman he got involved with; never could make another commitment."

Jordan heard a muffled intake over the phone and knew that she was crying.

"Ok then," he said brightly to change the mood. "Let me know when your arrangements are in place, and I'll make sure I'm at the airport to meet you. Don't worry about a thing."

"Jordan, you're the best. Thank you. I'm really looking forward to seeing you again. Though I wish it were under better circumstances."

"You and me both—just get yourself here and we'll take it from there."

****

The airport was coming into view, and Jordan exited off the highway, concentrating fiercely, as he had a nasty habit of missing his turning. After parking the car, he made his way to the arrivals section inside the airport.

He saw her before she saw him. Considering the years that had passed and the fact that she'd raised a family with little time for her own needs, she'd obviously taken good care of herself. She looked fabulous, with blonde hair rolled up in a chignon. Huge hoop earrings framed her elfin-like face. Unlike the casual attire of the travellers in general, she looked as if she were about to attend a business meeting. Her slim navy-blue suit fitted her as if it were custom made, the slit in her skirt reaching her knee, discreetly showing off a shapely calf. Her shoes were soft leather, very fashionable yet still a good choice for flying. He always focused on what shoes he was wearing when he flew anywhere, as his feet inevitably swelled up like the chef's best soufflé. Jordan had developed a keen eye when appraising women, although his hectic schedule allowed little time for him to establish and develop any lasting romantic liaisons.

Wheeling a small case and with a travel bag slung over her shoulder, she suddenly spotted Jordan and hailed him from the other side of the luggage carrousel. Unable to harness the flood of tears, she clung to him as soon as she'd passed through the barrier.

"Oh Jordan, isn't this ghastly? Do you think Luke could have murdered that woman?"

"Well, it certainly looks like it, and you know better than anyone all about that temper of his. It wouldn't surprise me in the least. I suppose we'll find out soon enough. Our company's lawyer, Gary, has referred his friend Sean, who's a top-notch criminal lawyer. Luke really got lucky. It would seem that he has a good team behind him. I have complete confidence in Sean, and if anyone can get Luke out of this predicament, Sean is the guy. Come on, let's get the hell out of here. All these people shoving and yelling, it's too nerve-racking. How do you feel about a bite to eat and maybe a drink to settle the old nerves?"

"Just what the doctor ordered. I didn't eat anything on the plane; didn't feel like it."

"Yes, I know what you mean. I'm not doing too well in that area either."

Jordan took her arm and, guiding her through the crowds, offered some words of comfort, although he was feeling far from comfortable.

"Try not to worry. We'll just have to hang in there and keep our hopes up that the police will be satisfied when they complete their investigation. As I said before, I have confidence in Sean; he'll put his best foot forward, we can be sure of that."

The waiter led them to a window seat, and each sat for a while quietly contemplating the situation. The Vancouver crowd was busily jostling each other, most of them at the end of their working day and in a hurry to get to their homes. Following their second drink, the situation seemed a little brighter and the pair perked up.

"Come on, let's get you to your hotel. You must be totally exhausted." Jordon took her arm and grabbed her luggage at the same time. "Why don't you hang loose for a couple of days to give yourself a bit of a breather? We can't do a thing with the investigation still ongoing. You may as well give yourself a break. Wander around for a while; get the feel of the city and the ocean before you arrange to go and see Luke. He's in such a bad place anyway at the moment. I haven't even mentioned that you made arrangements to come to Canada. Take the opportunity to zone out for a bit. You know I'm here within a stone's throw.

"I have a great apartment overlooking English Bay, and as I keep saying, you're welcome to stay there if you want. I have a guest room with adjoining bathroom. In fact, why don't you revisit that idea as soon as you get yourself together? It's too early for you to even think about how long you'll be staying, when you're going back to UK. Just give it a bit of time."

"Thanks Jordan, you're an angel, and I might just take you up on that. I've booked only a few days at the hotel, but it would be easy to change the dates. I've already mentioned to the booking clerk that I may need to make changes, and there's no problem. Let's just see how things go. Luke may still have feelings for me, but that's not to say he'll welcome seeing me in these circumstances. He may well send me packing."

****

Jordan had been right. Susan was actually enjoying the area, in spite of the circumstances. Her hotel was great, one of a chain and just steps up the street from English Bay. She was actually getting a better night's rest and her appetite was picking up, as attested to by her clean plate after devouring a wonderful hotel breakfast. She'd practically scraped the shine off the plate as she inhaled her bacon and eggs, with country fried potatoes and a side of brown toast with marmalade. And much to her amazement, she found herself actually ordering another round of toast.

Refuelled, Susan was all set for a good day's walk, with substantial walking shoes and a flask of water. Leaving her room, appetite fully appeased, she determined to make a good day of it, as off she headed for Stanley Park.

Sitting on a large rock at English Bay a while later, the magnificent North Shore mountains rising up in the distance caught her attention. A narrow strip of ocean separated them from downtown Vancouver. Joy of joy, there were the harbour seals Jordan had told her to look out for, cavorting a short way offshore. What a picture they made.

Finally tearing herself away, she continued on her three-hour walk around the famed seawall that encompassed all of Stanley Park. She had read of a plaque embedded in the cliff near the historic Siwash Rock, a huge granite projection off the seawall, surrounded by legends of the Indigenous people of Squamish in British Columbia. The plaque had been placed in remembrance of the man who had dedicated 32 years of his life, from 1931 to 1963, to building the seawall. James Cunningham was a park board member and master stone mason, and his life's work had not died with him. But the constant lashing of the incoming tidal waves, particularly virulent in winter months, ensured an ongoing project requiring constant repairs and maintenance.

It was a day to remember for Susan; every moment was thoroughly enjoyed. She was beginning to feel she really belonged and was definitely one of the crowd, finding herself stopping at regular intervals for a chat. The people were friendly and open, obviously very happy in their environment. She absolutely loved it.

Meandering back along the beach, Susan was suddenly aware of how hungry she was. *Must have been the strenuous day of walking*, she thought as she headed up the stairs to a little restaurant-cum-bar adjacent to her hotel. It was a circular structure with windows all around, offering a wonderful view of English Bay. Thinking she would order an early dinner, she settled on the house white wine, West Coast seafood chowder with chicken strips, fries, and salad to follow.

The waterfront was busy with people strolling. Little boats bobbed offshore, and fabulous cabin cruisers headed purposefully out to sea. What a pleasurable scene it was, with an equally pleasurable dinner, leaving Susan thinking she'd have to adjust her eating style. Certainly she'd need to limit her intake or be in trouble soon with her weight. The thought of being forced into a larger size and the expense of new clothing would put a stop to her greed, she hoped. *But another helping of fries wouldn't hurt, would it?*

She didn't think she could wring much more out of the day, and upon opening the door of her hotel room, kicked off her shoes and flung herself into the nearest chair to contemplate events and percolate her plans for the next day. Her eyelids were blinking with fatigue. Reluctantly leaving the comfort of the chair, she tidied up and headed for the shower. An early night, just curling up with her book before zoning out, was looking very attractive.

Even though she was actually switching off and beginning to relax, she was still anxious about seeing Luke so soon. She needed a bit more time and had asked Jordan not to mention she was in Vancouver.

*Jordan's right,* she thought again. *I'll go and talk to Luke when I feel more up to it. I'll try to find out where things now stand between us and whether there is any chance of getting back together, if and when he gets out of this mess. One thing's for sure: I'll help him in any way possible. That's if he'll let me, of course.*

Having made a decision, she felt mildly better about the situation and drifted off to sleep the sleep of the dead.

# Chapter 17
# Susan

Susan walked slowly to the café where Luke had finally agreed to meet her. She was besieged with doubt as to how she would be received. She had cajoled and argued with Luke until she'd finally persuaded him to see her. Having got her own way, she was now wondering whether she'd done the right thing. In retrospect, maybe it would have been better for them to meet when the investigation was further along and there was some kind of daylight ahead.

*On the other hand,* she reasoned, *isn't it better for me to be there at the onset, offering some support and a few words of comfort? Surely it will give him a boost of confidence to know I'm with him all the way.*

He looked up when he heard her coming, and for a brief moment, his eyes locked on hers. Her heart flooded with compassion for this man who now averted his gaze—head held down, unable to look at her directly, so filled with remorse was he. All the stuffing knocked out of him, he was but a mere shadow of his former self, hardly resembling the man she had known and loved. It filled her with shame when she thought of how she had pressured him into meeting with her. It had not been her intention to undermine or diminish him in any way—quite the contrary.

Moving briskly to the table, she reached for his hand and sat down quietly, allowing him time to come to himself, while the tears washed his cheeks. Straightening his body, his tormented eyes finally met her gaze as he considered her quietly. Then with the old familiar shrug, he opened his heart to her. And in the doing, they were able to speak of the way things had been, how they'd shared their hopes and dreams, and how foolish they had been to treat those times so shabbily and let them slip through their fingers. Finally, in the talking, they were in accord, both knowing they'd never lost their feelings for each other; they had always been soulmates and would always be so.

He flagged the waiter down and ordered coffee for both of them.

"Do you want anything to eat?" he said, looking at the menu. He seemed completely recovered, more at ease.

"No thanks, not really hungry. Just the coffee for me, please; I haven't stopped stuffing myself since I arrived. I'm really starting to pile the weight on again. Do you remember how I was a bit on the porky side? Well, I'm getting there again."

He seemed amused. "No, you were never porky, and you look as terrific now as you always did."

His look was intense and, sensing her embarrassment, he studied the cup in his hand.

Sipping their coffee, they exchanged small talk before Susan jumped in head-on.

"Luke, if we get through this, how would you feel about a completely fresh start, maybe here in Vancouver? Do you think Jordan would like working side by side with you?"

"It's something we have talked about, and I must say, I've always liked Vancouver."

His face clouded as the old familiar bitterness assailed him. Susan knew instantly that she had lost him again. She should never have brought it up. It was far too soon to be discussing relocating to Canada.

"Anyway, don't you think it's a bit premature to think about stuff like that? Right now, I'm being hung out to dry, anyone can see that. I've been scurrying in and out of the police station like a damn rabbit trying to outrun a ferret."

Standing up abruptly and dropping some cash on the table in the process, Luke looked over his shoulder as he began to leave.

"Thanks for coming, love. You'd best find yourself a better bet than me. Looks like I'm well and truly scuppered on this one. You'd be advised to move on."

The investigation could go either way, and Luke wasn't prepared to have her wait for a lost cause, should things not pan out as they wished. Life had a way of throwing curves, and he was well versed in dodging them, but this was the roughest one yet. No—there was no way he would have her involved.

He turned abruptly and her heart went out to him, but she could find no words of comfort to offer at that time, nor was she given the opportunity, because she was looking at his retreating back.

She had gone straight back to the hotel, and the feeling of hopelessness was to the fore when she thought of the way they had parted. The image of him walking away was still in her mind's eye. Their talk had gone so well, and then when she'd hinted at the possibility of a new life for both of them, if they got through the next few weeks, the old Luke had surfaced with a vengeance.

He'd been so brusque and defensive. But in retrospect, he'd always been that way. He was and probably always would be a difficult personality. Bad traits had been exacerbated by poor living and always having to fight throughout his younger years. A non-existent childhood without any of the privileges that normal children took for granted. Most people would have changed in the same way he had.

Both had found common ground in the hardship of their lives, a hand-to-mouth existence that neither would ever forget. Susan had been loved by her parents, and Luke's mother had thought the world of him, but his father was a piece of work and a confirmed alcoholic who seemed to hate his son.

Even thinking about the past consumed Susan with sadness.

*But, of course,* she reasoned, *who knows what goes through the mind of a drunk whose only motivation is in finding the next drink. It doesn't matter if it's your father, husband, whoever. If the ones you love and who profess to love you have a substance issue, then all bets are off.*

Susan had stayed at home because her mother needed her. They were poor, but they did have a humble roof over their heads. She recalled her father with fondness. He had no vices; his only thought was to be a good provider for his family. He had been a docker in London and a hard-working man until the day that girder had fallen on him and crippled him for life. He was never to work again. There was little compensation for him, and it fell to her mother to support the family. The situation had cut the heart out of a simple man. He was never able to get the upper hand on his feelings of inadequacy that, as the head of the household, he had let the family down.

As soon as Susan was old enough, she found herself a job helping out in a café overlooking the Thames. The food was good and plentiful, and she had the added bonus of being fed on the job. The establishment was well known amongst the men who worked on the boats or on the Thames in one capacity or another. They all liked Susan and consequently, her tips were generous, easing the financial situation at home.

It was while she was working in the café that she had first met Luke. He'd come in for lunch with a mate. There was an immediate connection between the two.

Several weeks later, he had appeared in the café on his own, sat at the same table as before, ordered the same lunch, and eventually had struck up the courage to ask her out on a date.

She smiled when she thought about that day. How uncomfortable he'd been when he asked her out. How unsure of himself, not a shred of confidence. He had all the cheek in the world when he was with his mates, but it was quite another matter when it came to taking a girl out on the town. But as time went by, he'd changed. They'd both changed. They'd met whenever they had the opportunity, and their attraction for each other had deepened with every passing day.

It nagged at Susan constantly because even though he made her feel like a princess, spending whatever small amount of money he earned on her, she saw no future for them. He had no prospects, no opportunity for advancement doing the job he did. Every time they parted and she returned to her miserably shabby home and her menial job, it weighed heavily on her, knowing deep down in her heart that she wanted more than he could give her. Going without, not having any of the pretty things a woman should have, and the inevitability of being weighed down with a family with never enough money to sustain them all properly, was a life that she didn't need and was not going to have.

"No," she would rage to herself, "I'm not going down that road all my life, just like my mother has."

Her father passed on, and although she hated to think that way, it was a blessed relief. The effort was killing her mother, and the expense of trying to look after his special medical needs as well as everything else were proving too much. Her husband's diminishing spirit and mental state had been taking its toll. She was not a strong woman, and Susan was sick of seeing her slowly fade away.

Not long after the funeral, Susan had broken off her relationship with Luke, telling him they were no good for each other. She needed more than he could offer. She hurt him deeply, she knew that, and would never forget the pain she had inflicted on him, but it had to be. At least, that's what she'd kept telling herself, even though her decision tore her apart.

The year was hardly spent when Tommy had come into her life. Dear, kind, solid Tommy, with a good union job and eager to offer her all the things she'd never had.

She took him up on that offer. They were married shortly after, and Susan had tried to put Luke out of her mind. She did, for the most part, but there was always a sliver of her that still hung onto him. She knew she would never really let him go. They were joined irrevocably. Cut from the same cloth.

\*\*\*\*

Suddenly, Susan felt chilled. Maybe it was the shock of seeing Luke again. Maybe she was just tired.

Her tea had grown cold, and she felt isolated and alone in the hotel room.

*I'll take a nice hot bath, have another tea, and get myself an early night,* she thought.

But still, she sat remembering, simply couldn't tear herself away from the memories and how it had been for them so very long ago. How special their long walks along the Thames had been. Hundreds of hypericum plants with their gorgeous golden flowers ranged along the paths following the river. The blooms had made the young couple's walks and picnics so magical from summer through the autumn days. They would stroll hand in hand, stopping only when they had found a suitable flat area to lay out their blanket for their picnic. The food always tasted so good, even though it was poor man's food—a hunk of cheese and bread with a bottle of water, and if they were flush, an apple or two, or some leftover fruit cake. But how it was enjoyed.

Those were different times. Then Tommy had come along, and life changed dramatically. He had been so good to her; she'd lacked for nothing. They had a lovely home and a family, a son and daughter.

One day, she had wheeled her two-month-old daughter along the Thames and once again enjoyed the warmth of the day and the miracle of the hypericum flowers, with their velvety stamens. The babe's rattle had fallen from the pram, and before she could reach down for it, he had stopped and picked it up for her. Their eyes met, both recognizing each other, both remembering and feeling the same old chemistry. Luke had looked hard at her and then her daughter, his face filled with pain and regret. Then the defensive guard was up and, turning on his heel, he was gone, up the path and out of her life.

Hurrying over to a bench, her legs as heavy as lead, she'd been grateful to sit down, and for the first time since they had parted, she cried. She knew she had no right to indulge herself in such a way; she was being disloyal to Tommy, but she couldn't help herself. In that moment, she knew that whatever Luke's deficiencies were, she loved him still. It had always been him and always would be.

*****

Dragging herself out of the chair, she headed for the bathroom. *I'll feel more like it after a good bath and a steaming cup of tea,* she thought as she ran her water. *I have to stop thinking about the past and move forward.*

It had been wonderful to see Luke again, even though their meeting had ended so badly. He'd worn well. He was as easy on the eye as ever, in fact, even better looking. His body had matured and filled out a little. Although the current circumstances were obviously taking their toll, he was still a very handsome man. She had been shocked to feel the old charge, amazingly as potent as ever.

*My Lord, he has the same hold on me as he always had, maybe even more so.*

She was meeting Jordan the next day. Thank goodness another diversion. She always found him so uplifting. He was going to show her around the tour boat and give her a rundown on the business he ran with Luke.

Sure enough, after a good night's sleep the next day, she felt more up to life, and after making a special effort with herself, went down to the pub restaurant in the hotel to sample another of the fabulous breakfasts on offer.

After picking up a few personal items from a pharmacy, she made her way through the town and down to the water where Jordan had the firm's cruiser moored. When she came into view, he waved to her from the deck. As she neared the boat, he beckoned her towards the gangplank and helped her to board.

It wasn't until they were sitting down in the lounge to the fore of the boat with a large pot of tea and some biscuits in front of them that Jordan, who was bursting with curiosity, could contain himself no longer. Susan had been sitting in her own world long enough, just gazing out of the window.

"Come on, then, enough of this gawking out of the window. Put me out of my misery and tell me how your visit went with Luke. I've been itching to hear all about it." Jordan's voice cut into her thoughts.

"Oh sorry, Jordan, I was miles away. I'm still trying to get my thoughts around the situation regarding Luke, and yes, you're right, we're still emotionally involved. Our feelings have not changed for each other. The minute I saw him, I knew it would always be him. I've known it all along. Just put it aside, didn't want to deal with it."

"Years ago, I bumped into him when I was wheeling the babe along the Thames, and it slammed me right in the face. I was not free to do anything about it at that time, but I am now, yet Luke is not available to me and may never be. I feel we were never meant to be together. Our timing has always been off, and now it seems that Luke has simply given up—resigned to the fact that he's finished. He's convinced that he'll be charged and convicted after the investigation and doesn't want to see me in the meantime. I was so depressed when we parted. I just can't see any good ending to this predicament."

Jordan could see she was really stressed and turned away momentarily to give her some space while she fumbled in her bag to get something to dry her tears. She buried her face in her handkerchief.

"I'm so sorry, Jordan. It's just that I feel so inadequate, so unable to help him, and I honestly don't know if he killed that woman or not. It's all so horrific. Give me a minute. This is disgusting. I have to get a grip on myself."

Excusing herself, she stumbled to the bathroom.

*Oh Lord, I think we'd better forget about the tea and cookies and get something stronger down us,* Jordan thought as he headed over to his amply stocked bar. Casting his eye over the bottles, he selected a brandy and a sparkling wine for later. A further search of the galley revealed, to his delight, a pot of wonderfully aged cheese imported from Cheshire in

England, which he positioned on a platter with an assortment of crackers and crisps.

When she hurried back, looking a bit shamefaced, he pushed a glass of brandy into her hand.

"Here, get that down. It'll help settle you."

That perked her up. She was looking a bit better, and her face lit up when she saw the spread.

He watched while she had a sip of the brandy and repositioned herself. She seemed fully recovered, so he forged on to make her feel better about things.

"Well, I personally think you two are jumping the gun a bit on this one. The fight hasn't really started yet, and you're already defeated. They are simply investigating, and nothing is carved in stone at this time. You need to remember that and think positively, otherwise you'll both go crazy."

"Yes, it seems that way, doesn't it? I'm so sorry Jordan, but honestly, I really don't see much hope. Luke was always a bugger with that horrible temper of his, and now it looks as if he could have cooked his goose on this one.

"Jordan, I did a lot of thinking about Luke before I went to see him. I love Vancouver, and I know he does. I was wondering if it would be possible to make a fresh start in Vancouver if he gets off. You've both been friends for so long and work very well together. I believe Luke was going to expand his business in London, but what about both of you building up the business here? Do you think that's a feasible option? If he gets clear of this, of course, and even wants to get back with me."

Jordan stared at her thoughtfully. "I did have talks with Luke some time ago about him coming to Canada and us joining forces here. He seemed quite receptive at the time, but somehow, what with both of us being so busy all the time, we never really got back to the idea. I think we could most definitely revisit it if and when this all gets cleared up. We're all young, and the timing is right to expand the business."

They sat quietly in the lounge of the cruiser for a while, each contemplating the idea. The gentle lapping of the water against the sides of the boat acted as a soothing balm on their senses as they sipped their drinks and sampled the snacks. The shadows lengthened and began their shimmering dance upon the water whilst lights were lit up in sequence along the shoreline.

Spontaneously leaping to his feet, Jordan offered her his arm. "Let's go and grab a light meal. There's a great little restaurant at the end of the promenade, with equally great food. Why don't we go there and just chill out for a while? We can finish off with a bottle of wine on the boat later. Or," with a wink, "maybe you'd prefer cocoa."

Susan smiled. "Yes, I'd like that."

"Which one would you like?"

She laughed. "It really doesn't matter. You've succeeded. I feel so much better, thanks to you. Wine or cocoa are just the trimmings on the cake. Oh, by the way, I've been thinking about your offer for me to stay with you, and I would really like that."

"Do you need any help with moving your stuff from the hotel? I'm a bit tied up during the day tomorrow but could help out in the evening."

"No you won't. I wouldn't think of it. It's absolutely no bother for me to move a few cases to your place. Just leave a note with any instructions. I promise I won't be a bother in any way."

Jordan dug in his pocket and pulled out a ring of keys.

"Here, put those in your bag," he said as he pulled off two keys from the ring. "Those are the keys to the apartment. The bigger one is for the apartment door, and the other one is the main door to the building. There's always cabs waiting outside the lobby of the hotel, and if I'm not available, grab one. Even though the apartment is just a few blocks away, you'd be advised to grab the cab, as you've got quite a bit of luggage."

Both felt their spirits rising as they made their way to the restaurant. The situation had taken on a more positive look. Maybe things would work out after all.

## Chapter 18
## Anne Arrives in Vancouver

Once again, Jordan was headed for the airport—this time to pick up Susan's girlfriend Anne, who was coming to Vancouver to visit her mother and also offer support to Susan. Both were in high spirits, and Susan hadn't stopped chattering since she got in the car, she was so excited about seeing her friend again. Even though traffic was light, Jordan was concentrating on driving whilst listening with half an ear, although he was intrigued by this woman he had heard so much about. He was looking forward to meeting her.

Jordan's car was sumptuously comfortable and a smooth ride. He was also an excellent driver. Susan reclined her seat, closed her eyes, and finally relaxed. Reliving her phone call with Anne, she realized how much she had missed her friend. They had commiserated with each other over the years, sharing life experiences, hopes, and dreams for the future. Life had certainly thrown its curves at each of them, but they had always remained closely bonded and were in touch regularly.

Susan had been entertaining the prospect of a visit from Anne ever since her own arrival in Vancouver. She really wanted her to meet Jordan. Her gut feeling told her they would hit it off immediately, and it was a marvellous opportunity to get her out for a visit. Not the best of circumstances, but at least they'd get to meet each other. On the one hand, there was Anne, a lovely woman in every way, and on the other, Jordan, the most eligible bachelor she knew. What better time to get the two together? She could say that she needed Anne's moral support, as it was such a dreadful time. It was certainly true that she would love to see her friend. She always perked up a bad situation.

****

Susan definitely wasn't a needy person and didn't want to come over as being one, but this was an opportunity she couldn't pass up if it meant introducing these two. Quietly she hatched her plan, deciding not to discuss it with Jordan until she had made it happen. She wasn't sure what frame of mind Anne was in, as she'd had a bit of a rough time dealing with the aftermath of her divorce. How her husband could have cheated on her was beyond comprehension. Susan found herself constantly turning it over in her mind.

*Anne's just about the most easy-going person I know, so agreeable. What an idiot he must be to have thrown her away just like that. Wonder if he now knows what he's given up by walking away.*

She had always thought that Anne was one of the most decent people and the kindest she had ever met. The two women had enjoyed a strong friendship for years and had shared some good times together.

Anne's father had married her Canadian-born mother after the war. They'd had many happy years in England, but when he passed away, her mother had returned to her homeland. Her older sister lived on Vancouver Island, and they had missed each other sorely through the years of separation. It made sense to spend their later years together, as they had always got along so well and shared many common interests.

Anne had remained in England, firmly entrenched in her marriage and career by the time her mother left. Neither had been satisfactory. Her marriage had ended in a nasty divorce because of her husband's frequent liaisons outside of the marital bed, and Anne's job situation wasn't looking too hot either.

*Poor thing, she's having a really bad run of luck—could do with a bit of a break,* Susan had thought as she picked up the phone to call her friend. Anne had answered immediately.

"Hi Anne, that was quick. You must have been sitting on the phone. It hardly rang."

"Well, it's not like I'm doing much. I've just been let go from my job. Made redundant, they said, but I know it was a personality conflict with the newly imported boss. We've had a few serious differences. Certainly doesn't make for a smooth flow in the office. The social life leaves a lot to be desired, too, being a new divorcée and all that."

She paused for a moment, obviously collecting her thoughts. "It's so great to hear from you, Susan. What's up? I've been wondering how you're holding up. Are there any further developments at your end?"

"Not really. The police investigation is still ongoing, and because of that, Luke doesn't want to see me. He's afraid of getting too pally or involved again and doesn't see the point in adding further complications while this is all hanging in limbo. He thinks it's best that we avoid close contact with each other. I suppose he's right in some respects, but I did tell him I'd be here and will stand by him."

"Well, just hang in there. Things have a habit of working out for the best, although it doesn't seem like that at the time. Listen to me! A right Miss. Optimistic aren't I? I was in the blackest hole before you phoned, but I'm right, you know. Things really do seem to happen for the best. We have to remember that."

"I'd really like to believe that, but in the meantime, I just want my best friend here with me for moral support. Anne, do you think you could manage to fit in a trip to Vancouver? This waiting game is telling on all of us. I've been staying at Jordan's. He's been wonderfully supportive, but even he is showing signs of strain. I feel like I'm starting to fall apart. And from what I've been hearing, you aren't doing so well. The best thing both of us can do is take a break and have some fun exploring—treat this like some sort of tourist visit."

"As I said, it's not like I'm submerged in anything, just sitting here contemplating my navel, so to speak. Actually, that's a great idea, Susan. Don't know why I didn't come up with it earlier. I could have got away from that awful job at the same time, before they got in first and got rid of me. Of course, I did get a little settlement from them, which I think I deserve, because of their unconscionable treatment, not to mention the years I've wasted with them covering their rear ends. It would also be very nice to get away from the stench of that foul divorce. It still burns my nostrils. Mind you, I can't begin to imagine how awful it must be for you. The waiting around would drive anyone insane."

"It could be a lot worse. As I said, Jordan has a great flat, and he's a terrific man. He's made me very welcome. I'm praying you'll come to Canada. I can't wait for you to meet him. I know you two would hit it off big time. Staying with him has opened my eyes to just how much both of you seem to have in common. You like the same things. You'd both get on like a house on fire. Even though everything is up in the air, you and I will have a really fun time, and Jordan knows just where to take us."

Anne was a little sensitive on the subject of men at the time, so she moved right along, not giving Susan the slightest encouragement on that subject.

"Well, as I said earlier, the timing is perfect. Since being laid off from work, I've been contemplating a trip to see Mum and her new man friend, Jim. So maybe that's the order of the day. Plus, you and I could both do with a lift. So in answer to your question, okey doke, I'll do just that. Don't need to bend my arm on that one. I'll ring Mum to let her know I'm coming and will give you a buzz in a day or so when I've made the arrangements."

Susan was over the moon. *Well, that was smooth and easy. Let's just see how this pans out. They really would be great for each other, and I can hardly wait to see her again.*

Smiling, she hung up and was just finishing the last of her glass of celebration wine when Jordan came in.

"Hi there, how's it going? Don't answer that, I can see. Don't you look comfy and happy. Had a good day then?"

He was always so considerate. Always thinking of her well-being, and he must have had quite a day of it. The boat business was picking up and getting a little hectic here and there. He had to prepare for the main season, which would be on them before they knew it. Between liaising with the London business, and making sure that Luke's man Doug and his own work colleague, Mike, in Vancouver, were on track with all the extra work they'd inherited, Jordan certainly had his hands full, "I'm doing well, thanks to you. I've just finished a glass of that lovely wine you left for me. I'm absolutely pampered."

"Well, I think I should be, too. I'll go and get what's left in the bottle—that's if there is anything left. You look pretty entrenched there. Be back in a jiffy."

He appeared promptly, carrying the bottle and an extra glass for himself. Filling both glasses, he sat down, enjoying the first taste of the sparkling wine on his tongue.

Susan put her glass down and leaned forward.

"Listen Jordan, I've just got off the phone with Anne. You remember her, don't you? She's my friend in England. I've talked about her occasionally."

"I would say more than occasionally. I feel she's part of my non-existent family, and I've never even met her."

"Well, it looks like you're going to get the chance. She's coming to Vancouver to stay with her mother and to give us some moral support. Anne has just been laid off from her job, and she's only a few months away from that messy divorce. Isn't that something?"

"It's great that she gets the chance to get the hell out of Dodge and," he grinned wickedly, "with the added bonus that she gets a chance to meet me."

"She should be here in a few days. She's going to give me a buzz when she has everything organized. I believe her mother is visiting a friend in Kitsilano, and the arrangement is that Anne can bunk in there for a while, and then they can both travel over to the island together. This will work really well for us. When we give her the grand tour, it'll take our mind off things; a bit of a diversion for us, don't you think?"

"Yes, I do, and fortunately, I could probably take some time out for lunches or dinner, whatever. I've been shuffling business around a bit, and as you know, it's been a bit frantic at work, but I've pretty well set things up for when we get busy again, and Mike is just great. He's my right hand. I'll just be having the odd conference call with Luke and Doug in the UK branch. This actually would be a good time for me to regroup before the onslaught again."

So plans were made, arrangements were put in place, and a list of possible day trips was put together. Both began to look forward to Anne's imminent arrival. A bit of a diversion was definitely something they both needed.

****

Once again, Susan and Jordan found themselves hanging around the luggage carousel inside the airport.

"There she is." Susan yelled frantically, waving enthusiastically with both hands.

Jordan's attention was drawn to a woman waving back at them.

*Holly smokes. Susan's description of Anne was definitely understated. She's stunning.*

Jordan was drawn to her natural beauty—not the magazine-cover type, but striking. Her face was shrouded by curls and cut in a way that made her look like one of those cherubim he'd seen on Christmas cards. He was blown away.

Anne drifted over to the other side of the carousel, flashing a dazzling smile at Susan, followed by a mild appraisal of her male companion.

Jordan rushed forward to take her carry-on.

"I have another couple of cases coming on the carousel. Look, there's one of them over there."

"Here, let me get it for you," and he positively dragged her suitcase from the carousel and placed it beside her carry-on.

"Oh, thank you. How kind. You must be Jordan. Susan's mentioned you many times."

"Only the good stuff, I hope."

Her outstretched hand slipped so easily into Jordan's. A sensation of warmth flooded him immediately as he beamed down at her. She was like a ray of sunshine, a soothing balm to frayed nerves.

"Oh, there's my other case, the orange one. I thought I'd better get something colourful and easy to see."

Anne was prattling, she knew, but couldn't seem to stop herself. She certainly wasn't going to encourage this good-looking man—well, not too much, anyway. Nevertheless, she too had felt some strong chemistry between them.

"I haven't really scheduled a return trip. Thought I'd stay for a while, really make a good break, although I am so sorry about the circumstances."

"Watch the luggage while I grab the other case." Jordan dropped the bag at her feet and leapt forward, grabbing a trolley én route. He left the two women hugging as if they hadn't seen each other in years. When he returned shortly, they were still at it, both bawling their eyes out.

"Just follow me, ladies," Jordan said grandly, grinning broadly at all the emotion. "Trolley's loaded; let's get to the car."

Making their way up the ramp to the car park, Jordan led them over and opened the doors for them.

After Susan was safely ensconced, he rushed around the other side of the car.

"Let me get that for you, Anne." Again, he was aware of an inexplicable sensation as he took Anne's arm and helped her into the back seat next to Susan—very perplexing for Jordan, who was generally immune to women's charms, being so clear-thinking and wrapped up in business matters.

"Now you two can chat up a storm. Do you fancy a quick bite to eat at my place? It might be nice for us all to have a little get-together before Anne goes over to Kits to her mother."

"That would be terrific. It would give me a chance to unwind and freshen up before I see Mum," Anne piped up. She was beginning to see how caring Jordan was. She was not used to a man treating her with such consideration.

"I'm still wondering if I should mention the job business or not. She tends to be a bit critical here and there, and losing my employment would just add to the pile, with me looking like a right failure, especially after the rotten marriage drama. Mum has consistently maintained that it takes two to make a marriage, and I must have fallen down somewhere. She definitely wouldn't understand about losing the job, either. I'm sure she simply wouldn't grab the concept that quite able people lose their jobs through no fault of their own. Yep, I don't have a good track record. So I think I'll just keep my mouth shut and not get into any of it."

Jordan was all over that—a dog with a bone.

"So does that mean you fancy a glass of wine before having a bite to eat, just to brace yourself for when you guys meet up—medicinal purposes and all that?"

"Oh, I'm sorry. I do go on a bit, don't I? It must be jet lag or something. Yes, I'd love a glass of wine, and thank you so much for helping me to get organized." Their gazes met intently in the rear-view mirror.

Feeling mildly discombobulated, Jordan steered the car out into the traffic.

"Then it's a done deal. Let's go back to my place. We can sit on the balcony with wine and watch the boats, and then I'll throw something tasty together for us." He caught Anne's eye once again in the mirror.

"You can look across the water at your mother's friend's place and figure out how to position yourself when you catch up with her."

"Oh, aren't you just the darling? Susan, why haven't I met this charmer before?"

"Because you've been too busy shovelling you know what, the same as the rest of us, while simultaneously trying to hang onto our jobs, and all that other good stuff." She was amused. The dynamics flying around the car had not escaped her.

When they arrived at Jordan's flat, he set up the balcony with wine and appetizers, while Susan took Anne into the bedroom she was occupying and showed her the adjoining bathroom, so she could freshen up.

"My goodness, what a great place this is, Susan. Has Jordan had it long?"

"Yes, he bought it some few years ago now—got in while the timing was right. Real estate prices have steadily risen over the past few years and will only go higher."

Jordan's voice burst through on their conversation.

"Come on, girls, we're wasting wine time here. It's going flat."

"Just give me a few minutes to freshen up." Grabbing her bag, Anne dashed for the bathroom. "Boy he's eager to get the party moving along, isn't he?" she said, glancing over her shoulder at Susan.

"Yep, that's Jordan, always in a rush to get the fun going."

Susan left her in the bathroom and joined Jordan. While they waited for Anne, they sipped their wine, each deep in thought, until Susan broke into the silence.

"So do you like her?"

"I think she's terrific, really terrific."

Susan was dying to know more, but at that moment, Anne came breezing into the room, smelling of something delightfully fragrant.

Susan had placed herself strategically on the short side of the table, leaving space for the other two to sit together facing full onto the water.

The wine and treats went down very well. Standing to refill the glasses, Jordan excused himself and disappeared, his voice then resonating from the kitchen.

"What do you girls fancy? I have pizza and salad, pasta and salad, chicken pie and salad."

Anne winked and grinned at Susan.

"Boy of boy, you certainly like your salad, don't you?"

"Have to keep this fine body of mine in good shape, haven't I?"

"Well, not too much room for improvement, from what I can see." The words were out before Anne really thought about them.

Jordan was now rattling around the kitchen in a state of utter confusion, having met his match.

"I can't believe I said that to him. Don't know what came over me. Sorry, Susan. This outrageous flirting stops now."

"Well, it's true, isn't it?" Susan stretched and yawned. "He's really something, isn't he? Actually a really super person as well. He's quite a catch. Never been able to figure out why he hasn't been snatched up by some scheming woman. Mind you, he doesn't give anybody much of a chance, being the workaholic that he is. I was really surprised at how enthusiastic he was about your visit. And," she added with a smirk, "he's going to take time off over this next week or so. He wants to show you around. We're going to have lots of fun."

They all shared a thoroughly tasty pizza and tucked into the huge bowl of salad a few minutes later, which Jordan had served with a flourish.

"Just to keep in prime physical condition," he'd added, throwing a lascivious wink in Anne's direction, which she refused to acknowledge.

It was only when the coffee arrived that Jordan noticed Anne's eyes were drooping and she could hardly hold her head up.

"Anne, why don't you stay the night here with us? You look beat—definite case of jet lag. You can take the spare bed in Susan's room or have my room, if you prefer. I'll kip down on the sofa."

"No," she cried. "I couldn't possibly put you out after all your efforts to give me a good send-off to my mother."

"I agree with Jordan," Susan said uncompromisingly. "You can take the spare bed in my room, and you should give your mother a call and tell her you'll ring her later tomorrow. Who knows," she said, looking at Jordan, "you may want to linger a few days—just hang out with us and simply have some fun."

Anne focused on Jordan. "Are you sure you're okay with that?"

"I'm more than okay. Gives me a chance to treat you to one of my special breakfasts tomorrow."

"Not more salad, I hope, tasty though it was. I must have gone through a bucket load. And since you've offered, yes, you're quite right, it would make sense for me to stay over. I hadn't realized how my life events have had such an impact on me, and what with the travelling, I'm absolutely done in. Thank you very much for all your kindness, Jordan, it's very much appreciated."

Jordan waved her to silence. "You're more than welcome, and as Susan said, you should consider staying on a while longer, if it suits you."

"Thank you, Jordan, I might just do that."

At that moment, Anne really did look like a Christmas cherub—golden curls, rosy cheeks, and an impish grin. Jordan turned towards the door smiling.

"It's my pleasure, glad to be able to assist. I'll get your bags from the car."

## Chapter 19
## Food for Thought

Jordan sat on the grassy bank sloping down to English Bay. The sun tinged the trees, casting an iridescent glow throughout their boughs as it sank slowly beyond the horizon. It was once again a beautiful sunset. A medley of colour stretched as far as the eye could see, swathing the tips of the offshore mountains in a rosy cloak, bestowing a magical quality upon them. He loved this time of day and had left work early so he could take a couple of hours out before meeting Anne and Susan for dinner downtown.

Anne had decided to stay a few extra days in Vancouver, and it had been great. He had enjoyed her company immensely. A ripple of pleasure coursed through him as he contemplated the upcoming evening—in particular Anne, who had been occupying his thoughts at disturbingly regular intervals. She really did seem perfect in every way, too good to be true. Their connection had been immediate from the first meeting, and even though she'd remained distant after the initial flirtations, he sensed she was warming to him. He was looking forward to spending some time with her and getting to know her better.

Jordan whiled away the next hour or so daydreaming and inhaling the evening's pleasurable activities, periodically focusing on the dogs running with their owners, or simply taking in the view. English Bay was a favourite of people and canines alike, as was the famed Sylvia Hotel located across the street. The hotel offered an old-world charm and a warm welcome to guests and their furry companions alike. Built in 1912, the Sylvia had been preserved and designated a heritage hotel in 1975. Ever enduring, she sat primly amidst the more modern structures bordering the promenade. Adorned in a mélange of colours, a vigorous Virginia creeper covered almost half of her structure—a permanent reminder of bygone opulence.

Jordan was drawn to the careless abandonment of the couples on the hotel's patio as they laughed and shared intimate sentiments. There had been too little time in his busy life for enjoying such intimacies, and as he absorbed the merriment around him, that fact was blatantly obvious. Yes, it had been all business and no play for far too long.

His father had been a major influence on the path Jordan had trodden, taking over his life completely when, at an early age, Jordan had lost his mother. Although not an unkind man, he was rigid in his beliefs and completely inflexible on educational matters. Jordan's father was a managing director of a boat manufacturing company, and as Jordan grew, he found himself being maneuvered by his father into a position within the same company, which did not sit well with him at the time. But while he had no intention of working in an office all his life, Jordan did nurture a love of boats and determined to learn everything he could about the engineering and structuring of seagoing vessels, with a view to working on the water in some capacity or other.

The opportunity presented itself when his father was nominated to attend the main annual boating event in London, where one of the company's boats was to be exhibited as the centrepiece in a major promotional drive. Much to Jordan's joy, his father, thinking it would be a learning experience for his son, requested that he accompany him to the UK.

It was at the exhibition that Jordan had met Luke. They made a point of staying in touch by meeting up at trade fairs and such. As their friendship grew, they formulated a plan to open a cruise business in Canada, the aim being that Luke would take care of the UK operation and Jordan the Canadian.

Initially, there had been major fireworks when Jordan had outlined his plans to his father. As a man who had always trodden the straight and narrow, never taking any chances, it took some time before Jordan's father had warmed to the idea of his son branching out on his own. Finally, on board with the idea and after understanding the full picture and realizing the potential, he had committed a large start-up fund in Jordan's favour. Consequently, Jordan had expended no time on romantic liaisons and personal pleasures over the years, so committed was he to success and determined not to let his father down.

*Well, it's been long enough, and I'm long overdue for a change in routine. I'm sick of being alone. No way am I going to let Anne slip through my hands easily. We'll see where this goes. This is a relationship most definitely worth pursuing, and I'll damn well make the time for it.*

Pausing to glance at his watch, he could see he would be late if he didn't get cracking. It was a hard scene to leave but his spirits were high as he made his way to his car.

\*\*\*\*

"What a truly lovely evening." Anne was positively glowing when they returned to the apartment, riding the roller coaster in her excitement.

"I absolutely can't remember when I've had so much fun, and what great food. The salad was to die for. But," and she smiled at Jordan, "I have to say, guy, definitely not as tasty as yours—not by a long shot."

Jordan was flattered. "Well, I must confess I do tend to live on salad. It's so easy to partner with a piece of salmon or chicken strips or whatever. It makes a quick and very nourishing meal, especially when accompanied by a round of herby garlic bread. I've perfected my salads over the years. I suppose it stems from always being on the run, trying to fit everything in on a tight schedule. Talking of schedule, what time do you want to leave tomorrow morning? I can either drop you off at the ferry or get a taxi for you."

Anne was leaving the next day for Vancouver Island. Her mother, Helen, had decided to go on back to the island, as Anne had extended her stay in Vancouver for a few more days. Apparently, more materials for Helen's house renovation had arrived, and Jim wanted to get on with the work. They were hoping to have it all shipshape before Anne got there. It had worked out well all around. Anne had phoned her mother the day before to tell her she would give her a quick call upon docking on the island.

"I thought I'd get the 1:00 ferry," Anne replied. "I'm flexible, though. Mum's only a stone's throw from the ferry terminal. I've let her know, and I'll give her a buzz when I arrive."

"OK, I can work with that. I have a really early start in the morning, so if you two ladies can get your own breakfast, etcetera, I'll be back later to pick you up. I can take an early lunch, as my afternoon appointment is pretty late in the day, but that's about it. I don't have anything else on that's pressing. Anne, I'll be pleased to drop you off at the ferry."

Susan looked from Anne to Jordan. Her eyebrows were furrowed. Jordan knew her well enough to see that something was troubling her.

"Does that not work for you Susan? Your eyebrows are giving you away again."

Susan smiled amiably. "No, it's just that I'd like to try to meet up with Luke. It's important he stay focused, and he's being so remote at the moment. I know it's because he's assuming the worst. But I still feel I need to keep trying. Anne, how would it be if you and I have a nice breakfast, and then Jordan can pick you up and you two can travel together? I'm sure you guys don't need a chaperone by now. You're both behaving so well."

A slightly abashed Jordan rose to the occasion.

"Alright, it's just us then, Anne. Maybe we could stop for a bite before you board the ferry."

He knew that Anne was always ravenous, with a huge appetite to be appeased constantly. Jordan had put it down to her unbelievably high energy level. Her system required constant fuelling, and yet she remained willowy.

"And as an afterthought," he said, face wreathed in a grin, "perhaps we should pack you a snack for the trip as well. You don't know when you'll get to eat again."

"Oh, stop it, for heaven's sake. Anybody would think I was greedy or something." Anne gave him a playful shove on her way to the bedroom to get organized for the upcoming travel.

****

The following day dawned bright and breezy, just perfect for a ferry trip.

The two women enjoyed an extended chat over tea after breakfast, with promises from Anne that she would be back from the island for a visit and to celebrate Jordan's birthday a few weeks hence. They were still chatting, having reorganized Anne's travel bags by squeezing in her recent purchases, when Jordan, who had left at dawn, appeared. Flushed and raring to get moving, he was obviously still running on the adrenaline rush of previous business.

It was a leisurely drive to the ferry terminal, with much less traffic than Jordan had anticipated. Anne was positively purring.

"Thanks for everything, Jordan. It really has been great meeting you, and thank you for acting as tour guide. I feel completely invigorated now, ready to face anything."

"No. It's me that should be thanking you. I thoroughly enjoyed taking a break here and there. Anne," he said earnestly, "I have a business trip coming up next week on the island and wonder if we could get together, maybe have dinner or something. Does that appeal?"

"Yes, it most definitely does. I'd really look forward to that."

Having left Anne at the ferry gate, Jordan felt his high spirits dim somewhat as he sped back to Vancouver. Business mode soon kicked in, however, as he continued on to his appointment.

\*\*\*\*

Jordan had originally planned for a one-night stay in Victoria but had extended it by a couple of nights, for both business and pleasure reasons. Anne had been delighted to hear that he was staying longer when he had phoned to confirm their timing for dinner, and they arranged to meet up in the harbour area on the evening of his arrival. Anne arrived early. Jordan spotted her sitting a few yards away on a bench and hurried towards her. No dinner reservations had been made; they simply mingled with the crowd and enjoyed exploring in and around the harbour for a couple of hours.

"How do you feel about that place over there for dinner?" Anne asked, suddenly feeling a few hunger pangs. Nudging him in the direction of the restaurant, she pointed to an ancient-looking pub across the street. Jordan took her arm as they strolled across the road. After they paused outside to view the extremely enticing menu, he opened the door for her and ushered her in. Both were met by a cheery older woman in an apron who showed them to a secluded corner table. The ambience was quietly intimate, with dark wooden furnishings and soft upholstery. Extending a warm welcome and sensing their need for privacy, the proprietor wasted no time with small talk. Smiling down on them, she lit the candle on the table, dropped off the wine list and menu and made a smart exit.

They were already firmly entrenched in conversation when she returned shortly after with a pitcher of water. Flashing another smile, she hastened away to the kitchen, clutching their orders. They dove back into enthusiastic discussion.

"So did you think any more about coming back to Vancouver for a while? You can't miss my birthday bash now, can you?" Jordan was smiling.

"No, I can't miss that. Susan reminded me about it. I thought I'd come back in a couple of weeks. I've met Mum's man friend, Jim, and must say I like what I've seen so far. He's very handy as well and gathered all the materials together for the renovations to the lounge and sunroom. They seem to be having great fun and appear to be perfect for each other. Still, although it may all seem rosy on the surface, who really knows how it will pan out?"

"Spoken like a true cynic," said Jordan. "Oh, ye of little faith."

"Sorry, I suppose I am a little cynical. Anyway, although quite a bit of the work was done before I got there, I am going to help Mum redecorate the lounge and sunroom. She's very excited about it, as it hasn't been done in a while. It's a super space for socializing, with plenty of room for quite a gathering if they feel sociable. She'll really make use of it once it's finished. She has a whole new lease on life. Also, can you believe it—she actually didn't lean on me at all about the mess I've been making of my life. I was really surprised."

"First of all, you have to stop blaming yourself for what has happened in your life. It happens all the time to more people than you probably realize. You meet the wrong partner, someone with a different agenda, and it's curtains on the relationship. It almost happened to me several times and would have if I hadn't been too busy with my job. In your case, though, situations are compounded by you getting a new boss who couldn't wait to get you out of the company—bingo, two bad arrangements. So, moving forward—about the arrangements at my place."

"Boy oh boy, and you say I'm a cynic."

But Jordan was not going to be side-stepped. "Naturally, you can stay at my place if you don't mind sharing with Susan. Of course, there are other options," he winked cheekily. "It's a big apartment, as you know."

"Well, darling, hate to burst your bubble, and much as I love you, I'll bunk in with Susan. It's just great that you don't mind us both being there, even if it is a very expansive apartment. What's the square footage anyway?"

"Oh, I can't really remember. I believe about 1,300 square feet. Premium space for Vancouver, but I bought just at the right time. Seriously, though, I really don't mind you staying there. I'm hardly in the apartment anyway during the day, and it'll be good to meet up with you guys in the evenings."

Once plans had been mapped out for Anne's return to Vancouver, Jordan filled her in on his business activities and hopes for the future of the company.

"So I'm crossing my fingers that you'll seriously consider extending your visit to Canada. When you come back to Vancouver, I'll give you a run-through of our business there. Wish I had more time on this trip to show you the new cruiser Luke and I were considering, and the area we had in mind to expand our little office here on the island. The plans have all been put on hold and are still up in the air a bit, with all the flack flying around. Damn Luke, he's really socked it to us on this one."

Jordan's face clouded momentarily obviously revisiting events, as Anne forged on hastily, not wishing to lose the mood.

"We have time for decisions, Jordan and we have more good stuff on the horizon, don't we? After all, your birthday bash is imminent. Oh, I've just remembered—I don't know how you feel about a dinner at my mum's tomorrow night, now that you've extended your stay by a couple of days? It's just a thought; although I have to admit," Anne grinned a trifle sheepishly, "I may have mentioned that I might be bringing you."

"Hmm, dinner, eh? You may have mentioned I was invited to dinner?" Jordan was teasing unmercifully.

"Alright, alright, yes, I did mention it, and Mum said she would love it if you could come. I'm sorry, Jordan, I should have asked you first."

"No problem, I was just pulling your leg." Jordan laughed. "And thanks very much for the invite. I'd love to come. I'll make sure I'm sporting my best bib and tucker."

"Phew, well that's a relief. You really will like both my mum and Jim. The two together are really inspiring and as I said, so much fun. He's been taking her everywhere in that camper van of his. What with that and the renovations they've both been up to, there's never a dull moment, and they're never short of something to talk about."

As an afterthought, she added, "Maybe you and I could have breakfast or meet for lunch and do some sight-seeing before visiting them in the evening? It's just a suggestion."

\*\*\*\*

The next few weeks were overwhelmingly busy for Jordan. His trip to the island had been very successful, and after speaking with Luke, he had taken the opportunity to secure a few weeks' grace on the purchase of the cruiser they had both been considering for some time. They had hopes that the deal would be revisited if the investigation concluded favourably. At least a firm consensus had been arrived at as to which cruiser would best suit their needs. Now, they just had to wait and see which way they were heading with Luke's situation.

Eventually, the eagerly awaited day arrived. Jordan came home and opened his apartment door to be besieged with birthday wishes as Susan and Anne chorused 'Happy Birthday'. Slightly out of tune, but it was nevertheless heart-warming after a hard day at work.

"We're really looking forward to dinner, and we have a few surprises here when we get back. And no peeking in the fridge," Anne added with a wide grin.

"Oh Anne, you really are incorrigible. Just can't keep a secret, can you?"

"Ok girls, no fighting. I'm off to the shower or we'll be late for our reservation." He looked from one to the other. "You did make a reservation, didn't you? Where are we going, by the way?"

"Of course we made a reservation," said Susan with exaggerated derision as both watched Jordan retreating to the bathroom. "We're not telling you where we're going. It's a surprise, and the really great thing is that Luke will be joining us at the restaurant. He's warming a little and prepared to socialize. He would have seen you anyway because it's your birthday, but I'm thrilled that he's prepared to join us all. I didn't have to push him either. He really wanted to come."

Jordan paused before closing the bathroom door. "I'm really glad to hear that. It'll give him a chance to think about something else for a while." *Let's just hope he'll behave himself and not fly off the handle or lose it for any reason,* he thought privately as he readied himself for the evening's frivolities.

\*\*\*\*

The birthday bash was the first of many happy get-togethers. Jordan was frantically organizing and reorganizing his schedule so that he would not miss out on seeing Anne. He was determined not to lose any opportunity. He knew it was important. He had not felt this way about a woman before.

The police investigation was still ongoing, and the diversions provided by day trips and evenings out were not only very enjoyable but also necessary to keep everybody from going crazy.

One evening when Anne was in the bathroom, Jordan took the opportunity to ask Susan how it was going with Luke.

"Well, as you know, our first meeting left a lot to be desired. I managed to get him to meet me again a few days after your birthday and once again tried to discuss options, should we get clear of this predicament. I would like to make a completely fresh start with him and with you here in Vancouver. I've given it a lot of thought. I love it here, and it would be the best solution. Luke won't get into this type of discussion at the moment, so time will tell.

"I really do feel by working together, we'd succeed, if we get the chance. I could even be helpful in some way in the business as well. I did take the opportunity to do some business administration courses while I was with Tommy. He looked after me so well, I didn't have to go back to waitressing. I felt I should better myself—one never knows what life is going to serve up, and I wanted to be qualified in something I could take up, should the need or occasion arise. I'm just putting it out there for possible consideration later on. I do realize, though, that everything is up in the air.

"One thing's for sure: Luke still feels the same way about me. I just hope we can finally be together. By the way, not to pry, but you and Anne seem to be quite an item. How's that going? She's even talking about moving here permanently."

"We've had some great times together, and you're absolutely right. We've both developed quite strong feelings for each other. It's funny you should mention the business because I asked Anne if she would consider taking over the office as manager, if she decides to stay in Canada. As you know, she's worked in office management for years and is more than qualified to take charge when I'm away—be the anchor, so to speak. Mike wants to work himself in more and get away from some of the paperwork, which would be a positive, and I'm pleased to say it looks as if Anne is giving my proposition serious thought. There's nothing for her to go back to in the UK now. Her mother is here, and since we've been hanging out together, the relationship has gone to the next level—serious enough to think about our future plans. I know it hasn't been long since we met, but we've definitely clicked. I've never felt this way before, and by some miracle, she feels the same way. I hate to think of her not being here." Jordan paused for a moment.

"Of course, everything hinges on what happens to our friend Luke. I've had discussions with him about the business, and he's indicated that if he's convicted, he'd like me to take everything over. Maybe wind up the UK company. We've had innumerable conference calls to London. Doug's doing a great job holding everything together and virtually running our London branch. He's hanging tight to see what happens. He also has roots here and is very amenable to the possibility of immigrating to Canada. He's keen to remain a part of things. He's been with us now for quite a while, certainly from the time the business really started to take off. I met Doug personally on several occasions. He's a nice guy. We could work well together.

"So whatever the legal outcome, we have a game plan worked out, with or without Luke. Just hope it's with him, of course. The name of the game would be consolidation of funds, with a subsequent expansion. It's great to hear that you've taken some office courses as well, because if we end up expanding our operations, there'll be unlimited opportunities. Definitely something we should keep in mind."

"Wow! You've certainly been busy. Looks like you have it all under control, whichever way things go. Mind you, Jordan, I've always had faith that you could hold things together."

"We just got lucky tying in with Doug, and then there's Mike here in Vancouver. I consider myself very fortunate that he's working with me. He has loads of experience in the business and was always ambitious and willing to learn when we worked together at the boat manufacturing operation—always talked about moving on and doing something for himself. Let's hope all our big plans fall into place and we can really take care of Doug and Mike. And," he added with some trepidation, "let's hope Luke is part of those plans."

# Chapter 20
# Held in Custody

One miserable, rain-soaked day, the body had been spotted by a crew on a small fishing boat. It was floating in the water a short way off shore. Shortly after the authorities had arrived, a large crowd began gathering, and as usual in such cases, the police were forced to remove the more aggressive of the individuals, who were gawking with all-consuming morbid curiosity.

On the day following the event, Luke had popped out for a coffee and a bite to eat. He grabbed a newspaper from the kiosk outside the café and unfolded it while waiting for his order. There was no missing the write-up—the press were having a field day with it. He suspected it would only be a matter of time before he was hauled back in again for more questions.

The waiter bustled back with his order and refilled Luke's coffee cup. The food stuck like cement in his chest, but he knew better than to start messing about with his diet. He had a very high metabolism, and it would not bode well for him if he missed meals. A throwback to his youth when there was no regular food on the table.

Later that night, as Luke sat miserably at home, he was startled by the phone ringing. It was Jordan.

"How're you doing, buddy? I'm sure you've seen the headlines, so I won't belabour the point. Rest assured, Sean's up on this. Listen, Luke, I can meet you later this evening if you want to catch a quick bite; might do you some good to have a change of venue."

"That would be terrific. I need to give myself a bit of a shake. Thanks again, Jordan. You're the best."

Luke was gratified to think that Jordan, who had been pushed to the limit, was still putting himself out to relieve the situation. A night out would be the best thing, as the situation was taking its toll on both of them. He also wanted to have a quick run-through on their business options, looking at the best and worst scenarios again. Jordan was his best friend, and he wanted to make things right for him.

****

The days passed, and nerves became more frayed as the expectation of a bad outcome became stronger. Luke began collecting a few more items for his emergency holdall. Pausing to sit on the bed, he felt disorientated—unsure of what he should take with him should he be summoned again by the police. Even though Sean had given him a variety of possible scenarios, he was still in the dark as to whether he could be detained overnight or longer, if he was called.

The day was another one reminiscent of the British climate, with the morning grey and overcast. Luke's worst fears had come to fruition. They were banging on the door, making their presence felt. Upon opening it, he was confronted by two police officers, who introduced themselves and produced their identification. After he showed them in, a brief series of questions ensued. As Luke had anticipated, they asked him to accompany them for further investigative enquiries.

The sun hid behind an ominous cloud barrier, once in a while peeking through just to tease the senses. But it was a watery, poor excuse for a sun that extended no warmth, and the atmosphere was exacerbated by the heavy dampness in the air. Luke shivered, the weather matching his mood as he prepared himself mentally for another rehashing of questions and answers back and forth.

Following approval to make a phone call, he dialled Sean's number. "Hi, Sean. Well, they've just come for me and I'm organizing myself to go with them. Don't know if they'll detain me overnight or not. I'll leave my overnight bag here by the bedroom door, and perhaps Jordan could pick it up later if I'm going to need it."

"Don't worry, buddy. I'm on my way. Don't let them start without me. I'll give Jordan a quick call and alert him."

"Thanks very much for everything, Sean. Even though I can be a bit of a so-and-so here and there, I really do appreciate what you're doing."

****

Jordan was in his office when he received Sean's call advising the police had taken Luke into custody. He was shocked, even though he had been expecting it.

Sean was in full business mode. "They've obviously seen the coroner's report—looks like the ball's rolling. I'm on my way down there, just leaving, in fact. Any chance of you grabbing Luke's hold-all? He asked me if it could be brought in to him. Apparently, it's just behind his bedroom door. Let's hope he won't be detained and need it."

"No problem. I'll come anyway and be outside. I'm on my way."

The two men met up briefly half an hour later, and Jordan handed over the bag.

"Any point in my coming with you? Might be able to help in some way," he said.

"No. I don't think they'd let you in at this moment. But don't worry, you carry on back home, and I'll give you a buzz when I get out of there."

****

"No. Call me at my office, I still have stuff to clear off my desk." Jordan was feeling the pressure and wanted to make sure no work was outstanding.

Luke was taken into the interrogation room. It was cold and sterile, and so were the investigators. Just when he was getting to screaming point, Sean arrived with gusto.

The atmosphere grew even colder after that, and if the direction of their questions was anything to go by, they were obviously treating it as a possible murder, with him as the prime suspect. They persistently came back to the bruises found on the neck and body of the woman. He was chilled through to the bone. Things didn't seem to be going well—definitely looking as if they considered he could quite conceivably be guilty of murdering the woman—it could go either way.

It was an exhaustive exchange, with Sean fronting the deluge of questions. Finally, the officers were finished with them. Luke was to be held in custody pending further investigation.

Exiting the room, the detectives closed the door behind them, allowing Luke and Sean a few minutes of privacy. Once they were alone, Sean went to work immediately, talking quickly to keep Luke focused.

"I know they were rough on you, but keep your cool. They always do that. It's just scare tactics to see if they can get more out of you. Just hang on and don't lose your temper at any of these sessions. Let me do the talking."

"Ok, ok. I know where you're coming from. I'll cooperate fully. Don't have much option, do I?"

*They've really got me hung, drawn, and quartered,* was all Luke could think as Sean's voice washed over him in waves, the lawyer pacing back and forth as he gave his client an in-depth briefing.

"It looks as if formal charges could be laid. I believe they think they have a case. They're putting a lot of emphasis on the bruising on the body and will obviously be talking to Crown Counsel. If it comes to that, it will be up to the prosecution to decide whether charges should be pressed. All we can do is wait. I'll update Jordan when I get back to the office, and I'll definitely be in tomorrow to see you."

The two men entered the room again, and Luke barely had time to remind Sean about his hold-all.

"I'll pop down for it and be right back. It's in my car. I had Jordan meet me just before I picked you up, just in case you were detained. Jordan wanted to wait and possibly come in to see you, but I told him to carry on." Sean turned and addressed the men. "Ok, if I pop down for it? I'll be right back."

"Ok," one of them acknowledged, "I'll meet you by the stairs. I'll get it to him."

Luke was then escorted back to the holding area, the heavy-set officer giving him a nudge when he slowed up. *Just to feed his ego,* Luke supposed. *Funny how the short bloke always has a chip on his shoulder,* he mused as they reached his cell. *Always trying to prove themselves.* Another slight pressure was applied to his arm, and he was led into the small enclosure.

The door clanged shut, and he'd never felt so alone in his entire life.

Throwing himself onto the narrow bunk in one corner of the cell, he realized instantly that his haste was ill conceived, as the bunk was brutally, bone-shatteringly hard. *Must have a board for a mattress,* he thought as he tried to reposition himself. *No question of getting any decent sleep on that.* Surprisingly, he did manage to nap for a few hours.

Jolted back to his senses by the sound of the gate clanging, he saw they were bringing in a tray of something unrecognizable as food. He was about to tell them what to do with it but thought better of that. *Better not rub salt in the wound.* He forced it down. Once he got past the first swallow, he felt more enthusiastic about it. *Not that bad*, he surmised when he'd cleared the plate. *I've eaten worse. Now's not the time to get finicky.*

He put the empty plate on the small table by the gate and went over to the sink. After rinsing his mouth and hands, he lay back down on the bunk, carefully this time, and closed his eyes.

If only he hadn't suggested that wretched, ill-fated trip. He had thought that getting cozy with the Buchanan family would open a few more doors for him and be good for the company. And, in theory, it would have been, but recent events would have the exact opposite effect on his business, if and when he was able to resume it again.

*Yep,* he thought bitterly, *this has really torn it. I may never get out of jail, let alone get back home. That damn woman, she asked for it and she got it, but it looks like she's finished me in the process.*

Their heated argument on the boat had evolved into a physical battle and was still vivid in his mind. He shuddered, recalling the feel of his hands on her. How could he have let his evil unbridled temper get the better of him?

\*\*\*\*

Jordan sat by his office phone, waiting for what seemed hours. Finally, it rang. It was Sean, and he sounded very frustrated.

"We'll just have to wait it out to hear whether they're pressing charges or not. But all indications are that they'll be talking with Crown Counsel, and it will be up to the prosecutor as to whether formal charges are laid. Let's hope we're not dealing with the latter, otherwise we'll be looking at a bail hearing. I don't want him languishing in there indefinitely. No good saying 'don't worry'—we could have a bumpy road ahead. But let's be optimistic, and I'll be in touch as soon as I have the picture. I'll be in there again tomorrow. Now, you get some rest, buddy. Nothing more we can do at the moment. Just let it ride. It's another day tomorrow."

Jordan felt a little more positive knowing that Sean was on the case. He was reportedly a very good lawyer, boosting Jordan's confidence. He liked Sean—he felt right for the case.

*No point in putting this off. I'd better give Susan a buzz and bring her up to date. When Sean says it's ok to visit, we'll have to get down there and provide some moral support to Luke. Damn his hide for bringing this on all of us.*

Later on, when he'd collected his thoughts and consumed a strong black coffee, he phoned Susan.

****

Luke had been detained overnight since being apprehended. They advised him to call his lawyer for another little get-together. As always, Sean picked up the phone almost immediately. *Hmm, he must have that thing permanently stuck to his ear.* Nevertheless, Luke was glad that Sean had always been able to make himself available. *I can thank my lucky stars that he's on an official break and able to fit me in; would have really been in the dirt without him.*

"I'll give Jordan a buzz," said Sean. "He may want to meet us there."

When Sean was ready, he put in a call to Jordan on his way down to the car park. "Brace yourself, friend. It looks like this could be it. They've got all they need by now. The good news is we can all stop dancing around each other now and get this show on the road one way or the other. Either charges will be pressed, or he'll be released. Let's hope it's the latter."

Jordan sat down, dazed. *Finally, the waiting is over.*

"Thanks, Sean. I'll get Susan, and we'll see you there."

****

Sean was giving Luke a quick briefing before going into the adjoining room when Jordan and Susan arrived. They sat together, watching through the glass while Susan's fingers bit into Jordan's arm.

Luke's eyes were sunken, his face drawn. He'd obviously used up his reserves. Jordan whispered in Susan's ear, "Hope he's going to be able to stand up to this. It's only just begun, and look at the state of him. He could have a long way to go, and he looks as if he's beaten already."

They sat forward in their seats, straining to catch what was being said, but of course they were out of luck. Susan whispered back to

Jordan. "Thank God he's got Sean backing him. Sean's really in his element, isn't he? He's obviously not taking any guff from Luke either."

Jordan shushed her to silence as the adjoining door opened and Sean and Luke were ushered into the interview room.

It was time for Sean to show his skills.

"If you fancy a cup of coffee, I'll go and get us some." Jordan gently freed his arm. "If I don't get some fresh air, I think I'll pass out."

"Thanks, Jordan. That would be great."

He appeared shortly thereafter, handed Susan her coffee, and settled himself down. By the time the inner door was finally flung open, the pair were practically numb with tension, in spite of a double dose of caffeine.

Sean appeared and made his way towards the distraught pair. His face was grimly set.

Their spirits fragmented, falling to earth like crystals after an ice storm.

# Part 3

# Chapter 21
## Germany and Thoughts of Home

Jonathan was forced back to England from time to time to meet with Mark or attend estate sales and such. It was always with a great deal of anxiety that he alighted from the plane in London, as the unwieldy deluge of memories inevitably besieged his brain. Try as he might, there was no way he could rid himself of them. Trips were therefore limited to short stays, because the longer he was in England, the more troubled he became—plagued with past associations, which even the passing of time could not dissipate. He was better off out of it.

Every time Jonathan returned to Germany after one of his trips, he was unsettled. Helmut found it upsetting to see his friend disappearing into his own world—a world inaccessible to anyone else. It was always the same, even though his mood usually lifted after a few days. Still, Helmut couldn't bear to see him so down and strived to keep him constantly on the run in between business matters, by organizing numerous events in an attempt to break Jonathan's melancholy. And he did; they always had fun—no doubt about that. It was good for Helmut as well because it gave him a break from the long hours he was giving over to the final studies for his degree, some respite from the worry of his job insecurity.

Finally, that special night arrived. Helmut had received his degree earlier that day, and the three friends got together in the evening to celebrate. They crowned Helmut king, and what a proud king he was. At last, after all the years of struggle, his dreams were really coming to fruition.

The friends had gathered in their favourite place in the Alte Markt in Mönchengladbach laughing and jostling with each other they rehashed the day's events. Jonathan, who now had all of his business ducks in a row, smiled from one to the other, his gaze settling on Helmut. His friend knew immediately that Jonathan had been up to something and was bursting with impatience to find out what it was. He could hardly contain himself.

"This looks about to be significant, my friend, so spit it out. I've known you long enough to read you like a book. What are you holding back?"

"You'll both be glad to know that I've found the perfect spot for the gallery in Bonn. It's absolutely great—the most perfect property. And here's the best: there is a marvellous apartment upstairs, which goes with the business…" He paused briefly, savouring the moment.

"Now before either of you utter a word, I want to run through some options/possibilities with you. I've had long sessions with Mark about this, and I think it's manna from heaven for all of us. You could both live in the apartment and manage the gallery while I'm off doing my thing at the auctions. As you know, I like to be on the move and love the thrill of the bid. It would appear to be a win-win situation for all of us. You always wanted to run a gallery, and here's your chance. The timing couldn't be better for all of us.

"So, what do you say? I know I'm springing this on you, but at least give me an idea of whether you'd be interested. If you are, we could all go and have a look at the premises. Don't think this great space will be on the market for long, although I must confess, I have fixed it so that I get first crack at it. It's right on the river, a gorgeous location.

"Now that Helmut has his degree, you're both more than qualified to manage the gallery and take care of things whilst I'm out of town. You wouldn't be short of work, that's for sure, once we got established, with the added bonus that you'd love it. If everything works well, we can even look at a shareholding arrangement in the business for you both. That would be a little down the road, of course. We'd have to see how business develops."

Jonathan kept rattling on with his sales pitch, although it wasn't really necessary for him to work so hard at it. The pair were completely blindsided, but it was entirely obvious that they were indeed very interested. Gertrude started to cry, and Helmut looked as if he were about to follow suit.

"My God, Jonathan, I don't know what to say, old friend. We'd love to look at the premises with you. We both love Bonn. As a matter of fact, we were planning on staying there for our honeymoon."

"Well, all being well, that should be quite soon."

Jonathan was grinning at them so much, his face ached. He rushed onward. "Anyway, one step at a time. Could you be available the day after tomorrow then, to look at the space with me and see what you both think of it? We could travel down there together, if that would suit you."

"I can go tomorrow, if that's not too early for you, Jon." Helmut was staring hard at Gertrude, soliciting support. "Want to get on this as soon as we can. Isn't that right, Gertrude?"

"In my mind, I'm already packed, Liebling."

Jonathan leapt to his feet and grasped his friends' hands.

"Great, it looks like it's in the bag then, doesn't it? I'll just shuffle some stuff around and tomorrow it is. Whose car shall we go in?"

"I'll be only too happy to drive. Just let me know the timing. And thank you, friend." Helmut's eyes were moist as he grabbed Jonathan's hand.

A huge sense of relief settled on Jonathan and a load shifted off his shoulders—a load that had been bearing down on him. It was great that everything seemed to be falling into place after all the planning. He was helping his dear friends and they were helping him. How much, they would never know.

\*\*\*\*

Helmut parked the car in one of the two parking slots assigned exclusively to the property. He grabbed Gertrude, and they clambered up the pavement, almost falling over each other in their eagerness to see everything. At the first sight of the flat, Gertrude shrieked with sheer joy. They could hear her 'oohing' and 'aahing' as she stood on the massive balcony, which ran the length of the building.

"Liebchen, just come and look at this deck. It's perfect for you to grow your herbs and whatnot, and there's room for us both to enjoy a glass of wine in the evening." Gertrude was alive with excitement.

Helmut, in his usual way, swept her off her feet and danced her all around the lounge, just as he had when they were children, never having lost their childish ways or their magic. Their spontaneous joy was infectious. They were enthralled, completed besotted with the place, as indeed they were with each other. Their worries of the previous few months had not tarnished their devotion to each other in any way.

Jonathan stood back and grinned, feeling as if he'd just won the jackpot. It was perfect for the happy couple. He left them for a few minutes to bathe in the moment and went to the main floor to draw up some draft plans.

"Hello there, friend." It was Helmut. He'd come to find his buddy.

Jonathan took his arm and led him down to the would-be gallery section. "What do you think of this area? Isn't it a perfect space for displays?"

The two men spent a few minutes planning the layout, and Jonathan made copious notes in readiness for inclusion in a master plan, which he'd already started preparing.

"Here, come with me," he said. "I want to show you something more, just to boggle your mind."

Jonathan led the way downstairs to a fabulous storage area. It was warm, clean, and dry, everything they needed for their venture and completely vermin-proof, as the building had been a fabric establishment previously. The risk of rodents moving in with their destructive habits was always high in areas near the river, but this room had been completely sealed, and the windows were top of the line, fully double-glazed, allowing no access.

"You can see how warm and dry this lower level is, can't you? And there are also ample exits out of the building, in case of fire."

"Wow, with all these features, we should get a good break on the insurance," said Helmut. "I know an excellent security company who could really fix us up at a reasonable price."

"Great, make a note of that, and I'll leave it to you to get in touch with them and put forward a proposal for us to go over—might be a good idea to get a couple of quotes, while you're at it."

Following business, Jonathan locked up, and the friends took a walk along the river. The entire area was a long strip of funky night clubs with mini dance floors, disco lighting, and space for small musical groups. The business strip also included an abundance of cafés, antique businesses, and collectibles of all shapes and types—a perfect location for a gallery.

Helmut was animated. "What about us annexing a small section of the property for local artists to display their work? What a draw that would be, as it is such an eclectic mix of businesses, residents and visitors here—something to tempt any and every taste. What do you think, Jon?"

"That's a great idea. The ball is in your court, Helmut. You have a clean slate to work with. If you and Gertrude see ways to improve and expand as we go along, let's hash it out and share ideas as we all move forward with this."

Helmut and Gertrude were ecstatic. They simply couldn't wait to get at it.

There followed a night of all nights none of them would ever forget, no doubt about that. The wine flowed. The vitality of their never-ending talk, youth, enthusiasm, in fact the whole kit and caboodle ensured it was a memorable occasion, concluding with the hugging and type of love only true friends know. They stayed in Bonn that night, all being more than a little inebriated. The next morning saw them piling enthusiastically into Helmut's Volkswagen. Despite the fact they were all nursing outsize hangovers, their exuberance was not to be thwarted.

****

Jonathan was tired, more tired than he could ever remember. He needed to rest, he knew that. It had been a hectic schedule. *One last heave,* he was thinking as he poured himself a strong German coffee and sat down to phone Mark. *He's going to be over the moon when I tell him the good news,* he thought, sipping his coffee appreciatively.

As Jonathan had anticipated, Mark was tickled to death that everything had gone so well and that Helmut and Gertrude had dropped into their laps as new managers.

"Honestly, Mark, you should have seen their faces when they saw the premises. They couldn't believe their eyes and can't wait to start getting everything up and running. They're really excited about the flat as well." Jonathan knew Mark would be out on the first plane he was able to book.

"I'll fly out the day after tomorrow, if that works for you?" he questioned, confirming Jonathan's suspicions.

Jonathan took a quick glance at his calendar. "Yes, that would work fine."

"Perhaps you and I can meet up in Bonn when I arrive, so that I can take a look at the place. We can grab a bite to eat on the way back to Mönchengladbach afterwards."

"Yes, that would work, and later at dinner, we could put our heads together—toss some ideas about and draw up an agreement for Helmut and Gertrude to review."

"Absolutely," Mark enthused. "After they've taken a look at it, you and I can fine tune it, if necessary, prior to us meeting up together. It would seem that we've landed on our feet on this one. I've heard so much from you about your two friends that I know I'm going to like them. In fact, I like them already. Do you mind booking me into the nearest hotel to you?"

"No need for that—you can stay with me if you wish. Of course, as an after-thought, if you'd rather have a bit of space, there's an excellent hotel just steps from here."

"The hotel would be fine, Jon. You'll need a bit of a break after we've locked up the deal, and besides, I'm going to be on the phone most of the time, getting some issues cleared up before our next board meeting."

"Yes, you're right of course, and I only have the one desk. This is only a small flat, but I find it very convenient just for myself."

Jonathan couldn't help feeling a little selfish but still he nurtured feelings of intense relief. The little flat he had taken on a long-term lease was his sanctuary. He valued his time alone, and it was a perfect retreat to escape from a killer business schedule.

Once they had settled the arrangements and finished discussing the agenda for their upcoming meeting, they signed off.

\*\*\*\*

Jonathan sat back, contemplating life in general. Yes, it had been exhausting over the past weeks, but very rewarding. It was great that everything was coming together. He phoned Helmut and told him the good news.

"Mark is really happy with the way things are turning out. I'm drafting up an agreement based on what you and I have talked about. I'll run it by Mark at dinner when he gets in. He's completely in accord with everything and looking forward to meeting with you both. We'll take a quick boo at the agreement before the meeting, so that you can both review it and be clear on everything prior to us all getting together the day after tomorrow. Does that work for you? Mark is all set to travel and will be arriving on Tuesday. I'm meeting him at the premises so that he can see the place. We thought we'd schedule a dinner meeting with you both, perhaps the following Wednesday, or if not, Thursday, if you're ok with that?"

"As Gertrude said before, friend, our bags are packed and ready to go. We'll be at the meeting whenever you decide. Give me a minute while I get a pen to put the details in the calendar."

****

Mark arrived in Bonn with gusto and, like the rest of the group, loved what he saw in the premises. The two men drafted the agreement over dinner, and Jonathan put in a call to Helmut to arrange a briefing for the following day with the young couple before they all got together formally.

The night of the gathering finally arrived. Everybody was, by then, on tenterhooks and anxious to get business finalized.

Mark's hotel had been very accommodating, with a small conference room and catering for the meeting. After all the introductions were made, the waiter bustled in and took their orders for drinks, while they studied the menu.

Mark scrutinized the young couple closely, really taking their measure. They were both feeling mildly uncomfortable, and even more so when he got to quizzing them.

"So, Jon was telling me that you two have plans to get married as soon as this is underway."

Helmut was determined not to be too intimidated by Mark and met his scrutiny head-on and with confidence. "Yes, we do have plans and you've made a wealth of difference to our lives. We can actually make firm arrangements now for the future, thanks to you both. I've waited for a crack at a business such as this all my working life. This opportunity is exactly what I have worked towards all these years. I am sure Jon would have told you about that. We are eternally grateful to both of you, and I can assure you, Gertrude and I will not let you down."

Mark beamed around the table at everybody. "I feel completely confident that you'll be a perfect fit for our business expansion. We consider ourselves very fortunate that you are both joining us. We'll all make a great team. Isn't that right, Jon?"

Jonathan nodded enthusiastically, and once the agreement was approved by all, duly signed, and witnessed, Mark left his seat abruptly and went over to shake hands vigorously. The ice was broken, and everybody began to relax.

"Well, now that's out of the way, let's get the table cleared off, order more drinks to celebrate, sit back, enjoy the evening, and cement our plans."

"Boy, he's really enjoying himself," Jonathan said, nudging his friend. Of course, by that time Helmut's face had glazed over with all the tension that had built up within him, not to mention the anticipation of the bruises on his ankle after Gertrude's constant kicking under the table.

Mark flagged down the waiter while smiling expansively at everybody. He just loved it when things came together, and was totally oblivious to the nervous energy Helmut and Gertrude had been exhibiting all evening.

It was agreed that Helmut would run the gallery, assisted by Gertrude, and they would be regular employees until such time as the project was underway. All being good, a little shop would be added to the business for the sale of surplus items and such from the gallery, things that would not be shipped back for inclusion in the showrooms in England.

It was further agreed that Mark would come out for a meeting again in the near future. The couple's status within the company would be revisited, with the possibility of the offer of shares in the business and maybe a partnership down the road.

Dinner was served with a flourish, accompanied by murmurs of satisfaction from all. The timing of the meal was fortuitous, as Helmut was becoming overwhelmed again by their good fortune. Food was a welcome distraction.

****

Some weeks hence, Gertrude and Helmut tied the knot. It was a simple ceremony with just a few special friends. Gertrude's parents travelled in from Cologne and were particularly welcome, as Helmut had no family, even though her mother howled her way through the entire ceremony.

It was held at a little historic church in Bonn. A reception followed in a neighbouring hall. An outstanding buffet to suit every taste had been set up and ran practically the width of the room. Helmut, of course, did it justice by sampling just about every dish on the tables, critiquing them as he munched his way around the displays.

The day was further enhanced by Mark attending and acting as master of ceremonies. His droll sense of humour and eloquence as a speaker soon had everybody in the room laughing and clapping. It was a flattering and gratifying experience for him. He was moved and completely bowled over with all the attention.

****

Over the following months, the branch really started to take shape and pay its way.

A separate space was sectioned off adjacent to the gallery for the local artists to hold small events exhibiting their work and offering some pieces for sale. There was also plenty of wall space with good lighting for hanging exhibits, and a display of surplus gallery items for sale.

The gallery was taking shape, soliciting much public interest and gaining momentum—a job well done. The newlyweds had worked relentlessly to make a success of the new venture, and it was paying off.

Following the first year of a consistently successful business, Mark returned to Bonn. Jonathan had set up the new Terms of Employment Agreement, and it was put in place. Helmut and Gertrude had reviewed their finances in the interim, the bank approving a sum to be loaned in conjunction with their savings. They were able to come up with sufficient funds to allow them a thirty percent share in the Bonn business, leaving Jonathan and Mark as majority holders. The option for full partnership for both Helmet and Gertrude was still open for future discussion.

Two years later, the Bonn gallery had begun to yield consistently impressive profits and was becoming very well known, particularly in the local community. It was a regular stopping off point for many repeat customers. While Helmut and Gertrude continued to work tirelessly, Jonathan was fully occupied attending auctions across the continent. Totally committed to keeping the UK business stocked, while sourcing suitable pieces for the Bonn store, he ensured a steady flow of business, and sales were increasing. Once in a while, Helmut attended auctions with Jonathan and had proved himself to be a very accomplished bidder and dealer.

Marketing played a huge part in getting the establishment up and running, and while Helmut was at the fore, Gertrude's earlier marketing studies for small companies were beginning to make an impression. She was constantly upgrading her knowledge and shining in that area, with a growing aptitude and a real liking for that part of the business. She was also totally committed to establishing good, solid contacts. The couple were putting every ounce of their energy into making a go of it, proving exceptionally successful. They loved every aspect of the running of the gallery and were in the process of setting up the little shop. Their lives were bright, and business looked very promising for the future.

Jonathan was filled with nostalgia, thinking of what his life would have been had he not lost Sarah. His loneliness was exacerbated by the happiness on his friends' faces. His thoughts turned yet again to returning home. The urge was strong to finish the work he had begun on his house, work that had been left in limbo all those years ago.

*Yes, it's definitely time to think about going home and getting back to those major renovations. They're long overdue. I need to finish what I've started,* he thought for the umpteenth time.

Maybe it would also be a fitting time to investigate the running of a little antique business in the annex of the property. Perhaps grow another arm of the company, which had already flourished beyond any of the partners' expectations with all of their various holdings. But not in the foreseeable future. He needed to get his personal life in tow. Still, definitely something to think about and keep on the back boiler.

What he really needed at this time was to get back to his base and his roots. Maybe get that dog who had been waiting for him out there somewhere so patiently all these years.

## Chapter 22
## Forgiveness

Gina was relaxing in her London flat in Henley-on-Thames. The lounge was large, with a window that covered an entire wall. But the breathtaking view of the Thames more than compensated for the lack of wall space. Thankfully, there was one wall of shelving, which housed the couple's books above a built-in library desk. Patio doors on the opposite wall led out onto a wrap-around deck that could accommodate gatherings of up to six and was in constant use when Gina and Ronald were in London.

Hanging baskets adorned the entire length of the overhang above the deck and were maintained year-round by the housekeeper. Her arrangements were spectacular, not only in summer but in winter also, with gorgeous shades of brown, gold, and crimson—a mélange of colour much admired by visitors. Being an avid gardener herself, the caretaker worked with added incentive, as she was allowed to share the account for her personal needs at the nursery that provided the plants. Gina also loved plants and was gratified to see the exquisite arrangements every time she returned to the apartment—a royal welcome indeed.

The couple had just arrived back in London from their Hertfordshire residence. Ronald was attending to business in the city, and Gina always found a visit to London an inspiring change. Her husband was in the shower, getting ready for the evening, a major production for him as he still respected the formalities and upheld all social aspects of the evening meal. His clothing was carefully chosen, and he was unfailingly impeccable when he appeared for the pre-dinner drink. It always pleased

Gina to see him looking so well turned out. She never failed to appreciate the effort he made, even if she was disillusioned with the rest of their marriage.

The balcony displays were as beautiful as always, filling Gina with joy at their gorgeous colours and perfume. Her gaze drifted towards the Thames, following the antics of a rowing team. The river purling under the even pressure of the oars and their gentle swish, swish sounds carrying over the waves added to her quietude. For once, the man at the helm had his mouth shut. Usually, his voice carried vociferously across the rippling tide as he issued his instructions to the team members.

Gina felt at peace with the world. It was a rare pleasure to feel so relaxed and contented, in contrast to the anxiety she and others had been feeling a few months previously, on that fateful day…

****

It was 2 April 1982, a time of year that should have been welcoming new growth, new life in the northern hemisphere. But no! Argentinian forces had invaded the Falkland Islands. Located in the southwest Atlantic, the islands had been under British rule since 1833, and their residents were predominantly of British heritage.

The fight for control of the islands had been ongoing since the late 1600s, with the United Nations intervening in 1965 and extending an invitation to Britain and Argentina to enter into peace negotiations. Alas, to no avail. The attack was the latest in a long history of invasions of the Falkland Islands and no less bitter.

It had not been anticipated that Britain would intervene, but the British Prime Minister, Margaret Thatcher, was a formidable force, one not to be underestimated. Gina thought for a moment about how far women had advanced within the working environment since the war years. A far cry from when they had been relegated back to the kitchen sink and their domestic duties after the war, some having transported planes during wartime. Because of the need for pilots, those women's expertise and participation in the war effort had been desperately needed, albeit tolerated temporarily. It was not deemed appropriate for women to be flying military aircraft, and they were employed as civilians only. But necessity had prevailed, and they had played a major role in protecting their country.

In the same spirit, the prime minister maintained that the Falklands were a British outpost and would therefore be protected—and she had forged on, regardless of mounting criticism. Merchant ships were refitted and a warship convoy assembled and dispatched with remarkable speed.

The Falkland War had come to an abrupt end when Argentina surrendered, having been grossly underequipped for such an ambitious undertaking. Lasting three months only, the war had nevertheless claimed the lives of over 900 British service personnel, Falkland Islanders, and Argentinians.

*Thank God it was over quickly, otherwise who knows how many more innocent lives would have been lost,* Gina thought. *There's been fighting and trouble throughout the world since time began. Will it ever end?*

In an attempt to lose herself in her writings and break her train of thought, she clutched a notebook of poems on her lap while simultaneously struggling to adjust the recliner, all of which proved to be a job of work. She knew from experience that it was an exercise in futility, and she'd eventually have to get on her feet if she wanted to change the chair's position. The shrill ringing in her ear interrupted her, causing the book to fall to the floor as she grabbed the phone. It was her son, Jonathan.

"Jonathan, sweetheart, how are you doing? I've been worried about you. Since you moved to Germany, we hardly hear from you, or see you, for that matter. Why are you living in Germany most of the time? And why has your house been in the hands of a caretaker for so long? It's been niggling at me, and I'm concerned."

His mother's deluge of questions was overwhelming, and when Jonathan finally got a chance to speak, it was very obvious from his tone that he really wasn't interested in her sentiments at that moment. Picking up on the vibes emanating from the phone, she was immediately stilled.

"Mum, I just felt I had to try and reach out to you one more time."

Gina was shocked. He sounded like a stranger, bearing no resemblance to her usually upbeat son.

"Jon, what's wrong? Tell me."

"First of all, you never saw much of me when I lived in London. You were always off somewhere else apparently more interesting, so I really can't imagine why you should be so concerned about my well-being at this late stage. You're my mother, for God's sake. I've needed your support all through the years. When Nate died, you and Dad died with him—but what about me? I'm your son, too. Didn't I deserve to have my parents in my life? Parents who were interested in my life, hopes, and dreams, supporting me in my endeavours—in fact, all the things normal parents do. Instead, you've never been available, never. You've set your lives up to the exclusion of your remaining son."

She listened in stunned silence, her son's words ripping through her, words couched in ever more desperate terms. But she knew he spoke the truth.

"I lost my parents a long time ago, and you might be interested in knowing that I also lost my sweet Sarah. She died at the time I left England for Germany. As if that wasn't ghastly enough, I had the added horror of seeing her body being dragged on from the ocean off Vancouver, where she had drowned. When she was taken from me so savagely, I lost the only thing that made any sense in my life."

Shocked and mortified, Gina gasped in horror, while Jonathan became increasingly more distraught, obviously heartbroken, as his story unfolded.

"I've been utterly alone through the years, forced to deal with the loss of the elder brother I loved and then Sarah. Her loss has been a lingering grief—it's ripped the heart right out of me. I've become obsessive about it. In fact, I've even wondered if I should seek professional advice. I certainly couldn't seek comfort from my parents, having become so alienated from you both. You simply had no room in your hearts for me through the years, so submerged have you both been in your own misery.

"The feeling of loneliness and being unwanted through my youth was overwhelming. You both shut me out while dealing with your own sorrow, and that never stopped. My work has become my life. I've been a driven man. The final bitter blow of losing the love of my life has been slowly eating me up these past years. It's all been too much, simply too much to bear alone."

Gina's was gripping the phone so tightly, her fingers were going numb, as her son's venting poured forth. She had never heard him like this before, so hopeless, so defeated.

"I was going to ask her to marry me," he almost screamed down the phone, "but you two were oblivious to that. You were never around, were you? Sarah and I had a stupid row, and now she's gone, lost to me forever. Oh God! I don't know why I'm even bothering to phone you. I'd better just get off the line."

"No, no, Jon. Please don't go," Gina almost shrieked. "Jon, please let me talk for a minute. You're right, oh so right, and I am so very sorry. Can you ever find it in your heart to forgive us? I'm so saddened to hear that lovely girl is gone—how tragic and how ghastly that, once again, you've had to bear your grief alone. I swear things are going to be different. Yes, we are your parents, and we've made a rotten job of it. I've worried about this situation for way too long.

"Your father has been so lost, so isolated in his wretchedness and shame since Nate went. The situation has gone on far too long—almost reached a point of no return. He's always blamed himself for Nate's death and felt he should have done more for him when he was alive. I was afraid for your father and didn't want to leave him alone, particularly on the yacht. I was in such fear of what he might do to himself. We hear of yachting accidents all the time, where owners have become distracted and aren't watching what they're doing.

"The past years haven't been fun for me either. I've been so lonely myself, and truly, I have missed you so much and the long talks we once enjoyed. I miss my home most of the time, although not those so-called friends of your father who descend on us regularly. They certainly leave a lot to be desired."

She paused for a moment. Jonathan could hear her laboured breathing as she struggled for the right words.

"You are right, of course, in everything you say. Our selfish, callous treatment of our son has been unconscionable. Please come home and give us another chance, and I promise from now on, we'll be more supportive. You are still very precious to us, and in spite of all, we both love you deeply. Changes will be made, I promise. I'll get through to your father one way or the other. This situation has been carried way too far."

Jonathan seemed to recover himself a little, and his mood lifted. More in control of the situation, he was feeling somewhat ashamed of himself for being so tough on her. She was an unselfish woman, he knew that, and in spite of how it appeared, deep in his heart, he knew she loved him greatly. It couldn't have been easy for her these past years.

"Ok, Mum, please don't get upset, it just makes things worse. I'm sorry to be so tough on you, but I've had it, I really have. It's been a long time now since Sarah died, but I haven't been able to lay it to rest. I can't seem to come to terms with the situation—just can't seem to move forward with my life.

"I've felt so wretched lately, and now that Helmut and Gertrude are married and making all sorts of plans for their new life together, I'm feeling rather like a fish out of water. Don't get me wrong, I don't begrudge them their joy together. I'm very happy for them, but it seems to have brought all my own previous plans to the surface. I should have been planning my life with Sarah. I've tried to get over losing her, but I can't, I just can't get her out of my system. This horrible sense of loss is always there with me. I'm not interested in any other woman, can't get into any kind of a relationship. Sarah was everything to me."

Gina's tears were cascading down her cheeks. Her heart went out to her son.

"Helmut and Gertrude have been fabulous these last few years. I don't know what I would have done without them. But they're a married couple now and have their own lives to live. I need to get my life together, with parents who are part of it. I need to come home to a family."

"Jonathan, I'm going to sort this situation out today. I'll not allow it to go on like this. Please give us another chance to make amends. I want you to come home, and I'll fix it one way or another. I've never stopped loving you and neither has your father. He just can't handle any kind of emotion anymore. I'm so sorry, so very sorry we have let you down so badly and were not there to help you through this terrible tragedy."

Finally, Jonathan had been able to free his mind of the accumulated debris. Suddenly, all was clear to him, and he finally knew the path he should take. He was going back to England, his home. And in doing so, he would not only help himself but also help his parents get back on track. With a bit of luck, they would be a family again.

"Mum, I've missed you and Dad so much. Let's all try to move on with our lives. While we've been talking, I've made a firm decision. I'm coming home. Helmut and Gertrude are well underway, and the business is on an even keel. I'll still be making regular trips to the continent, but I'll get back to working on my own home in between times. Now that we've finally opened up to each other, let's help each other."

Following the promises and goodbyes, Gina fumbled when putting the phone back on its receiver. She sat for a long time before calling her husband down from the upper floor.

As soon as he walked into the room, he could see his wife was traumatized. Her tears had dried on her face, and her cheeks were streaked and eyelids swollen. She would never have normally shown herself in such a state, as she was a very private person. Her face was grimly set, and a miasma of gloom hung in the room. He knew it was serious business.

"Ron, please sit down. I want to talk to you."

Gina's voice was strained and there was no mistaking her tone or body language. Without saying a word, he immediately sat by her side.

She talked. Oh, how she talked—of the love they had shared, how they had met and how very much they had meant to each other. Incipient tears threatened, in spite of his efforts to keep them at bay. He was deeply moved, her words forging into the walls of the massive iceberg that had become his heart, the iceberg he had created all those years ago. He had tried to clamber out of that icy cage but had found himself unable. And her words continued to flow forth.

"I miss the man I married. I feel as if I am withering and dying slowly along with you. Your vitality and the excitement of our partnership have disappeared beyond a screen of artificial living and an endless round of empty socializing. We're no longer spiritually together. Over the years following our son's death, you've become unreachable, cocooned within yourself."

He made an effort to interrupt, but she waved him to silence.

She spoke of the loss of their firstborn and the negative impact he'd had on their lives in his later years, and then she spoke of his death, a subject that had never been raised.

"Ron, I have loved you forever, it seems, but I've watched you go away from me, the love and comradery we enjoyed squashed like a vague memory. Everything I have ever wanted is sitting right here beside me, and yet you're out of reach. You have to stop blaming yourself for what happened to Nate. Our son was old enough to know the path he had chosen, and you did everything you could have done to change that. All those years ago, you left me, and I want you back.

"You know you've always been loved by me, as you were by Nathan. He was just one of the many who lost their way, but at the end, he found his way back to you, and now," she added with emphasis, "now, we owe a debt to our one remaining son, and we need to make up for shutting him out all these years.

"That was Jonathan on the phone just now. He told me that Sarah is dead. She drowned, and that was why he left England so suddenly. That's also the reason his house has been left empty all this time, why he simply built his life in Germany. He was unable to talk to us about anything and has been in misery all this time, trying to make a go of his life. And what have we been doing? We've been off on one binge after another, trying to find fun and laughter in our lives again, and while we've been at it, we've thrown away the thing that should have mattered most to both of us: our son! We've acted disgracefully. We'll be lucky if he can ever forgive us for shutting him out the way we have.

"Jonathan called to say he needs us, and by God, we're going to be there for him now and for the rest of our lives. I've lost one son. I'm not losing the other. He's coming home, and his parents are going to be there to welcome him, and I sincerely hope you're with me on this, because it's our last chance to make amends and to retrieve what's left of this marriage."

Ronald moved towards her, reaching out, but she moved back, distancing herself from him.

"No, Ron. Don't you dare distract me. I'm saying what needs to be said and should have been said a long time ago.

"Please think about all of this, and remember Nathan loved you till the end. In that last moment, he had eyes only for you. You know that."

She was crying again, uncontrollable sobs. Struggling in the pocket of her robe for her little embroidered handkerchief, she turned her face from him and moved across the room towards the stairs leading to the upper floor. Her husband was unable to comfort her, so consumed was he in his own resurfacing grief.

"I'm going to my room now, and I won't be joining you for dinner. I need to be alone for a while. But please think on what I have said. I'm looking to you to work with me and make changes to this diabolical state of affairs. I hope and pray you realize how tenuous our situation is. We have almost lost everything of any worth. If we lose our son, we lose each other and our marriage."

Leaving the notebook of her writings on the floor where it had fallen, she hurried to the privacy of her room.

Tears fell from her husband's downcast eyes, blurring her words as he read them, words that broke his frozen heart as they cascaded across the page at his feet, and he cried until he could cry no more.

**LOST YOUNG MAN**

*The young man confronts his father yet again,*
*Every day their relationship feeling the strain.*
*Differences growing in vigour and verve,*
*The young man no longer his family will serve.*
*Head held high down the road of no return,*
*Too young for any living wage to earn.*
*Days, months, years and the living so poor*
*To go home seems not an option anymore.*
*So easily he becomes a part of the scene*
*Craving the feelings which make life seem serene.*
*Too late to turn the clock hands back.*
*Too late to get back on the right track.*
*The mature man lies in the gutter of no use,*
*Body worn and torn, wrecked with drug abuse,*
*And then moments before the lost man dies,*
*His father reaches for him and the young man cries.*

He went to her room and held her. The screaming in his head subsided, and the prayer in his heart, so long unanswered, burst forth as hope. They remained in each other's arms until awakened by the birds chirping and waiting on the balcony railing for their breakfast.

A new chapter in their lives was about to be written.

# Chapter 23
# The Homecoming

Shortly after arriving in England, Jonathan spent a few days at his flat in London and met up with Mark on business issues. He was glad not to be experiencing any major anxiety upon seeing the familiar places. Only an underlying sadness accompanied him as he moved about, handling company affairs. He was not in any hurry to meet up with friends or contacts—plenty of time for that later. But he was in a hurry to get down south to his house and move forward with his plans.

His first sight of the house had him transfixed in its usual way. He never failed to marvel at what a lovely home it was. How very fortunate he had been to acquire such a property. Going from room to room was a cathartic experience. He did, however, make a point of giving the library a miss. Seeing Sarah's face would definitely prove too much and despoil his good resolutions and intentions of getting on with the matters at hand.

The housekeeper had done a great job, and the house had been well looked after in his absence. It was immaculate. Even the contractors were clean workers, having left no debris around the premises. Having a yen to see the garden while the light was still good, he took the back door leading outside, still having no taste for visiting the library, which boasted a perfect walk-out to the garden. Its traditional patio doors faced onto the paved area and beyond into the grounds.

He had been intending to leave his visit to the garden until the next day when he was fresh, but as usual, it lured him forward. Moseying down to the little brick summer house, he saw that the wisteria still had not bloomed—not surprising, because the vine could take up to five years after planting to produce its first flush. Nevertheless, he might be lucky to see a few flower trusses later in the year, as it had been put in the ground a while before he'd left to live in Germany. Even without the flowers, the leaves were a gorgeous fresh green, and he knew that the summer house was a perfect host. The vine would be seen at its best, as it was such a prolific climber and could ramble at will. It would be spectacular when it got under way—just a matter of patience. It pleased him to see that the grounds had been well maintained in his absence.

The travelling had been gruelling this past week. He thought it must have been the strain of organizing himself for his return and a permanent stay. It had caught up with him very quickly, much more so than usual and, fatigue now overcame him. He had been going flat out at work and really needed this break.

Following a light dinner, he decided to have an early night and was gratified that the old sense of contentment began to settle on him. He was calm, a feeling that had eluded him for a very long time.

The next few days were bliss. He was even able to get to the library briefly, although he did not remove the dust sheets. His caretaker and friend had shown her compassion and intuition once again by covering the picture above the fireplace in a delicate drape, which he also left in place—plenty of time for removing that when he had toughened up a little more. Shirley really was a lovely woman and an expert housekeeper, and her excellent care of his house had lifted some of the worry off his shoulders. She had even worked as an intermediary between him and the contractors, on occasion. He was looking forward to taking her to dinner and thanking her properly.

****

All too soon, it was time to return to London, and it didn't take Jonathan long to get back into the groove. A few days after his arrival, he found himself passing by an old club. He paused to look at the poster of the upcoming entertainment. The picture was of a woman standing by a piano, obviously a guest performer. Stopping dead in his tracks, he recognized Sarah's mother, Rose. She was still as beautiful as ever.

*A mirror image of her daughter, had she still been here,* he thought savagely. *How like Sarah she is, except that her hair is platinum and coiled up in a chignon.* Bitterness overwhelmed him with such a grip that he found himself succumbing to the wretched thoughts invading his brain.

*This has to stop now,* he thought, giving himself a jolt. *Stop wallowing in self-pity and think about somebody else for a change. What about this poor woman? It looks as if she's still separated from Stewart, could even be divorced by now—what a depressing thought. Rose has shared the love of a lifetime with her husband, but the daughter with the heart of an angel is now gone, and the other managed to destroy the very love that had held them all together. How damned ironic that she should be alive, when my Sarah is gone.*

\*\*\*\*

Rose and Stewart had separated; divorce had not been discussed. While Rose remained in the family home, Stewart had disappeared into the confines of an old-boys-network club, in which many ex-servicemen had taken rooms and continued to live a life of opulence and past grandeur, playing chess or poker, or simply bullshitting their way through the evening over a glass or two of Glenfiddich, or whatever else took their fancy.

Although used to socializing, Stewart tended to keep himself to himself. He belonged with the woman he had loved from the moment he first set eyes on her, but that woman was now lost to him and had returned to a life on the stage, singing. He felt hopeless, completely out of his depth, and unable to rectify the situation.

Rose was, at that time, appearing at a club regularly frequented by the ex-servicemen; it was a favourite venue for them. They loved to hear the old songs, and for Rose, it was a joyous trip down memory lane, although her sadness was reflected in every song her doting audience requested.

****

Jonathan shuddered and pulled his hat further down. He realized that it was Rose and Stewart's wedding anniversary, and there she was, looking absolutely gorgeous, about to make everybody else feel better about living when she herself must be drowning and at her lowest ebb. He shivered at the injustice, and his heart went out to her.

*Damn it, damn it. I'm coming back for the eight o'clock show. I'll at least take her flowers and spend some time with her. In fact, I'll phone Mum and Dad and see if they're up for our reunion tonight. We can all offer some support now, when Rose really needs it. We can have our reunion at the same time rather than waiting for next week for our get-together. We could have a real bash this evening. I just hope they'll be able to manage it tonight and won't have something else planned.*

The thought of reuniting with his parents and the boost they'd all be able to give Rose elevated his mood and spirit.

Full of good intentions, he stopped at the little flower shop on the corner, at the end of his street. The florist knew him and gave him a warm welcome, waving enthusiastically as she saw him approaching. She'd been there for years, and Jonathan had been a regular customer when in London. He valued a fresh arrangement on his table at regular intervals. After an exchange of the latest local gossip, he bought flowers for Rose and for his mother, in anticipation that his parents would be able to make it. *If it's not possible for them to come, I can always get the flowers delivered to Mum the following day,* he thought as he rushed down the street to prepare himself for the evening. By the time he reached his apartment, he was motivated and ready for anything.

Flinging his coat over the chair, he grabbed the phone and dialled his parents' number. Fortunately, his mother answered. He relayed everything to Gina, who was overjoyed at the thought of a festive evening, not to mention seeing her son again.

"We don't have anything planned, and I know your father will really enjoy this. Rose is a lovely singer. It's been years since we last heard her. In fact, I think it was a few months before you left for Germany. I just want to say, the most important thing for us is to see you this evening. I know your father wants to say how very sorry we are. He's determined to make amends."

She hesitated. Jonathan knew she was struggling to find the right words—particularly difficult for her, as emotions were running high, and English was not her first language.

"Don't worry, Jon, we're on track and won't let you down again. We both love you very much. Nothing will stop us from being there this evening."

"That's absolutely terrific. I'm sure it'll be a good evening. What a reunion. I'll hold two spots for you both. We should hang up now so that we all have plenty of time to get ourselves organized for the evening."

****

The club was crowded when he returned that night, but Jonathan had phoned ahead and made a reservation. He was led to a really good spot a little back from the stage. He had requested one of the bigger tables, as he wasn't quite sure how many would be in the party. The florist had done him proud, and he was armed with two beautiful and very large arrangements for the ladies; fortunately there was plenty of room on the table for them.

As soon as he was settled, he ordered up a bottle of champagne in the hopes that Rose would be able to join him for a drink between songs. His eyes roamed the room as he sipped his drink, appraising the growing crowd. Apart from the older regulars, there were quite a few younger groups. The mood was infectious, the entire room charged with excitement. Grandparents, parents, sons, and daughters were all gathered. Rose was obviously still very popular, judging by the wide range of people in the audience.

Her voice was as pure as ever, as she recalled the heady nostalgia of the war years in her choice of lyrics and glided with ease through each of her requests like the true pro she was. Her smile widened when she saw Jonathan, and as soon as she was able to take a break, she made her way over to his table through the many handshakes and wishes.

Wrapping her arms around him in warmth, she gave off a very exclusive fragrance as they hugged. Jonathan poured them each a glass of the champagne once she was settled in her seat, and her face lit up as he presented her with one of the bouquets, which he had hidden under the table. He had chosen a bouquet of peachy pink roses, being careful not to get red blooms—red roses should, after all, come from her man and lover. He had no wish to remind her of anything that would make her unhappy. His mother's bouquet was a mixture of colours he knew she would love. Vibrant blooms matched her personality.

"These are for you. I just wanted to mark the occasion. Although you hide it well, I know how sad you must feel inside."

Tears glistened in her eyes; it was as if he'd read her mind. But she picked her words carefully and deliberately.

"I've loved Stewart most of my life. He was and is the only man I've ever really known. He was everything to me, and now he's gone. Jane put too many demands on us, and when her evil moods took over, they overwhelmed everything and everybody, including us. It's a terrible thing to say, but it was only upon her death that we were able to start healing, although the damage was done by that time. She had trampled our lives and torn our love for each other to shreds."

Jonathan was stunned, trying to assimilate what he had just heard.

Rose was scrutinizing him closely. "Are you alright?"

Barely able to speak, he whispered. "No, I'm not, I'm definitely not. Did you say Jane is dead?"

"Yes."

"I'm sorry, I thought because you were upset, you mixed the names up."

"No, I didn't. It was very unfortunate. As you know, my daughters looked very much alike, and Jane deliberately duplicated Sarah's appearance, right down to dyeing her hair black so that you could hardly tell them apart. Then she ingratiated herself with Luke, who she knew was smitten with Sarah. You were aware that Luke had a thing for Sarah, weren't you?"

Jonathan nodded numbly, feeling some of the old jealousy and anger rise within him momentarily.

"Jane lied her way onto Luke's boat, telling Sarah some yarn about Luke being unable to take her to Vancouver Island. As it happened, Sarah also had a pressing business engagement at that time, so she couldn't take time off anyway. Her message cancelling out of the trip didn't reach Luke. Her young assistant was supposed to deliver the note of apology but apparently forgot, being tied up with her latest boyfriend. Anyway, Luke being the womanizer he was took Jane with him. Apparently, a row began shortly after they left Vancouver for the island. There was a scuffle, and she broke away from him, ending up going overboard and subsequently drowning. At least, that was Luke's story, and he stuck to it all through the police investigation, which was quite drawn out. It was only brought to a head when Jane's body washed ashore off Vancouver some days later.

"The police obviously conducted a very stringent background check when she was found. Stewart and I were asked for statements. There had been some serious digging around for information, because when we were questioned, they constantly directed their queries to Jane's mental state. So they were aware of her background, and we filled in the gaps for them.

"When they took Luke in for questioning, the story was all over the papers—a very unfair state of affairs. Luke's previous lady friend, Susan Brown, formerly Chalmers, travelled from England to be with him. She publicly announced that she would stand by him no matter what the outcome, and she did. She said she had always loved him and would support him in any way she could, to the bitter end. So that was nice anyway. We can only hope he was telling the truth throughout the proceedings. He was actually crying when they took him into custody, but Susan was as good as her word and was later photographed by the news people holding his hand.

"Anyway, after some bandying around, it never was established whether Luke actually pushed Jane intentionally or not. All I know is he got really lucky. There was some confusion about the bruising on Jane's body, which certainly didn't help Luke. That was a crucial issue during the investigation, and they kept going back to it. It really didn't look too good for him, and they were pushing for charges. We can only assume the Crown prosecutor was not in favour, as the case was weak, and without enough evidence, they would never secure a successful prosecution.

"It was all so ghastly and sad. You really have to wonder if Luke was as bad as he seemed. The papers had him drawn and quartered. It's easy to judge people, but we really don't know what's going on in their minds. I'm quite sure Jane stuck her neck out. She provoked everybody. I still prefer to think it was accidental though. She probably just went overboard when they had their scuffle, as Luke had said. I can't think he deliberately pushed her, so I'm giving him the benefit of the doubt. I don't bear him any ill will, because we'll never know for sure what exactly happened on that boat. I just hope that young man can put this behind him and move on with his life.

"Susan and Luke came back to England when it was all over. He sold his business, and eventually they all moved to Canada with Susan's mother and the kids. The children were older, but they still needed supervision. Apparently, it was a permanent move and Luke was going to work with his partner in their business in Vancouver. Even Luke's work colleague packed up and went with them, so it was a clean break for all of them. So there you are. There are bright spots after all.

"Sadly, Jane's pernicious behaviour finally caught up with her, and we've all had a hard time recovering from this. Years of worry, and then her death added to the pile, and my Stewart gone from me. I don't know if I'll ever get him back—if we'll ever recover from this."

Her voice broke and, becoming overwrought again, she bowed her head and fought to regain her composure.

"My poor Jane, so tormented and to end up like that. They thought she had been in the water for over a week. You know, we have to make allowances for the way she was. She was sick. She couldn't help herself half the time… Oh dear, I have to get myself under control. I still have a couple more numbers to perform."

Jonathan stifled his own shock and confusion for a moment. He was feeling ashamed at having upset her. Stretching over the table, he picked up her glass and pushed it into her hand.

"Here you go. Take a gulp of that. It will make you feel better." He paused, then continued. "Rose, you know our family situation. My brother Nathan destroyed our family. My mother and father have lived together but have been estranged for years, pushing everything they held dear away from them. My father just gave up and lost himself in travel, and my mother felt compelled to follow him.

The amazing thing is we're back together again. My dad has finally let go of all his pain, and we're all working together to pick up the pieces. In fact, they're coming here tonight for our family reunion, and to offer you all the support they can. What do you think of that? Isn't it going to be grand? So please take heart. Stewart loves you, he always has, and I know he'll come back to you. Just you wait and see."

Having recovered her composure, Rose hugged him to her. Turning her attention to him fully, she was aghast at his ashen features. He looked as if he were shell-shocked and about to pass out, even though he was making a supreme effort to cheer her up.

"Did you not know Jane had died, Jonathan?" she queried. "It was in all the news. It was a shock to all of us when you and Sarah broke up and the situation seemed irreconcilable, particularly when you disappeared the way you did after your disagreement. She has refused any male company ever since and only planned to go with Luke because he was headed to Vancouver Island. She thought the sea air would clear her mind and give her a chance to get herself together before meeting her friends in Victoria."

*So it was Jane and not Sarah who died.* Realization was beginning to hit Jonathan. *Sarah is alive!*

"I can hardly believe what you're saying. My darling Sarah, I thought she was gone. She'll never be able to forgive me, even if I'm lucky enough to ever see her again. I should have taken more time in Canada and seen what the outcome was. I simply didn't see the point—she was dead, as far as I was concerned."

He was looking at Rose beseechingly seeking her understanding.

"I just couldn't take any more when I saw what I thought was her beautiful body floating, so distorted. I just couldn't handle the situation and folded, and now I don't stand a hope in hell of ever getting her back."

"What do you mean, you saw Sarah's body?" Rose was squeezing his arm.

"Well, it was when I was in Canada on business…" Jonathan then relayed how he had gone to Vancouver hoping to reconcile with Sarah. How he had seen the body being taken in by the coast guard and then attended to by the coroner. Because of the tattoo and general likeness, he'd assumed it was Sarah.

"Oh my Lord, you poor boy—we had no idea what was happening with you. Sarah had the tattoo removed when you broke up with her. She knew you always hated it. Jane copied it prior to going on board with Luke, and what with darkening her hair, she really could have passed for Sarah, especially under the circumstances and given the state she was in when she was discovered. If the truth came to light, maybe that's what the row on the boat was about. Maybe Luke found out suddenly that it was Jane and not Sarah. Honestly, the girls looked identical when they copied each other; they used to do it when they were very young kids."

Rose's voice trembled as she bravely took a hold of herself. "Jonathan, I can see how this happened; it's easy to understand why you thought it was Sarah."

"Well, it's too late now. It's all too late now—can't go back after all these years. I've blown it. I should at least have found out what happened. I owed that to Sarah. I've thrown away the only person who gave balance to my life."

Jonathan was distraught, acting badly. He knew it but couldn't stop lashing himself. "My own fault. I've lost Sarah and thrown away these years and all the good times we could have had together. I worshiped her, we belonged together, and now she's unavailable to me." He was inconsolable.

"Now you just listen to me, young man. Get yourself together. You haven't lost her, you never did. She's remained constant to you unfailingly through these years. She's dedicated her life to her work and is a very successful individual but avoids any personal relationships like the plague. Jonathan, as a mother, I know my daughter, and I know you two are right for each other. You were meant to be together.

"When you disappeared, Sarah was beside herself with sorrow and regret. She simply couldn't believe that your stupid row had separated you and was amazed that it caused you to leave the country, and for so long. She thought you were coming back for her, and she waited and waited, then finally threw herself into her work. She also closed her heart to any other possibility of a relationship with any other man."

Jonathan was aghast. "I just assumed instead of acting like an adult, and then compounded the issue by taking off, as far away as I could get. But it was the tattoo that threw me off, that damned, wretched tattoo. I took it at face value. How could I have been so short-sighted? I was so sure it was her. On the rebound, I seized the opportunity to transfer and open up a new branch in Germany. As you know, the country has always been very familiar to me. I spent so much of my growing up years staying there with friends at vacation time and later on, my business dealings. I arranged with Mark, my partner, to base myself on the Continent, had my house maintained here, and simply relocated to the Rhineland. Germany has always been a home away from home for me, and I have good friends and contacts there, so it made sense to make it my base away from England and the memories.

"Mark and I had talked about opening a branch for a long time, and if ever there was a right time, it was then. I've had a good and reliable person looking after my house and taking particular care of my Sarah hanging in my library. I couldn't bear to look into her face. It just broke my heart to look at the painting, knowing she was gone. And that's the way it's been for me."

"Well, that's not the way it will continue to be if I have anything to do with it. Sarah's coming here tonight to see my performance and to mark the occasion, and you'll see her. Don't blow it this time. I'm counting on you."

"Sarah's coming here tonight? You mean I'm actually going to see her again?"

Jonathan's thoughts were scrambled and confused at the thought of seeing Sarah after all the past years. He prayed to God that he would be capable of giving a good account of himself. Throwing his arms around Rose, he was overwhelmed with gratitude to her, for her understanding and for creating the daughter he dared hope would give him another chance.

Pulling away gently, she straightened herself.

"Now, I have to get back. The audience is getting restless. You have to get a grip on yourself. Why don't you nip into the men's room and swish some cold water over your face. You look dreadful." In parting, she kindly wagged a finger at him: "Remember what I said—don't blow it when she arrives."

Jonathan took another gulp of his champagne, terrified at the thought of the upcoming reunion. He was sure that if Sarah did come, there was not a hope she would bother even crossing the room to talk to him.

*I'd better do as Rose says and go and rinse my face. May as well give it my best shot.*

Much refreshed a few minutes later, he was feeling more resigned to the situation and in control of himself and moved towards his table.

Rose had been waylaid by some people at a neighbouring table and was just leaving them when he seated himself. She made her way across the room, then glided up the stairs and onto the stage, waving and smiling, acknowledging her audience and their enthusiastic applause once again as she walked towards the piano player.

# Chapter 24
# We'll Meet Again

Rose hadn't lost any of the grace she'd always possessed as she returned to the stage, pausing periodically to chat to people as they held their hands out to her. She was indeed a true star, with all the allure to reel in her admirers, bringing her hands to her face in mock modesty as her audience let out a roar of welcome and appreciation.

Jonathan turned away for a moment, his anxious gaze drawn to the club entrance. He'd been waiting with huge apprehension for Sarah to arrive, and when she did, he was stunned. She paused in the doorway to look around the room. Her beautiful face, unlined from the years that had passed, instantly tightened, registering shock as her eyes fell upon him. She stood mesmerized for a moment, before moving slowly towards him. Stopping abruptly directly in front of him, she stared in disbelief, absolutely incredulous. He rose unsteadily, his hand firmly on the back of the chair for support, and then spontaneously grabbing both of her hands, looked down at her, his eyes drinking in every detail of her features.

"I'm so sorry, so very sorry for all these years we've missed." He was distraught. "How can you ever forgive me? Your mum has just told me what happened. I thought you were dead and it was your body I saw in the water. I even saw the butterfly tattoo in the same position as you had yours done. I was so sure it was you. I never even considered it could be anybody else."

"What do you mean you saw me in the water?" Sarah was confused.

"I had originally gone to Vancouver, hoping for a reconciliation. I knew you were travelling with that Luke fellow and that you had plans to stay with friends on Vancouver Island. I was going to try to see you and really hoped we would be able to get back together again. I just fell apart when I thought I was looking at your beautiful corpse floating and so distorted by the ocean. I couldn't handle it and had to get away, out of the country."

Repeating himself as he had earlier with Rose, he stumbled, on pouring his heart out to her, his voice rasping with the effort and lack of breath.

"You know I was always leery of Luke, never liked the chap, shifty individual, always trying it on with the women, and when he focused on you, I was jealous, I don't mind admitting it. The thought of you travelling with him was intolerable. I imagined all sorts of horrors, and then when I saw you in the water…" His voice trailed off into the abyss. "I'll spend the rest of my life trying to make this up to you, if you can possibly forgive me and give me another chance." He was begging and didn't care.

Sarah listened, striving to make some sense out of his ramblings. Finally getting the story via the circuitous route, she hugged him, although she was having a hard time accepting how stupid he had been not to have followed up and checked out the facts. At least he could have found out exactly what had happened! But there was no way she was going to pursue the matter at this time, seeing how absolutely beside himself he was. This moment was precious, not to be lost to them. She refused to allow it to be ruined by delving into the reasons why they had been apart for so long. There would be plenty of time for that. She would just thank God for now that they were back together again.

"Be quiet. We'll talk about this at a later date. I can't get into it now and what did and did not happen. It's too depressing. Let's just enjoy the evening and be thankful we've found each other again. We have the rest of our lives."

Jonathan could hardly believe his luck. She was back in his life, and it looked as if she was giving him another chance. Pure joy coursed through him.

Rose's dulcet tones filled the room as she burst into song, cutting Sarah off in midstream. No sooner did one song finish than the audience shouted out their requests for another. There was a brief lull in the volley of requests, then suddenly, a deep, mellifluous voice, all too familiar to Rose, echoed throughout the room.

"How about 'We'll Meet Again'? I'm sure you know it."

Feverishly blinking through her tears, she attempted to beckon him onto the stage. Even with the encumbrance of his cane, Stewart managed to get up a fair gait, handling the stairs carefully. She sang to him and for him only, from the depths of her heart. The audience were silenced, mesmerized by the sheer unadulterated love emanating from the stage.

Sarah was frantically diving for a napkin to mop the flood of tears rolling down her cheeks.

"Oh Jon, isn't this heart-rending? I'm afraid I'm making a bit of a fool of myself. Will you excuse me for a few minutes please?"

Sarah was not alone—many others were also delving into their pockets for something to dry their eyes while she made a hurried exit to the ladies' room.

Jonathan was relieved to have a few moments alone to regroup. There was too much emotion floating around, way too much, and he was fighting to get on top of his feelings. Fiercely concentrating on Sarah's retreating back, he then returned his attention to Rose, finally recovering his composure—a recovery short-lived, for suddenly, pushing their way through the tables, arms outstretched to their son, were his parents, faces aglow with happiness.

Gina lit up the room in a red Grecian-style dress with an enormous corsage clinging for dear life above her ample bosom. She dropped one arm momentarily to give Ron a quick squeeze of much-needed encouragement. He was more than a little apprehensive as he approached his son and was confronted by Jonathan's serious expression. To his intense relief, it suddenly morphed into a smile that seemed to spread from ear to ear.

Gina, true to form, was in full swing—a ship with all sails unfurled, her thick accent ricocheting off the walls of the room.

"Sweetheart, we've failed you miserably, but we're here now, both of us, and will be forever. You poor boy, we are both so sorry, so very sorry about your sad news, and that you bore this loss alone, without your parents."

His father also grabbed hold of his son and held onto him as if he were about to lose him forever.

"Son, I've made a mess of our lives, but I've finally come to my senses. It took us almost losing each other before it happened, though, and for that I'm bitterly ashamed. I hope to God you'll give us another crack at putting things to rights."

His mother was still on a roll, and Jonathan was valiantly trying to get a word in edgewise.

"Oh Jonathan, I'm so sorry, so sorry, that lovely girl, we were so fond of her."

Jonathan finally managed to intercept his mother. "But Mum, Mum! Will you give me a chance to speak, for pity's sake?"

He pulled two chairs out from under the table for them.

"Please sit down, both of you, and please listen to me."

Gina's mouth was firmly shut, and Ronald too was mute, both obviously wondering what was coming.

"Everything is resolved. I made a terrible mistake. I have only just found out from Sarah's mother that it was Jane, the sister, who I saw drowned in the ocean when I was in Vancouver. I assumed it was Sarah, as they looked so much alike. That was when I ran like the idiot I am and relocated to Germany to get away from the ghastliness of it all. It's so sad about Jane, but Sarah's here, and I thank God for that and, can you believe it, she's giving me another chance! She's just gone to freshen up; she'll be back in a minute."

Jonathan's eyes were bright with anticipation as they all waited for Sarah to reappear. Finally, after what he thought was an inordinate period of time, there she was at his side. And what a huge reunion ensued.

His father grabbed both of them, practically taking their breath away in his expansive hug.

"Thank God you're safe and sound." Turning to Sarah, he said, "You two are going to see much more of us in the future, and I regret bitterly the time that has been wasted. Jonathan, how about us all taking a trip on the yacht to Provence? We didn't have much time together on your last trip there. I'm sure you missed some of the sights, and I know your mother is itching to take you around to see everything, and maybe the white horses again."

"What a super idea, Dad. That would be really terrific. What do you think, Sarah? How would you like to combine it with our honeymoon trip? I'm not letting you slip through my fingers again."

"Oh, Jon, I'd love that."

"Talking of fingers," he added, taking her hand firmly in his, "you know when we were in Amsterdam with Helmut and Gertrude all those years ago?"

She interrupted him. "Of course I remember. How could I ever forget? I've been living off memories like that for years. I thought something was going on, with you preening and strutting around as if you were the cat's whiskers. I just knew you'd been up to something at the time."

"Well, I had, and why in God's name I didn't get on with it at the time I'll never know. I'll forever regret not firming up on us then. I was going to ask you to marry me. I didn't because I thought I would wait for the exact moment. Anyway, we get another crack at it, and before the week is out, you'll have the most gorgeous ring on your finger."

"You didn't. Tell me you didn't buy me a ring in Amsterdam all that time ago and you actually still have it after all this time."

"I did, and I most certainly do still have it. In fact, I've changed my mind. I'm not waiting another day. I'm grabbing a taxi right now, and I'm going to my flat to get it. I'll be back in twenty minutes."

He was as good as his word. Rushing in not long afterwards, clutching his little parcel as if his very life depended upon it, he ran towards her, zipping through the tables like greased lightening lest they got separated again.

Sarah's face was flushed with excitement. Everything was happening at once.

"Look, Mummy and Daddy are coming back from the stage. Let's tell them the good news."

Rose and Stewart were hanging onto each other, both remembering another time when they had clung to each other so tightly all those years before, just as they were at that moment. Rose had been pregnant, and Stewart was on the run from the hospital. Both were hurrying from the bombs to start a new life, and here they were again, clutching onto each other for dear life, only this life looked to have much more favourable odds. It was filled with hope and promise.

Stewart held Rose's arm firmly to steady himself but even more so her, as her eyes were filled with tears of pure joy and she couldn't see worth a damn.

"Take your time," he whispered. "If we both hit the deck, we'll never live it down."

They made their way carefully down the last of the stairs, Stewart swinging his cane out in front of him with practiced ease, carefully seeking support on each step until they reached level ground. They headed towards their daughter and friends, the pair of them smiling like Cheshire cats, their hearts full of joy.

Then the clapping and whistling from the audience began as all rose of one accord. The six family members gathered around the table, and the champagne flowed. Stewart pulled Rose closer and presented her with a little package.

"Darling you always said you would like to match your keepsake. You can open this little gift now, just as long as you promise you won't turn on the waterworks again. There's been enough caterwauling tonight, enough to last a lifetime. Happy anniversary, love."

Rose's hands trembled as she opened the little red velvet box, and all of Stewart's threats fell on barren ground.

Inside, sitting on a bed of satin, was a pair of Victorian-style earrings, so exquisite, their lustre dazzling. They were adorned with rubies and seed pearls, exact duplicates of the brooch she loved so much.

Everybody clapped and extended their best wishes by raising their glasses to the ecstatic couple. They had hardly settled themselves down when Jonathan rose to his feet, his eyes never leaving Sarah's face as he tapped a spoon on his glass for attention.

"I have an announcement to make everybody. I have decided I'm not missing the boat again."

"Hear, hear," voices around the table murmured, all knowing what was coming. The rest of the audience were craning their necks to see what was going on, and there was a clatter and scratching of chair legs as all turned to watch.

Going over to Sarah's side, he knelt down at her feet and took her hand.

"Please, Sarah darling, will you marry me? And before you answer, will you please find it in your heart to forgive me for wasting so much precious time? Furthermore, I'm not taking no for an answer," and he grappled in his pocket for his prized possession.

"I've no intention of saying no. In fact, it's about time, don't you think? Yes, I'll marry you, and yes, I forgive you. Now where's that ring you've made such a hoo-ha about?"

Jonathan proudly presented it and placed it on her finger.

"Oh Jon, it's quite beautiful."

"And so are you. And so are you," he said, pressing her to his body so tightly, she could hardly breath.

Everybody spoke at once, voices raised with excitement. It was decided that after Sarah and Jonathan were married, they would begin their honeymoon on Ronald's yacht, and all six would take the vacation of a lifetime to Provence to toast the newlyweds and celebrate the reunion of all three couples. What a trip that would surely be.

Ronald stood gallantly looking down at Gina. A lascivious smile spread across his face, a smile brimming with intent.

"May I have this dance, beautiful lady?"

Gina fluttered her eyelashes at him, and they glided onto the dance floor, holding each other more than a tad too intimately for old married folks.

Rose and Stewart sat smiling at each other, having never stopped holding hands. Finally breaking free, Rose took off her earrings and replaced them with the new ones, seeking everybody's approval, although those left at the table were very obviously distracted by other matters…

Sarah and Jonathan gripped hands tightly, afraid to let go of each other. Gazing into the eyes of his soulmate, Jonathan pulled Sarah close and whispered in her ear.

"Well, I've certainly learnt my lesson. Never pays to assume, does it?"

# Epilogue

To assume in the matter of love is to risk losing forever all you hold dear.